The teenager had a scared look on his face as he held his finger to his lips." You gotta be quiet, lady. They might hear us," he whispered.

Uh, oh, I thought. Another weirdo. Well, might as well play his game.

"So what's this all about?" I whispered.

"Lady, you're in a lot of trouble. That sign for the gas goes up once a year—*and this is the day!*"

AMAZING™
STORIES

DAY OF THE MAYFLY
by Lee Enderlin

TSR, Inc.

To Leon and Rena:
Who started it, then encouraged it.

Distributed to the book trade in the United States by Random House, Inc., and in Canada by Random House of Canada, Ltd.
Distributed in the United Kingdom by TSR UK, Ltd.

Distributed to the toy and hobby trade by regional distributors.

AMAZING, the AMAZING logo and the TSR logo are trademarks owned by TSR, Inc.

First printing: February, 1986
Printed in the United States of America
Library of Congress Catalog Card Number: 86-50151
ISBN: 0-88038-263-5

9 8 7 6 5 4 3 2 1

TSR, Inc.
P.O. Box 756
Lake Geneva, WI 53147

TSR UK, Ltd.
The Mill, Rathmore Road
Cambridge CB1 4AD
United Kingdom

BARGAIN GAS

Days like that particular May 1 made me wish I had bought a convertible instead of the Charger Hatchback I was driving. The DJ on the radio had been saying that the temperature was an almost perfect 71 degrees. The few clouds punctuating the sky were there just for effect. I couldn't have picked a more perfect spring weekend to drive up to northern Vermont to see some college friends— friends with whom I'd regularly gotten in trouble (laughing uproariously each time) with almost every sorority at Utica College in upstate New York. Joanie and Marie were, I was sure, friends for life, even though we hadn't been able to get together since we graduated a year ago.

Both of them were dutifully impressed with my new car, my terrific job as a commercial artist for an advertising agency in New York City, and my tiny, but incredibly expensive, Greenwich Village studio apartment. "C'mon down and visit me sometime. It's crowded, but I'd love to have you. There's an awful lot to do in the city."

"We will, Lisa, we will."

"Where do you park that thing in Manhattan?"

A giggle. "Do you realize they charge a fourteen percent parking tax in New York? *Fourteen percent!* God, it costs thirteen dollars an hour just to park in some places! I don't even make thirteen dollars an hour!

"I leave the car at my mom's house in White Plains. It's kind of inconvenient, but I couldn't resist it. It's my weekend getaway vehicle. I wouldn't have been able to come up and see you without it."

And I wouldn't have been driving through the heart of the Catskills on my way home on that gorgeous Sunday afternoon, either. Interstate 87, taking the high road. It was a much more scenic route than I-91 as well as being more convenient and just plain faster.

It's about a five-hour drive from Burlington to White

Plains and even figuring the better part of another hour to get home from my parents' house, I expected to arrive at my apartment sometime around six that night. Plenty of time to relax awhile before having to worry about facing the rat-race again tomorrow morning. Already, I missed Joanie and Marie. So now that I'd made the trip, I knew it was going to be one I'd want to make often.

It was somewhere past the Port Henry turnoff that I first noticed the sign looming huge over the highway ahead. Its black and yellow message rose at least forty feet over my head: UNLEADED 49.9 GAL. THIS EXIT. Almost a third what I'd have to pay in the city. Fortunately, my needle was reading darn close to empty. Another eighth of a tank to go. Even if it was diluted with cheap alcohol, it was still too good a bargain to pass up. So I pulled off the highway and soon turned into a little town called Ashley Falls.

Ashley Falls, I discovered, was screwed into the side of a mountain, isolated from its neighbors in an odd sort of way with nothing but mountaintop to the west and a steep drop to the east into a valley not much bigger than the highway that squeezed through it. North and south ran tight, snaking roads whose main purpose was feeding the entrance and exit ramps to I-87. The thought struck me as I rounded the exit ramp that there was so little traffic around here that maybe the gas was left over from 1973.

A few more signs made sure I didn't get lost trying to find the gas station with the unbelievable price. My big city background started me wondering what I'd be forced to buy for the privilege of tanking up at 49.9. A case of Dry-Gas maybe or a couple of six packs of Coke or something. Maybe it'd be something useful after all.

The station itself consisted of three pumps in front of a tired, filthy building. A tilted sign over the door read HARRY'S. On the left side of the building, beside a pair of garage doors, sat a tow truck of dingy white and maroon with the same name emblazoned across the back. Next to it was a smaller pickup painted in the same motif.

A middle-aged man with his excess weight stuffed into a pair of oily overalls approached the car. My eye was caught by a curious button on his lapel. About two inches in diameter and light blue, no words, just a picture of an insect with lacy, oval wings and a long, slim thorax and abdomen. I didn't recognize it though.

"What'll it be, miss?" He smiled a friendly grin, exposing yellowing teeth.

I killed the engine. "Fill it with unleaded, please."

"Certainly."

The attendant stepped around the back of the Charger and uncoupled the hose from the pump. A moment later, the hose was feeding the tank. Harry's employee (or was it Harry himself?) engaged the "automatic" lever on the trigger, leaving the machinery to operate itself. "Would you mind opening the hood, miss? I'll check yer oil."

Here it comes, I thought. The car's only a month old and I know very well that it doesn't need oil. Still, it may be fun to listen to his spiel. I reached down and pulled the hood release. It popped open with a thump.

There was one thing I absolutely had to ask, though. I leaned out the window so I could be heard.

"Say, how can you sell this stuff so cheap?"

"Oh, ever' once in a while, we get a load that can't be sold. Usually some station upstate goes outta business or simply can't hold no more or somethin' like that. Then they offer it real cheap to little, outta-the-way places like this just to dump it. They don't want word gettin' around the real populated places that cheap stuff's still available somewhere. I gotta admit, though, this is awful cheap even for that way of doin' business. I coulda charged seventy-five cents and nobody'd know the difference, but I figger the folks who suffered when I hadda charge a dollar fifty deserve a break, you know what I mean?"

I sure do. Admirable of the man. I smiled in agreement. Maybe he's not going to rip me off after all.

The fat man disappeared as the hood rose. A couple of

moments later, he came back around to my window, wiping the dipstick on a rag so dirty I found it hard to believe it could clean the stick enough to get an accurate reading.

"Yer oil's okay, miss, but I think you may have another problem. Yer radiator indicator light been goin' on?"

I had to stop and think. "No, I haven't noticed it."

"Well, you've dropped a pretty big load of coolant out here. I think maybe you better take a look at it." He stepped back, inviting me out. Naturally, I was quite suspicious, but I knew I really should take a look at what he was talking about. I unbuckled my belt, opened the door, and stepped from the driver's bucket seat. Harry, or whoever he was, walked behind me.

A large Y-shaped puddle of green slime was beneath my engine. "This's a new car, ain't it?" I heard the attendant ask through my dismay.

"Huh? Oh, yeah. Only five hundred miles."

"Happens sometimes. The weld on the cap prob'ly ain't no good. No big deal."

That at least was good news. "How long will it take you to fix it?"

The attendant laughed. "Me? Oh, prob'ly forever. I don't do that kinda work. I know someone who does, but he's busy today."

"Well, since this is kind of an emergency, don't you think you might be able to persuade him to do just this one job?"

"Nosiree. You see, today's a local holiday as well as bein' Sunday. We celebrate May First, Mayday y'know, in Ashley Falls ever' year. Everything's gonna be closed tomorrow, too, around here."

"How come you're open?"

"Ain't, technically. Just doin' some repairs on my own vehicles." He pronounced it "vee-HICK-uhls."

And "hick" is a pretty good term for him, too, I thought as I grimaced at the puddle. "I don't suppose there's a Dodge dealer nearby."

"Nearest one's 'bout thirty miles from here in Chester. But shoot, they'll be closed today, anyway. Even if they're not backed up to two weeks from next Shrove Tuesday with reg'lar stuff. How far you drivin'?"

"White Plains."

"Never make it. That'll overheat ever' ten, fifteen miles or so and she'll spill her cookies all over again. You'll never be able to buy enough coolant to keep her goin'."

I turned away, shaking my head. For the first time, I noticed a young boy, maybe about fourteen or fifteen, standing in the doorway to the service station. He was leaning against the jamb, watching me idly. He was almost as dirty as the man standing beside me but with that lean, gangly look teenagers get. His sandy blonde hair hung down in clumps around his eyes and ears.

I turned back to the attendant. "Well, I'm not sure what to do."

The man wiped his rag down the dipstick again and leaned over to stick it back in its hole. "If you don't mind my sayin' so, miss, I think you're kinda stuck. It really don't look like yer gonna get this car automotive today, if you know what I mean."

"Terrific." I looked around the town of Ashley Falls. From its position among the hills, it must be almost constantly in shadow. I shivered slightly. The sky that was so perfectly blue a few minutes ago had turned into a nondescript gray slate. There was now a distinct chill in the air. Figures. I must have muttered it half out loud.

"Excuse me, miss?" the fat man said.

"Oh, I was just wondering if there was a place to stay around here. A motel or something."

The attendant laughed at me for the second time today. This time, it didn't strike me as so friendly. "What's so funny?"

"Sorry, miss. I didn't mean to make fun. It's just that this town's so small, the closest thing we have to a place to sleep overnight is the park. And you don't have to pay."

"I hardly think that's suitable."

His voice mellowed a bit in apparent sympathy with my plight. "Okay, listen," he said as he plucked the gas nozzle from the side of my car and returned it to the pump. "I'll get in touch with someone who can help you. Wait here while I make a phone call." Before I could acknowledge his order, he turned and headed back toward the station's tiny customer lobby. The kid jumped back from the doorway into the shadows of the building as the older man approached. I turned back to my car, resting my hands on the upraised lip of the hood. I looked closely at the seam around the radiator and the cap. Offhand, I saw nothing out of the ordinary, but then, I'm not a trained mechanic. I ran my hand around the cap, but it felt oddly dry. I would have thought I'd pick up some kind of liquid from the leak.

"This cap seems awful dry here," I called out suspiciously.

Harry stopped abruptly, short of the doorway, turned back to face me, and stood there rubbing his hands on his rag. "Huh? Oh, uh, yeah. Yeah. Of course. It's prob'ly the seam underneath. Or, uh, maybe you kicked up a sharp rock or somethin'. We'll get it fixed. Whatever."

He turned back and went inside. With a mutter of disgust and frustration, I slammed the hood down.

I leaned against the hood of my crippled auto and, slightly chilled, crossed my arms in front of me. Suddenly, I heard someone yelling inside the station. It was the mechanic. "What the hell you standing about for, boy? I gave you a job to do. Now do it!" There was a slight scuffling sound, then the noise of metal being moved behind the garage doors. A minute later, the mechanic returned, wiping his hands on that same oily rag.

"Father Jonathan'll be here in a minute," he called. "He's on his way."

Father Jonathan? A priest? What are they going to do? Hold Last Rites over my poor little car? What am I supposed to do with a priest, for crying out loud? He darn well

—
10

better be wearing a mask and carrying a blowtorch!

"You'll like him," the fat man was saying. "He's quite a refined gentleman."

"He'd better be something. I don't really think a priest is what I need right now." I looked up at the man and behind him, standing in the doorway once again, was the teenager. The boy quickly put a finger to his lips and gave me a silent "Shh." Then he pointed over to the side of the building as if to say, "Meet me over there later."

I looked at the fat attendant. "Are you Harry?"

"That's right. Pleased to meetcher." He stuck out one greasy palm, then withdrew it when I hesitated. "Listen, miss, I understand yer dilemma here, but there ain't much you can do about it. If yer stuck here overnight, yer stuck here. That's all there is to it. We'll getcha back home tomorra, don't worry none 'bout that. Ashley Falls is a friendly little town. Besides, you might just enjoy our little festival tonight. Might's well make the best of a bad situation, as they say. I'm sure you'll get everything straightened out with yer employer and all."

That reminded me. There were people who had to be told. And the man's attitude certainly had mellowed some. I relaxed a bit and said, "I'm Lisa Ames. I do have people I'd like to call. Have you got a phone here?"

"Yeah, sure, but it's outta order."

I saw a tattered booth at the corner of the building. There weren't any signs on it except for the ancient blue-and-white PUBLIC TELEPHONE.

"I think I'll give it a try anyway. It'll only cost me a quarter." As I started to walk toward it, Harry grabbed my arm rather brusquely.

"I said it was out of order."

All my growing anger and frustration at the situation popped out. "And I said I would give it a try anyway." I yanked my arm from his grip rather expecting him not to let go, but he did. I reached back into my car and grabbed my pocketbook. As I walked over to the phone, I rummaged through the change purse and found only a couple of dimes and a nickel. I dropped those into the coin slot and got the reassuring sound of the dial tone. The phone didn't appear to be out of order at all. I dialed "O".

Two rings later, a voice answered. "Operator."

"I'd like to place a collect call to White Plains, operator. Number 232—"

"Excuse me, miss. I'm afraid this is a private exchange and we're closed down for the holiday."

"*What?* I've never heard of such a thing."

"Yes, ma'am. Ashley Falls is still serviced by a private company with its own exchange. And the switchboard is shut down. A couple more hours and you wouldn't have even gotten me, just a recording."

"But this is an emergency . . . "

The operator's voice was strangely nonchalant. "Is anyone in danger?"

"Uh, no. My car's broken down and I've *got* to get help."

There was an audible sigh from the other end. Of relief or disgust, I couldn't tell. "Well, I'm afraid you'll just have to use a phone that's tied into the Chester exchange. Father Jonathan has one. I'm sure he'll let you use his."

Odd how it comes back to him all the time.

"Yeah, sure," I said, dejected. "Thanks."

"You're welcome."

I didn't get my change back either.

I returned to my car to find Harry waiting with a knowing smile on his face. "Why'd you tell me it was out of order?" I asked.

"To save you the trouble. It's easier than trying to explain Ashley Falls's phone system."

"It would be nice to let someone know what's going on."

"I'm sure, Miss Ames. That's why I called Father Jonathan. He'll help you out with all that. You'll get it taken care of, don't worry." The smile grew wider. But somehow it wasn't at all reassuring.

My eyes wandered back to the doorway. The teeanger was gone. I shrugged ruefully and smiled back at Harry. "Thank you. I suppose you're right." I looked down at my watch. One thirty-three. "I guess I'll wait outside here. It's such a beautiful day." Fact of the matter is, Harry, I don't want to go inside. Don't ask me why. "Please don't let me keep you from doing anything important."

"Oh, you're not, miss. Not at all. Don't worry about it. Can I get you a soda?"

"That'd be nice, thanks."

"Coke be okay?"

"Great. Classic, if you've got it."

"Sure, if you prefer that."

Harry waddled back into his station and returned quickly carrying the Coke. He handed it to me and said, "Here you are. Father Jonathan'll be here soon."

I thanked him and sat sideways into the open car door, slumping against the backrest. The Coke tasted surprisingly sweet. Sure enough, the can said "New Coke."

A slight breeze had sprung up, punctuating the drop in temperature. I shivered again and pulled myself farther into the car. This was just terrific. A brand-new car breaking down literally miles from nowhere. Probably a whole day lost from work and, from the sounds of things, maybe even two. With a little luck, I might be able to persuade Harry to tow me to Chester and have that leak plugged tomorrow. At least by having the Dodge dealer do the work, it'll fall under the warranty. A phone call in the morning before I set out should resolve that.

As I lifted my head to take another sip of soda, I noticed movement inside the station. It was the teenager again—this time staring at me and waving both hands over his head. I thought I saw a look of desperation or even panic on his face, though it was hard to tell through the grubby glass of the service bay windows. Once he saw that I'd noticed him, he again pointed to the side of the station by the tow truck. Only this time, his gestures were

---

13

more animated, more urgent. I looked around to see if he was gesturing to someone else, but there was no one. He had to be signaling to me.

Okay, what's this all about?

Suddenly, an arm reached across the back of the boy's head and sent him sprawling into the garage door. Despite the filth in the windows, I could see the boy's face twist in pain. Harry, his amiability gone, appeared and grabbed the youth by the collar, yanking him back into the service bay. He was yelling at the youngster again, but this time I couldn't tell what he was saying. Well, none of my business.

I was just taking a sip from the almost empty can of Coke when a green Chevrolet Citation pulled into Harry's lot. It was probably six or seven years old, well used but not well tended. This had to be Father Jonathan.

The Chevy slowed to a halt and a tall black man, probably in his mid-thirties, emerged. Instead of the clerical garb I had unconsciously expected, he was dressed in a tweed sport coat, tan dress shirt, brown slacks, and well-polished loafers. His tightly curled black hair was graying slightly—and rather handsomely, I thought—at the sideburns. On his lapel was the same odd button as Harry wore, but his had a pastel green background. He was smiling widely as he approached me.

"You must be the young lady Harry told me about." He had dark, shimmering eyes that somehow reminded me of a deep, swirling whirlpool. His baritone voice was warm and mellow.

"That's right. Lisa Ames. How do you do?" I extended my right hand to meet his. He shook it vigorously.

"Jonathan Matthews. My pleasure."

"Excuse me, but I thought Harry"—I felt a little uncomfortable at using the man's first name so casually, but I had no other way to identify him—"referred to you as 'Father Jonathan'."

His grin widened even more. "Oh, I imagine he did.

Everyone in Ashley Falls calls me that. Actually, I'm not really a priest. I'm a minister and, technically, I suppose they should call me Reverend Matthews, but they've always called me Father Jonathan. My dad was known as Father William and his dad was Father Alfred." He smiled again and shrugged in a way that brushed aside the subject as unimportant. "So tell me about your troubles, Lisa."

"Well, Father, I—"

"Father Jonathan," he corrected me.

"Excuse me?"

"Father *Jonathan*," he repeated. "I rather prefer the entire salutation. 'Father' alone is pretentious and makes me sound like a papist." Then, realizing he might be talking to a Roman Catholic, he apologized, although his voice had held no malice. "Pardon me if—"

"Not at all. As long as you treat people as individuals, I don't care what you think of their religion."

Father Jonathan was thoughtful, nodding his head. "Very well put. Very insightful. I'll have to remember that for a future sermon."

Harry had joined us by this time, wiping his hands again on the ubiquitous rag. Father Jonathan said, "Ah, Harry. I'm surprised you're not at the festival."

"I will be soon, Father Jonathan. Just thought I'd take advantage of a quiet mornin' to change the oil in my own cars."

"Can't blame you. Now what exactly is this young lady's problem?"

"Well, she's blown a lot of engine coolant. Looks like her radiator popped a seam or somethin'. Jerry Kosinski's gonna have to reweld it, but I don't think he'll be able to do it today."

"Oh, heavens, no. He'll be running around quite like a headless chicken." Father Jonathan turned back to me. "He's in charge of this year's festival. It's quite an honor. I'm afraid he won't be available today."

My heart dropped a notch. I guess I had thought this

15

man was going to solve my problem.

Harry spoke again. "I ain't too sure about tomorrow, neither, it bein' a holiday and all."

"How long will the job take?" Father Jonathan asked.

"Oh, I'd guess the weld itself'll take less than half an hour. Then you gotta let it set awhile. Don't know fer sure how long. You'll have to ask Jerry."

"Well, maybe I can talk him into getting this young lady on the road tomorrow. I don't think he'll mind too much." Father Jonathan turned to me. "I'm afraid, though, you're stuck with our hospitality for the next twenty-four hours. We'll do our best. You're most welcome to spend the night in my home. I've plenty of room. And I won't take no for an answer. You won't be imposing at all."

His smile eased the pain somewhat. I thanked him and said that my relatives would have to be told. He amiably agreed. "And you're having the devil's own time getting through the local switchboard, aren't you? Well, we'll see to it," he assured me. "Are you in a tremendous hurry to do so? I'd like to show you our little festival. It's not far. The fairgrounds are only five blocks away."

I had to admit no one was expecting me until five or so tonight, maybe even later. What harm could there be in waiting? Besides, small town celebrations can be a lot of fun.

"Fine." Father Jonathan smiled widely again. Just then, the cloudbank passed by and the sun emerged again, but somehow, it still didn't seem quite as warm as earlier.

"I'll need your keys, miss," said Harry. "I'll put your car in the bay and leave it there until Jerry can get to it."

"Oh, sure. Just let me get my things out."

I walked around to the back of the Charger and slipped the key into the lock. The hatchback popped open. I leaned in for my overnight bag, then stood up and slung it over my shoulder. As I slammed the hatchback shut, I turned back toward the gas station and saw him again.

The teenager was back at the service bay waving frantically at me once more, making very exaggerated pointing gestures at the tow truck. I stared at him a moment, puzzled. Harry must have noticed my inattention, because he turned to see what I was looking at. The youth melted back into the gloom of the building.

How the devil does he expect me to get away from these two? Obviously, he doesn't want Harry to see what he's doing.

I dropped the overnight bag in front of me as I spoke to Harry and Father Jonathan again. "Uh, I'd like to use the facilities before we go the festival. Have you got a Ladies Room here?"

"Oh, sure," Harry answered. "It's around the side of the building. Unlocked. We don't need locks on the bathrooms around here." He chuckled slightly as at some unfathomable dirty joke. I was increasingly repelled by the gas station owner but was startled to find myself looking toward the minister as my protector.

It took me a minute to slip the ignition key off my "I Love New York" key ring. I handed it to Harry. "This isn't going to harm the engine, is it?"

"Heck, no. It's only goin' twenty feet. Not likely to overheat in that distance. Father Jonathan, would you like a cup of coffee while you wait?"

"Sounds fine, Harry."

"Help yourself. It's in the office. Say, would you mind openin' up the bay door for me?"

"Not at all."

Father Jonathan walked to the service bay as Harry climbed into the driver's seat. Somehow, I felt as if my car was being violated. No one else had ever driven it before.

I tossed my pocketbook over my shoulder and picked up my overnight bag. I started walking toward the tow truck.

The car's engine fired up behind me. "Miss Ames!" I heard Harry yell. I turned around and faced him.

"Yes?"

"The restrooms are on the other side."

17

"Huh?" I looked around, acting a little lost. A large sign reading RESTROOMS stuck out from the corner at the far end of the building from the tow truck. It was really difficult not to see it and I must have looked really stupid. "Oh, thank you." I changed direction and walked slowly to the right side of the service station. I heard the service bay door open and Harry drive my Charger inside.

I turned the doorknob on the restroom, held the door open for a moment, then closed it without entering. I dropped the overnight bag on the ground outside the building, but thought better of it. If Harry or Father Jonathan should emerge, they might get suspicious. I yanked it back up and dashed quickly around the back of the building.

The teenager was at the other end, his back facing me and peering around the corner toward the tow truck. I called out to him. "Hey, kid. What's going on?"

He jerked upright and turned quickly toward me. He was wearing an oil-stained T-shirt that between the stains read PROP TY OF ALCA Z ST PRISO. His dingy blue-jeans were equally grimy. He, too, had that same weird insect button pinned to his chest. Another blue one.

He had a scared look on his face as he held his finger to his lips. "You gotta be quiet, lady. They might hear us," he whispered.

"Harry and Father Jonathan?"

"Yeah. They'll kill me if they catch us."

Uh,oh, I thought. Another weirdo. Well, might as well play his game.

"So what's this all about?" I whispered.

"Lady, you're in a lot of trouble. That sign for the gas goes up once a year and this is the day."

The teenager was gulping air often, almost with every other word, in his haste to blurt out his story. He reminded me of an excited young child trying to describe a sudden accident to his mother. His eyes were flitting about, constantly looking behind me as if he were expecting someone

———

to come around the corner.

"See, they put that sign up just for the festival," he told me.

Part of the festivities, I imagined. Spreading the joy around. "Yeah, so?"

He took a deep, trembling breath. "They do it to get victims! It's a trap!" he blurted out.

The boy seemed on the verge of crying. As I looked at him fighting tears back, I remembered an incident when I was eight and lied to a teacher to get out of being punished for some slight indiscretion. But the lie ate at my conscience, and I cried all the way home, releasing my guilt in my tears.

This kid made me remember that. But what could he be feeling guilty about? Victims? "I don't think I understand," I told him.

"I don't either, really," he admitted. "But this festival isn't what they say it is. For God's sake, you can't go with Father Jonathan!"

"But my car's broken down. I can't go anywhere else."

"There's nothing wrong with your car. At least, there wasn't. There is now. My dad—uh, Harry—stuck an awl through the bottom of your radiator. That's why you've got no fluid."

"An 'awl'?"

"Yeah, it's sort of like a screwdriver only it's got a pointed end. You use it to start a hole for screws and nails so they they stay in place until they get seated proper."

I crossed my arms and eyed the boy suspiciously. "How do you know that's what your father did?"

"'Cuz he's been doin' for it for years."

"What for? Extra business?"

"No, lady, I already told you. To get victims for the festival."

"What's this festival all about then?"

"Look, I haven't got all afternoon to sit here and argue with you. If I'm not back in that garage in about two sec-

---

onds, my dad'll come lookin' for me. I'm telling you, lady, that you're in an awful lot of trouble and you might not get out of this alive even if you do exactly what I tell you. And you sure as hell won't get of here alive if you go with them. They'll kill you."

I wanted to scoff, but those last two words just hung in the air, like leaves refusing to blow away. If I'm in some kind of danger from Harry and Father Jonathan, then wasn't the kid risking himself to help me? I asked him about that. His answer was not reassuring.

"Yeah, that's true, lady. And I can't explain it all to you now. You've just gotta believe me. This is all crazy, I know, but *I* ain't. I've got my reasons."

I was puzzled, suspicious, and a little apprehensive. Obviously, this kid was in real fear for himself and, apparently, me as well. But why? Would I have a chance to find out later somehow?

"Jimmy, where the hell are you?" Harry suddenly bellowed.

The teenager raised his right hand and stabbed the air in front of me with his finger as he spoke. "Lady, I'm leavin' right now. You wanna save your skin, you jump into that van behind me." He poked a thumb over his shoulder. A half-rusted Ford van sat in tall grass at the back of the gas station.

"I'll be back later to explain it all to you." Jimmy ran over to the tow truck. "Coming, Dad! Just emptyin' the trash."

"That take you all day?"

"Somethin' was stuck!"

"Yeah, your brain! Now get a move on!"

I heard Jimmy run around to the front of the building and slip back into the service bay. The van he had pointed to was ten feet away, its rear door facing me wide open, beckoning. Someone here was crazy, but just who, I wasn't exactly sure.

Who could I believe? Harry? He had lied to me about

———

the phone. Was he lying about the radiator, too? He sure had hemmed and hawed enough when I noticed the cap was dry. Did that mean anything? Unfortunately, standing behind this garage wasn't going to answer that question. Father Jonathan seemed okay though, but then, I'd only spent a few moments with him. Jimmy had seemed genuinely afraid of something, and his story about luring victims into Ashley Falls certainly gave me the shivers, but surely it couldn't be true. Or could it?

Time was running out on me, too. If I didn't reappear in a minute, would Harry and Father Jonathan come looking for me? Would they suspect something if they found me standing around back here? Was there even something to suspect? I *had* to decide what to do!

Oh, come on now, Lisa, use your head! Think! Wouldn't it be best to get the answers to those questions from the adults instead of from some maybe-wacko teenager? Of course it would!

I returned to Harry and Father Jonathan. *(If you as the reader agree with this choice for Lisa, go to page 75.)*

I think I would have given up chocolate milkshakes for a week just to have five more minutes with Jimmy. It was just too damn frustrating not to be able to hear out his whole story about the festival. The van stood quietly nearby.

So what would be the harm of hiding in the van and waiting for Jimmy? Harry probably was a damn liar. So I stay here a few minutes, find out what else the kid has to say, and if it turns out that Jimmy's full of nonsense, I'll just go looking for Father Jonathan. I have to find out more about what Jimmy is so afraid of before I confront Father Jonathan—and Harry—again.

I thought I'd better hide in the van. *(If you agree, turn to page 155.)*

THE PROCESSION

"I think we better walk," I told Jimmy. "I hate to leave my car behind, but we're more mobile on foot. Which way do we go?"

"I don't know yet. The guys in the cars could be anywhere. The actual ceremony hasn't started yet, so they might be wandering 'round all over the place lookin' for you or any other outsider that wanders in."

"Ceremony? What ceremony?"

"Don't worry about it, lady. You're gonna miss it. Now wait here while I look 'round and find out where everybody is."

Jimmy scampered off into the black nighttime shadows, and I started to wait, wait, wait again. It's funny, but I never thought you could be bored and frightened at the same time. I hunkered down into the long grass growing alongside Harry's Service Station. At least this time, Jimmy probably wasn't going to take all day getting back to me.

It seemed an awful long time, but it was probably only about ten minutes later that I noticed that a small piece of sky had taken on an odd, fiery appearance. A little corner in the southwest at first, then gradually it moved north. Waves of dancing reds and yellows flickered constantly like some sort of earthbound Aurora Borealis. I watched the strange phenomenon for almost an hour as it slowly grew in size and intensity until it took up most of the western sky just along the horizon. My view was obscured by a line of houses and because of that, it took me some time to realize that the source of that light was not very far away— perhaps as little as a few blocks.

There was no sign of Jimmy, so I stood and walked out to the gas pumps. The light was definitely close by. I looked up and down the street both for Jimmy and some rationalization for going exploring. I found the latter. I promised the absent Jimmy to stay away only a few minutes—just long enough to find out what was going on. I crossed the street toward the line of houses.

Keeping in mind what Jimmy had said about search cars, as well as the terrifying possibility of running into Harry and Father Jonathan, I slipped into the starlit shadows of the backyard of a small Cape Cod. I passed quietly through its yard into the yard of another home facing in the opposite direction. Once past that house, I found myself on another residential street. Before I crossed, I made sure nobody was in sight.

The glow in the sky grew brighter as I continued west. I had gone past two houses already without even a glimpse of a light in any of their windows. In fact, none of the houses on any of these streets had any lights on. Odd, I thought. Literally everyone in town must be at this festival tonight. Maybe the flickering I was following in the sky had something to do with that ceremony Jimmy said was going to start.

I moved swiftly across the street and walked bravely through the front yard and into the back. When the dog started barking, I almost had a heart attack.

It was tied to a tree somewhere to my right. It must have been some kind of black lab or something like that because I sure didn't see him until he began announcing my presence with a bark that should have attracted half of Ashley Falls. In fact, I could barely make out his outline now even though I knew where to look.

I dropped to the ground, barely daring to breathe. I was sure the lights in the house the dog was protecting would go on and I didn't know whether to hug the ground and stay still or try and duck behind something. The nearest corner of the house was only a few feet away, but the back porch was nearer the dog—some twenty or so feet from where I lay. If a porchlight went on, I'd surely be caught in its beam.

I could hear the dog straining at the end of its chain to

---

get at me, the unseen menace.

I rolled over toward the house, directly under a blacked-out window. I thought that if a light *did* go on, I would be out of sight.

Why the hell wasn't anyone coming to investigate why the dog was still barking? In fact, why the hell weren't any lights even going on? Were these people at the festival, too? But it didn't matter, because in a few minutes Rover gave up, probably figuring he had scared me away. I heard his chain rattle as he settled down to go back to sleep.

Slowly, I stood and retraced my steps back to the street. It was still deserted like virtually everything else in Ashley Falls. Maybe if I was careful, it would be safe to stay on the sidewalk. Besides, I might even run into Jimmy since he was apparently the only other person in this town besides me who wasn't at the festival.

Continuing my search for the mysterious light, I strode quickly down four or five more empty blocks—with not so much as a car going by—until I found myself outside an Anchor fence around what was obviously the town fair-grounds.

There was the source of the strange light. I stepped behind a large oak tree and ducked down, watching the macabre scene.

Along the sides of the grounds were the usual wood and canvas game and crafts booths that are the hallmark of hundreds of such fairs every year. They were arrayed in long rows like strangely shaped tombstones facing inward toward a huge open area in which apparently the entire population of Ashley Falls was standing.

The curious light in the sky was being caused by the candlelight procession. Every resident of the town old enough to hold a candle had one in his or her right hand, held high, and filling the night with a dancing glow—a cityful of St. Elmo's fire. The townspeople were facing away from me and the candles used the backs of their heads as artists' easels to create a grotesque array of twisted, leering, red-

---

and-yellow "faces" staring in my direction. I felt a shiver begin in my shoulders and work its way to my knees.

The townspeople were all facing an empty stage at the far end of the fairgrounds. It appeared to be about six feet high and was ringed on three sides by a series of four-foot-tall candlesticks topped by bulbous lenses of orange glass and bathing the stage in an eerie light. The varnish of the stage reflected the orange light back up into the night, intensifying it, and creating a focus for the mob's attention without allowing a clear view of what was happening.

The throng stood motionless and quiet, apparently waiting for something, perhaps the ceremony that Jimmy had mentioned. I waited with the people of Ashley Falls.

Soon an expectant whisper moved through the crowd. The people at the rear stepped aside to create an aisle through the crowd. At the beginning of the aisle, by the entrance to the fairgrounds, a dark figure appeared. It was Father Jonathan.

He was dressed in some kind of somber clerical robe. Black and flowing down to his feet. Some gold embroidery around the cuffs. I couldn't tell much more about it in the dark. Unlike the others in the crowd, his hands were empty; they held not even a candle. He had a serenity and a majesty that needed no props. Smiling but silent, he walked toward the stage as fast as the crowd would let him.

I caught a glimpse behind him of four more people, all empty-handed. Two men and two women I think, though I couldn't see them very well in the manmade twilight. They disappeared quickly into the crowd, leaving me with no idea of who they might have been. Probably some other townspeople, the Festival Committee maybe, or that Jerry Kosinski guy.

They do it to get victims! Isn't that what Jimmy had said? With those almost-tears in his eyes?

Come to think of it, those people were walking just like a bunch of zombies . . .

Oh, come on now, Lisa, you're letting your imagination

run away with you. No, you're letting the imagination of a fifteen-year-old run away with you!

I was so intent on the scene unfolding before me that I never heard the footsteps behind me. A hand on my shoulder was the first indication that someone knew I was there. I gasped involuntarily and jumped about ten feet in the air.

"Jesus Christ, lady, will you please shut the hell up?" It was Jimmy. "I figured I might find you poking around here."

He must have read the relief in my face. "Yeah, you're lucky it was me who found ya. Anyone else would have had you up there in no time."

He nodded toward the stage. I looked over and saw that Father Jonathan had not yet reached the stairs at the side.

As I crouched down behind a tree, I demanded, "Where have you been? I waited a long time for you." Somehow, I felt I had to justify my actions to the teenager.

"Unfortunately, I ran into my father and his buddy Jerry in the procession. They stuck a candle in my hand and told to get in line just like everybody else. It took me a while to get sorta lost in the crowd. But once I did, I got my ass over to the gas station to get you and guess what?"

"I wasn't there."

"Right. And since I hadn't see you around Father Jonathan anywhere, I figured they hadn't caught you and you hadda be sure."

"Sorry," I said with some exaggeration. Then I saw that Father Jonathan had reached the stage stairs. "Jimmy, what's going to happen up there?"

He sat beside me, not even looking at the stage. A grimace crossed his face.

"That ceremony ain't a real pleasant thing. You'll be real sorry you saw it if you stick around, believe me."

"Why? What happens?"

Jimmy looked over my shoulder at the crowd. He didn't answer for a minute. "We really shouldn't talk here. Let's go back to the garage. I'll tell you all about it there."

I felt a momentary anger that this kid never seemed to think it was the right time to explain what the hell was going on!

But then the eerily-lighted stage caught my eye and I said, "No, not now. I want to watch what's happening." I saw Father Jonathan move onto the stage. There was about him a regalness—even a beauty—that I found fascinating, that spoke to something in my heart. *(If you agree, turn to page 45.)*

Then I realized that Jimmy was right—it was simply too dangerous to stay at the fairgrounds. I stood and, in a half-crouch, followed Jimmy back to Harry's Garage. *(Turn to page 167.)*

THE MAYFLIES

I wandered into the kitchen and found Father Jonathan busy with the last details of supper and watched him for a few minutes. Whatever Jimmy had been trying to tell me was obviously nonsense. Father Jonathan was one of the most polite gentlemen I'd ever met, and quite handsome, too. With all the activity going on over at the festival grounds, he still had time to fix an incredible dinner, and for a stranger, no less. Prime rib, baked potato, salad, everything. I watched him in the kitchen as he tossed the lettuce in the salad bowl.

"Is there anything I can do to help?"

"Not at all, my dear. Everything's in the oven. The most difficult thing left to make is the salad, and there's nothing to that. What kind of dressing do you like? You can have any kind as long as it's Italian."

I smiled at his good-natured humor. "Italian will be just fine, but I've got to insist on one thing. I'm doing the dishes later."

It was his turn to laugh. "Oh, no, you're not. I don't often have a chance to show off my cooking, and I'm certainly not going to make you work for your dinner."

I understood his feelings. I enjoy cooking, too, but rarely get the chance. When the few opportunities arrive— usually holidays at my parents' house—I try to make the most of them.

I felt as if I'd been a friend of Father Jonathan's all my life. I was relaxed, comfortable, and felt right at home. I sat at the kitchen table and looked around. I was impressed. It was as immaculate as Felix Unger's, but Father Jonathan certainly wasn't any sort of fuddy-duddy. Most of the single men I knew lived like bears. I always seemed to be cleaning up after one boyfriend or another.

My host had the windows open, and a slight breeze was blowing the curtains around. The sounds I heard earlier had disappeared—probably just some house noises. I had no intention of interrupting the relaxed mood I was in by asking something that was going to sound rude. So I asked instead, "How do you have time for this? Don't you have to be at the festival soon?"

"No, not for a while yet—around seven-thirty or so. Admittedly, though, dinner is a bit earlier than usual. Of course, in my business, I sometimes have to settle for a quick sandwich."

"I suppose that's true."

"So I make up for those times by fixing something special when I have the chance, and I love to share it. Usually I fix Chinese, but I didn't have time today."

It was just as well. I hate Chinese.

"What I really like to make is breakfast. Eggs and toast and bacon, or ham or sausages and orange juice. Now, that's breakfast. But what do most people stick in their stomachs in the morning? Cocoa Puffs, doughnuts . . . nothing but sugar. It's a wonder we're all not diabetic."

I smiled at Father Jonathan's lecture. I never ate breakfast myself—probably just as bad from his standpoint.

He finished with the salad and began ladling it into the bowls. A few minutes later, the prime rib was ready and he joined me at the table.

It was during dinner that, at my prodding, he told me about the teenager. "Uh, Father Jonathan, I have some things I wanted to ask. Mostly about Harry's son—Jimmy, I guess his name is—but a couple of other things, too."

"Oh, yes, Jimmy. Poor boy." Father Jonathan sat back, his eyes furrowed deeply. "You see, Lisa, Jimmy has some serious problems. It all goes back to a couple of years ago when his mother died. She had some pretty serious problems herself. Drank rather heavily. More than once I was called over to the house to, well, mediate some volatile situations. No one ever got hurt, but the potential was always there. I'm sure you understand what I mean."

I nodded.

"She was also given to moods of extreme depression, mostly when she was sober. It seemed as if there was always trouble at the house. Quite unfortunate, really, because in many ways she was a very fine person." Father Jonathan sighed, staring at his plate and only playing with his food.

"The drinking gradually became heavier and heavier, and she continued to refuse treatment. The depression, of course, grew deeper and deeper, and the arguments became more violent. Harry quite frankly feared for his son's life. Jimmy is a strapping young man, but you can imagine, I'm certain, how difficult it is to safely restrain an irrational person wielding a knife. To his great credit, Harry got the guns out of the house years ago. Otherwise, there's no telling what might have happened."

I felt a little awkward listening to the story. I was ravenous, but it seemed rather callous to eat while I listened to what Father Jonathan was telling me. Also, I wasn't really sure if this was any of my business. Was Father Jonathan betraying the confidentiality of clergy? Deep down, I'm sure he wasn't, but still, I was an outsider.

"Jimmy was very close to his mother, despite her problems. I suppose he felt he could help her if anyone could. Like most kids his age, he was pretty sensitive—still is, really. He was only fifteen at the time. . . . "

"How long ago was this?" I asked between mouthfuls.

"Oh, a couple of years."

"He stills looks fifteen."

"Yes, he doesn't quite look his age. I'm sure you must remember what it was like to be fifteen."

I laughed. "It wasn't all that long ago, Father Jonathan."

It was his turn to laugh now. "I didn't mean it that way, Lisa. I was just making a point," he said with a grin.

"I know." I smiled back to let him know I was only feigning injury.

"In any event, Harry felt he had no choice but to get a divorce."

———

31

"I imagine Jimmy had a hard time dealing with that."

"Actually, no. Apparently he was mature enough to understand that it was probably the best thing for his parents and that his relationship with his mother wouldn't change. In fact, he knew he could live with her if he felt he had to keep an eye on her, so to speak. I know Harry seems somewhat imposing and perhaps a bit Archie Bunkerish, but the fact is that he showed an awful lot of patience. Finally, though, even he couldn't take it anymore. I think Jimmy understood that as well. No, the divorce wasn't the start of Jimmy's problems. As it turned out, in fact, the divorce was never made final anyway."

"Oh?"

"Jimmy's mother couldn't deal with it. She felt it was an attempt to take Jimmy away from her, so she took matters into her own hands."

I dropped my fork and gasped slightly. "Suicide?"

Father Jonathan had finished his dinner. As he told his story, I wasn't even aware that he had been eating, although I was acutely self-conscious about my own dinner. I still had half a plateful of prime rib remaining.

Father Jonathan picked up his dishes and brought them to the sink. I hurried my last few gulps.

"Don't hurry on my account," he said reassuringly. "We've plenty of time before the festival."

I slowed down. I was thoroughly enjoying my host's cooking. "This is delicious, by the way."

He turned and smiled at me. "Why, thank you. One of my great joys in life is hearing that from my guests. Would you like anything else?"

"Perhaps a little more tea."

"Of course." He poured it for me, then continued his story about Jimmy's mother.

"Just before the court date for the divorce, maybe two or three days, she picked up Jimmy from school."

"Was she drinking?"

"I'm afraid so. Jimmy said later he smelled gin on her

breath. Anyway, she picked him up in the family car and drove him out to a small pond, which is rather isolated. She drove along a deserted road out there."

"Didn't Jimmy suspect anything?"

"He said they just talked. Despite her drinking, she was quite rational. He figured she just wanted to drive around a little and talk.

"All of a sudden, with no warning at all, she swerved off the road and into about eight feet of water. The windows were open, and the water just poured in. The car sank like a rock. Jimmy yanked his door open and tried to get out, but his mother was holding him inside."

"You're kidding me."

"I'm afraid not. She tried to hold him there so that he'd drown with her. Well, as panic-stricken as he was, he managed to break free and swim to the surface. He dove back down to try to save his mother, but she just fought him off. Later, the police found that she had buckled herself into the seat and tied it off with wire. Naturally, Jimmy was quite devastated."

"I can imagine." I felt crushed hearing about the tragedy, even though I really didn't know the family except for the few moments with Harry and Jimmy earlier.

"Well, not only was Jimmy shocked by his mother's suicide and by the fact that she tried to kill him, too, but there's also this lingering feeling of guilt that he failed her somehow. Like I said, he always believed he could straighten her out eventually. I'm afraid it weighs quite heavily on him. Still."

"I—I'm sure." I began removing the remaining dishes from the table and carrying them to the sink. Father Jonathan took them from me and carefully placed them into a pile of white suds.

"I won't have time to clean them tonight," he said, "but it's always easier if they soak awhile." He turned to me and motioned me away from the sink.

His story about Jimmy explained a lot of things, but not

everything. "So why would Jimmy tell me that you're looking for 'victims,' as he put it? He scared the daylights out of me!"

"I'm certain he did. I'm no psychiatrist, so I can't give you all the professional explanations for it, but the fact is, he simply hasn't been the same since his mother died. He dropped out of school as soon as he turned sixteen—which was no surprise, since he had stopped doing schoolwork months before and was in danger of flunking out anyway. He and his father couldn't get along anymore, whereas prior to that, they got along reasonably well."

"So why did he pick on me?"

"I imagine it was some kind of—well, I don't know what you'd call it—flashback? Guilt transference? He, uh, isn't always rational. Quite harmless . . . so far . . . but I'm afraid he needs professional help. Ashley Falls can't really provide that."

"I wouldn't think so. It's a small town."

Father Jonathan hesitated. He was still holding the dish towel, rubbing his hands thoughtfully. "That isn't quite what I meant. Harry doesn't exactly make a rich man's salary. He can't afford to give Jimmy the kind of help he needs. It's unfortunate. I've offered to help, but Harry's a proud man. He won't take charity."

"I guess that's a pretty old story."

"I'm afraid so. I just hope nothing happens before Jimmy gets over it. Maybe time will afford the help that his father can't afford to pay for. We can only pray."

He draped the dish towel over a cabinet handle and sat back down at the table. "Now, you had some questions for me?"

I held my head down. After hearing about Jimmy, I really didn't think my hearing strange sounds was very important, but I had mentioned having other questions earlier and now my host was pursuing it.

"It's really nothing, Father Jonathan. I, uh, simply thought . . . oh, no, it's nothing really."

"Come, come, my dear. If there's anything I can do to help, please tell me. It's not easy being among strangers. Please let me take the place of your family tonight, all right?"

How could I refuse him? Jimmy was quite obviously wrong about Father Jonathan.

"It's just that I thought when I was upstairs that I heard some . . . funny noises."

"Noises? What sort of noises?"

I shrugged. "I don't know. I'm sure it's nothing."

"No, no, please. I want to help."

"Well, it sounded like, well, kind of like moaning."

"Moaning? What sort of moaning?"

I felt really foolish. I could feel my face burning from blushing. "Like a person moaning." I couldn't look him in the eyes.

Father Jonathan's voice took on a cheerful note. "Oh, that. It's just an old furnace that squeaks. I admit it's a bit eerie at times, but I've gotten used to it. I'll bet you heard it in the shower. It happens every time you turn on the hot water."

I nodded sheepishly and smiled back at him. "I sort of thought so."

"It sounds very odd downstairs. You should hear it. Here, let me show you what I'm talking about."

He stood and walked toward the door leading to the basement. He stood aside and let me pass in front of him down the stairs, then flicked the light switch on behind me, and the cellar came to life.

There didn't seem to be anything special about it at first. The stairs descended into a single room that was nicely finished with wood paneling and appointed with a sofa, an easy chair, and a coffee table that matched the paneling. The ceiling was covered with white tiles that hid the pipes.

"This is where I bring people who want to talk out problems," Father Jonathan explained. "Sort of my second

---

35

office."

I looked around, and my host immediately guessed what I was looking for.

"The furnace is over here."

He turned left at the foot of the stairs, away from the finished room. I followed him dutifully as he led me behind the staircase to a tiny room that was closed off from the rest of the cellar. I saw Father Jonathan pull a key ring from his pocket and insert a key into the door.

"Right in here," he said as he stepped back again to let me pass.

Father Jonathan was such a thoughtful host that it would have been impolite not to indulge him in his little tour.

I stepped into the room. Just as I realized that someone was huddled in the corner, I heard the door close behind me. There was no mistaking the sound of the tumblers turning in the lock. I stood there in shock for a brief moment.

I turned back to the door. "Hey, what is this? What are you doing?" I yelled. My only answer was the sound of Father Jonathan's footsteps stomping back up the stairwell. I rattled the knob, then balled my fists and pounded hard on the door. "Hey! Hey, let me out of here!" I heard nothing from the other side. After several seconds, my hands started to hurt. I stopped pounding and leaned my head forward against my crossed arms on the door. A tear welled up in my eyes. What in the world could Father Jonathan be up to?

Then I remembered that I wasn't alone. I looked at the huddled figure and realized it was Jimmy! He was slumped against the wall, his head rolled back away from me. His hands lay at awkward angles at his sides, palms up. His mouth hung open slightly. Was he even conscious or just faking it? I stared at him fearfully, but I saw no movement except for his breathing.

I approached him cautiously, expecting him to leap up any second and reach for my throat. I wiped the tear from my eye and smeared the back of my hand with mascara.

I knelt beside Jimmy and took hold of his head, shivering violently with fear. His eyes fluttered as he tilted toward me. The right side of his face was covered with blood! I almost fainted.

"Jimmy, what—what happened?" I managed to whisper.

His voice was scratchy, like someone who had just awakened. His eyes were opened only slightly. "Aw, my dad beat the crap outta me when he figured out I had talked to you back at the garage."

"How'd he find out about that?"

"He didn't. He just sort of assumed it."

"Where else are you hurt?"

"Just my head."

I steeled myself and looked closer. There wasn't much of a gash on his temple, but there was a nasty bruise, and the skin was broken enough on the surface so that it had bled pretty badly. It was all caked up now, turning darker red as it dried. I winced and choked back my rising dinner.

"Does your dad always punish you like this?"

"Only when he wants to knock me out. He hit me with a frying pan."

Jimmy was beginning to wake up, but he was squinting hard, and I imagine he must have had one terrific headache. He held his hand to his forehead. He was obviously too weak to move much and therefore wasn't a threat to me. My apprehension faded. In fact, I felt sorry for Jimmy, with the pain he must be going through. It was killing me that I couldn't do so much as offer him an aspirin.

"You're lucky to be alive," I said. It was dumb, but it was the only thing I could think of.

"Yeah, well, Father Jonathan'll take care of that later at the festival."

"What are you talking about?"

He looked at me, and it didn't take much to recognize the frustration in his eyes. "You mean you still don't

37

understand?"

I leaned back against the wall beside him. "Yes, I do. He told me all about your mother."

Jimmy shot upright. "My mother? What did he say about my mother?"

I had only been in town a few hours, and already it seemed I was on a first-name basis with a skeleton in every closet.

"About her suicide," I said quietly.

"Her suicide? Her *suicide?* Why, that stinkin', lyin', murderin' bastard!" He jumped up and started swinging his fists in the air.

"Jimmy, you'd better calm down. You'll start bleeding again."

He stopped waving his fists, but he wouldn't sit down. "What exactly did he tell you?"

I grabbed him by his pants leg and gently pulled him down as I repeated the story Father Jonathan had told me over dinner. When I finished, he looked sullen as he stared at the floor. "None of that's true, you know," he said when I finished.

"It isn't?"

"Nope. My mother never drank. My father does, though. And you're gonna find out why before tonight's over."

"Where is your mother, Jimmy?"

"Oh, she's dead, all right. But she didn't kill herself. They killed her. At last year's festival. Because she wanted to put a stop to it."

"Put a stop to what?"

"To what they got us locked up in here for."

"Jimmy, you'd better start telling me what's going on. Right from the beginning."

He sighed deeply and pulled his knees up around his chin. "Well, the beginning is like hundreds of years ago or something, I guess. It all has something to do with the Underground Railroad back in the Civil War days. One of the slaves, some ancestor of Father Jonathan's, I suppose, came up from the South with this power he had to . . . oh, this sounds so stupid."

He lapsed into silence, and I had to prod him. "C'mon, Jimmy. You've got to tell me what's going on."

"It's pretty crazy. Really."

"I think I have a right to know."

"Look, I tried to warn you this morning, but you wouldn't listen. Now you're telling me you got a right to know. It's a little late for that."

"Then tell me what happened to your mother."

"First you gotta understand what happens at the festival. Father Jonathan has the same power that that slave had. He takes a group of people who drive into town to buy my dad's gas and brings 'em up to that stage you saw, and I'm telling you, he sucks the life out of 'em with that power of his."

I wanted to scoff, but he started crying again as he had earlier this morning, behind the garage. Tears welled up in my own eyes as I began to comprehend my situation. Jimmy had one important fact that tended to corroborate his story. He was locked in here with me. Somehow, I didn't think we'd be in here if we weren't in a heck of a lot trouble.

"I don't know why the whole town goes along with it. Maybe they're afraid of Father Jonathan. Maybe they like it. I don't know. But every once in a while, someone tries to put a stop to it. And they end up on that stage like the people who drive in for gas. They have some kind of philosophy about it—something like these people are only in Ashley Falls for one day, just like mayflies only live for a day or some crap like that."

I found myself listening more and more intently to what Jimmy was saying. His voice was gradually sliding into a whisper as his loss of blood caught up with him.

"Anyway, my mom wanted to stop it. I never talked to her about it, but I heard her arguing with my dad about it.

She kept saying that the festival was evil enough, but why did he have to get involved in it, suckering in people with that sign? My ma was one of those afraid of Father Jonathan, and my dad's one of those that likes it, I guess.

"I don't know the exact details, but apparently, on the day of last year's festival, she had some kind of fight with Father Jonathan. The next thing I knew, she was up there with about four or five other people on that stage, and Father Jonathan put her through the ceremony."

I didn't have to be told what that meant.

"How long you been in this room?"

"Most of the afternoon, I guess."

Jimmy slumped back again into the corner. His eyes closed, but I could tell he hadn't lost consciousness. It was obvious, though, that his outburst had left him badly weakened. I was sorry now that I had pushed him so hard for the information.

He remained quiet, regaining his strength, I guess. I dropped down against the wall, suddenly feeling weak myself. I closed my eyes, trying to reconcile the differing stories of Father Jonathan and Jimmy. Father Jonathan had been so cool, so urbane, so apparently sincere. . . .

But it was Jimmy's face that was battered. I tried to stifle a sob, but it was impossible. I was certain now that Jimmy was telling the truth. After all, I know what the old saying is about actions, words, and their relative importance. Why Father Jonathan had bothered to keep me amused during dinner, I couldn't even guess. Maybe he had just been playing an evil game of cat-and-mouse.

Oh, Momma, Momma, what have I gotten into?

That thought tumbled over and over in my mind, as if it were a talisman against fear.

Suddenly I heard someone at the door, fumbling with the lock. I jumped up, startled, but Jimmy never flinched—more because he was expecting it, I think, than because he was too injured to move.

The door opened and revealed Father Jonathan. Behind

him stood Jimmy's father, Harry. He was carrying a shot-gun, aimed right at us.

"I'm afraid, my dear, that the time has come," Father Jonathan said. He never lost that friendly, gentlemanly, soothing tone in his voice. He strode into the room carrying a small hypodermic needle.

"What good is that going to do?" I challenged him. "I heard you call my parents on the phone. They know where I am."

"Wrong, my dear. You heard me talking to today's Dial-A-Joke. Would you like to hear it? It wasn't very good. I'm afraid you'd be disappointed. I hope you enjoyed dinner, however. The least I can do for our Life-Givers . . . or may-flies, if you will . . . is to provide them with a decent meal. It gives them more strength to transfer to me later."

I backed off as he approached me, but there wasn't much room to retreat. Father Jonathan walked toward me, not hurrying, aware that I was trapped. Harry stepped inside the door and held his gun on me. I stepped to my left, putting Father Jonathan between us, but just as quickly Harry took a step to his left. When I couldn't go any farther, Father Jonathan approached me and reached out for my arm. I yanked it back, avoiding his grasp. Any thoughts of resistance were swiftly stifled, however, when Harry began waving his shotgun even more menacingly.

"You wanna git yer head blown off?" he growled.

My breath began to hitch violently, and I could feel my face contort as I began to cry. "Please, no, don't. I'll do anything you want. Just don't kill me, okay? Anything!"

"It's not so bad, my dear," Father Jonathan said quietly. "It's rather pleasant, actually. Don't be afraid."

He grabbed my arm roughly and jerked it toward him.

"No, no," I pleaded, and then began screaming. "No! No!"

Father Jonathan poked the needle gently into my arm, then put that needle into a shirt pocket and produced another one from the same pocket. This one was obviously intended for Jimmy.

As he knelt over the youth and took his arm, Jimmy spat at Father Jonathan, who patiently wiped the wad of saliva from his face. Harry stomped up behind him, ready to intervene if necessary, but Father Jonathan waved him off. Harry growled down at his son.

"You never was worth anythin'."

"I'd rather be with Mom, anyway, you fat bastard." Jimmy was barely audible now.

I felt a little dizzy, and the room started to spin slightly, like the first stages of a heavy drunk. I rocked back against the wall, but just as quickly as the dizziness had come on, it disappeared and was replaced by a feeling of lightheadedness and disorientation. I had no problem seeing and nothing was blurred, but somehow everything stopped registering, nothing had any meaning.

It was sometime later—I had no way of knowing how much time passed—that I felt myself half-stumbling up the cellar stairs and out of Father Jonathan's house. There didn't seem to be many people around, but I couldn't tell for sure. Somehow, I knew Jimmy was behind me.

A smooth, deep voice was uttering reassuring words to me, but I couldn't really make them out. The voice sounded like a lullaby in a foreign language.

I was dimly aware of walking a very great distance. I don't know how I held out. Maybe it wasn't as far as I thought. Time was inconsequential. I had no idea how long I had been walking. I simply plodded along numbly.

Suddenly I found myself in the midst of a large group of people, but I couldn't make out any faces. They were there, staring right at me, but they simply didn't register. Somewhere in the distance—or was it perhaps right beside me?—were a thousand pinpoints of light dancing to their own individual rhythms.

I waded through the sea of people, unconsciously following the hands that were tugging me along. Eventually the

---

bodies thinned out, and I was being led up some wooden stairs. A pair of hands turned me around. The pinpoints of light were waving in a seemingly endless tidal surge, back and forth.

I knew Jimmy was standing beside me—to my right, I think—and there were a few more people standing along the edge of the stage on the other side of him, but I had no idea how many.

I felt a pair of hands cup the top of my head. A deep voice chanted unintelligibly in a singsong fashion. Suddenly the volume and pitch of the voice's obscene song rose measurably. There was a loud response from the sea of light, and I was aware of a brief, brilliant flash. In that instant of brightness, I saw a sea of tiny insects with long, tapering abdomens and lacy, oval wings, some flying, some breeding, but most merely lying on the ground, their wings fluttering uselessly, as if they were dying. Some didn't move at all.

Somehow, I knew one of those dead insects was Jimmy's mother, Harry's wife.

The brilliant flash disappeared, and I realized that if I had wings now, they'd be fluttering uselessly. The annual Mayfly Festival of Ashley Falls was coming to its climax.

I was aware of a great, throaty roar of approval swelling from the crowd in front of me, and blackness descended over my drugged mind. My legs buckled, and suddenly I was kneeling on the stage, aware of only two things—first, that my life was easing out of me like a train slowly pulling away from the station at the beginning of a long, long trip.

And second, that Father Jonathan was stepping up behind Jimmy.

THE END

CANDLES IN THE NIGHT

Father Jonathan had reached the stage and turned to face the crowd from the top of the stairs. Several other people—the ones who had been walking behind him down the aisle, I think—moved up the stairs past him and went to the center of the stage. Father Jonathan lifted his arms into the air. I expected him to look up to the heavens, but he didn't. He just kept staring out at the crowd.

The people of Ashley Falls responded to Father Jonathan's gesture by raising their candles over their heads and yelling something I couldn't catch. When the cheering died down, Father Jonathan lowered his arms. He paused a moment, then walked across the stage to stand behind the first person on the edge of the stage. He was a man probably in his late thirties or early forties. He stared straight ahead of him, seemingly unaware of the crowd. Again, Father Jonathan held his hands over his head momentarily. This time, the townspeople were silent.

I watched fascinated as Father Jonathan lowered his hands slowly and deliberately over the sides of the man's head. He cupped the man's ears tightly and looked up above the crowd. He quietly muttered something I couldn't make out. I was too gripped to ask Jimmy if he knew.

Suddenly, the man slumped forward to his knees and every candle in the park flared for a few seconds, casting a brilliant glare on the scene. A sea of orange-yellow faces was watching the macabre play in front of them. I could have sworn that a flash of light emanated from Father Jonathan, too, but my attention was distracted by the candles and I couldn't be sure.

The man in front of Father Jonathan fell completely to the floor, as if his skeleton had been turned to liquid. A great cheer arose from the crowd as the candle flames reverted to normal. The other people on the stage never moved, standing like statues overlooking the crowd. If they were aware of where they were, they never showed it.

I was riveted to the ghoulish scene, not at all revolted but strangely attracted. Jimmy, however, felt differently.

"You happy now?" he said harshly. "That guy's dead. That's his wife standing next to him and their kid next to her and I guess her grandfather at the end. They came in about an hour before you did. They went off with Father Jonathan before I had a chance to stop them.

"Keep watching, lady. Soon Father Jonathan'll pass through the crowd touching everybody and mumbling some priest stuff. That's when the Transference of Life takes place. It's what keeps everybody in this damn town from gettin' old." A sob tore from his throat.

Father Jonathan was stepping behind an attractive brunette wearing shorts and a halter top.

"Doesn't she know he's there?" I asked, horror-stricken.

"Probably not. They use some kind of drug, I think." Then Jimmy paused for a moment before asking, "Haven't you seen enough yet, lady? This is exactly what I'm trying to keep you from getting caught up in. Now let's get the hell out of here!"

"No. I want to stay."

"What?" he shrieked, then he said more quietly, "You're kidding!"

I was silent as Father Jonathan went throught the same ritual he had followed a moment earlier, and the woman slumped to the floor of the stage. There was a definite flash from all the candles and Father Jonathan this time. No denying it. The crowd yelled in unison.

I don't know why; I just answered, "I'm staying."

"Lady, you're crazy!"

Jimmy stood and took a step toward me. He reached out to grab my arm. "C'mon, let's get outta here."

I took my eyes off the scene unfolding in front of me. "No, damn it. I said I'm staying." I yanked my arm free.

Jimmy was just as adamant. He reached out and jerked me toward him. "No, you're not. You're coming with me. Even if I have to drag you."

He spun me hard and sent me pitching headlong into the ground. I wasn't hurt, but I was certainly shocked. I started to roll over, but Jimmy was on me like a flash, snatching me by the upper arm and yanking me back to my feet.

"You don't seem to realize how much danger we're in," he whispered harshly. "I sure as hell didn't risk my life all afternoon just so you could get us both up on that damn stage."

He shoved me backward but didn't release his grip. In fact, he clutched my blouse even tighter and started to drag me away from the fence. "Now, c'mon, we're gettin' out of here before it's too late."

He was much stronger than I expected, and when I twisted and turned to break free, my blouse ripped, exposing a bra strap. I stopped fighting instantly, before I ended up half-naked. When he realized I had stopped struggling, his grip loosened slightly. I walked beside him in silence, awaiting a chance to break free.

Suddenly, I spun and whacked him hard across the face with my open palm. The suddenness of my attack caught him by surprise, and he staggered back, releasing my blouse. Before he had a chance to react, I gave him a backhand to keep him off-balance.

But not for long. He looked around quickly, then bent over, and swiftly picked up something in the darkness. It looked like a rock.

"Lady, I'm not BS-ing ya. We're gettin' out of this place together if I gotta knock you silly and drag you out by myself."

Shocked at his vehemence, I started to back off.

He followed me, step by step. I had no idea why, but I knew he was just picking his moment. I watched him tensely, hoping to judge my dodge just right.

He lunged and I jumped.

He went past me out of control and tripped over a thick tree root that was only half-buried. The rock went flying out of his hand.

I jumped on his back, hoping he wouldn't be able to simply toss aside my 105 pounds. For a second I wondered why this was happening when—supposedly—Father Jonathan was supposed to be the danger. But right then, all I could do was react to the immediate threat.

I'd always sort of wondered how I would do if I had to defend myself. Scared as I was, I found out that I had the inner strength to kill if I had to. I was ready to beat Jimmy's head into the ground. Maybe the adrenaline was clouding my capacity for rational thought, but, dammit, I was just plain mad now and I wanted to show this kid who was going to hurt whom.

But whether I would actually have done it, I never found out.

Jimmy was on all fours, shaking his head and acting as if he had been hit on the head. I tightened my grip around the back of his neck and felt an electric current suddenly snap through my arms. It wasn't at all painful, just a ticklish sort of tingle that spoke of hideous power.

Surprised, I yanked my hands back . . . and Jimmy slumped over, unconscious.

I stood over him, my rage gone now. I brought my leg over his back and stood beside him, wondering. Had Jimmy hit his head on the ground when he tripped over the root? I certainly hadn't hurt him badly enough to knock him out. I never even had the chance to lift his head up, let alone smash it back down again.

Then I became aware of footsteps crashing toward us. I started to run, but smacked right into a plump body. It was Harry. He wrapped his bearlike arms around me and held me tight to his chest.

"Well, little girl, it looks like we finally found you," he said triumphantly. He lifted me off the ground and I kicked and screamed and tried to bite him, but he kept his arms out of danger. I felt one of his arms let go but before I could take advantage of it, he had stuffed a gag in my mouth. I felt a momentary panic, but I kept kicking.

Another man emerged from behind a tree in another direction. Wordlessly, he picked up Jimmy and led the way as Harry dragged me back into the fairgrounds.

Through my struggles, I could see that Father Jonathan was about to perform the ritual on this year's third Mayfly, the little girl.

As Harry worked his way through the crowd, I could hear growing murmurs of interest all around but never a sound of protest. I closed my eyes and prayed that I would wake up from this nightmare immediately.

The two men climbed the stairs and Jimmy was dumped unceremoniously at Father Jonathan's feet. Harry shoved me to my knees and then pulled the gag from my mouth.

" 'Nother mayfly or two," he said.

Father Jonathan stepped away from the little girl and looked down at Jimmy. The teenager's eyes were still rolling around in his head. He really looked as if he had been clobbered.

"Did you do this?" Father Jonathan asked Harry.

"Nope. Found him that way when we found her."

"Did you do it?" he asked me.

I nodded and started to cry.

"How?"

"I don't know," I blurted out between sobs. "I just touched him."

"Oh? Interesting." He was staring at me with a funny look in his eyes. "I think you should stay with me. Harry, take your son to my house."

I had been feeling strangely apart from everything that was happening, but then I saw the crowd staring at me and I suddenly became very self-conscious.

Harry reached down and dutifully lifted Jimmy into his arms. He gave me a puzzled look as he went down the stairs and turned back into the crowd.

From the stage, I could see most of Ashley Falls. It was simply black. There wasn't a single light anywhere, except here at the fairgrounds. In a moment, I heard a truck being started up. Harry's. The two headlight beams suddenly knifed through the inky night like a pair of surgeon's scalpels, then they moved off.

I expected the festival to end now that I had intruded. Instead, Father Jonathan guided me to the back of the stage and softly told me to be patient. He then returned to the little girl and old man still standing at the front of the stage. I continued to watch with interest.

Five or ten minutes later, the Mayfly Festival of Ashley Falls drew to a close. The fourth victim, the old man, was left on the stage, his shoes dangling over the edge. Father Jonathan stepped to the front of the stage and gave a brief speech in his mellow voice that penetrated to the crowd at the rear of the grounds.

"My children, I am afraid we must alter the ceremony somewhat this year because of incidents beyond our control. The Transference from the Life-Givers, this year's mayflies, will not take place tonight."

There was a distinct mutter of disapproval from the people of Ashley Falls.

"Hear me out, please!" Father Jonathan continued. "This is only a temporary delay but a necessary one, believe me. The Transference will take place here beginning at one p.m. tomorrow afternoon. Please sing with me now, then return to your homes and come back tomorrow."

Father Jonathan began to sing a song I had never heard before. Actually, it was more of a chant than a song, and it increased in volume as more and more of the people put aside their disappointment and joined in. For some reason that I couldn't fathom, I found myself sharing in their disappointment.

I stood at the back of the stage wondering what was

going to happen to me now. I tried to make myself as small as possible, hoping they'd just forget about me.

And then it ended. Just like that. The crowd finished the chant and then slowly broke up. Little groups from the edges moved away first, then gradually, the entire town went home. Lights began returning to Ashley Falls—car lights, then a few houselights, and before long, the streetlights returned. Like a great dazzling spiral moving from the center out, Ashley Falls returned to life.

The whole time, not a word was uttered. The only sound came from the cars driving off.

Two men drove a van across the grass to the front of the stage. They jumped out, opened the rear doors, and began loading the bodies.

I watched the scene silently, fascinated in the same way the rodent watches the cobra. Staring death straight in the face, with no way to fight back.

Father Jonathan stood on the stage until the crowd had completely dispersed and the two men had finished their ghoulish job. When the last person was gone, he finally turned to me.

"You really surprise me, Lisa," he said as he approached me.

"Oh?"

"I've never before come across anyone else with The Gift."

"The Gift?"

"I take it you don't know."

"No, I don't know anything."

He took a deep breath. There was a tone in his voice somewhere between sorrow and resignation. "I think we'd better have a talk, my dear." He walked to the stage stairs, and I followed.

We drove in Father Jonathan's Chevy to his house. It was huge, a mansion, in fact, painted white with blue trim, and beautifully kept up.

I felt pretty strange being with him after everything I'd

witnessed this evening. Not quite fearful, but apprehensive and . . . and waiting. I knew I was on the verge of some kind of new discovery about myself. A discovery that left an empty feeling of foreboding deep in my stomach.

We pulled into his driveway and, not surprisingly, Harry's truck was there, although when we entered the house, he was nowhere to be seen.

Father Jonathan wouldn't talk to me immediately. He excused himself and went upstairs to get out of the black vestments he was wearing. Ten minutes later he returned in a pair of tan corduroy trousers and light blue dress shirt. I looked for a little alligator, but there wasn't one.

He went through the usual host amenities. At my request, he returned from the kitchen with a diet soda. Then he poured himself a drink of Kahlua and brandy over the rocks. He offered me a taste when I commented on how unusual it was and when I demurred, he smiled and called it his "chocolate thunder."

He took a very large first sip.

Sitting across from me in his living room, he somehow reminded me of a concerned adult preparing to have a serious conversation with a young child. From a roomful of beautiful antiques, he chose a stickback rocking chair to settle in. Then he began his story.

"Perhaps I should begin by telling you how I discovered I had The Gift, Lisa. I wasn't too much younger than you are now. About nineteen, I believe. It was such a long time ago, it's hard to remember."

"Father Jonathan," I interrupted, wanting to get at least one point settled, "if you don't mind my asking, when was that?"

He laughed politely. "I don't mind at all, my dear. It was 1854."

Turn to page 53.

THE GIFT

"Hey, niggra, what you doin' out there? Get your ass movin'."

The whip cracked once on Jonathan's naked back as he stood before the woodpile. The slave took a deep breath and lifted the axe once again. Already this morning, he had split half a cord of wood for the master's house. It was only midmorning, but the sun was beating down unmercifully and even here in the shade, the temperature was nearing ninety degrees. But as hot as it was, it was time to start stockpiling the extra wood that would be needed for heat on the Hansen plantation in the winter.

Jonathan watched as the master's son, Edward, strode haughtily back to the porch, whip tightly rerolled in his right hand. He sat down in a rocker and a pair of young black children resumed fanning him. Jonathan remembered that job from the days when, as a youngster, he used to fan Edward's father. That was when the plantation had been fun, when there were fish to catch, frogs to chase, food to steal from Beliza in the kitchen. Before Jonathan understood what life was like for his parents. He never dreamed that the minor chores he was given then would grow into a lifelong job of monotony and repression.

Jonathan raised the axe and swung once more.

The master was old now and not interested in much besides dying. Edward, the future master, was taking control of the plantation. His father had been harsh at times, in a sort of nonchalant manner, taking for granted that occasional pain was both necessary and normal.

But Edward was another matter. Cruelty was all he understood and all he dispensed.

Jonathan wedged his axe into another log, lifted them both as high as he could, and slammed them, much harder than necessary, down on the tree stump in front of him. The two-foot log split neatly down the middle.

Hours later, he was done for the day. Edward hadn't bothered him again. He had disappeared shortly after reprimanding Jonathan and hadn't been seen the rest of the afternoon.

Tomorrow would find Jonathan back at it again. And the day after. Until the job was finished. But now, it was time to quit. Jimbob, an older slave with short, graying, curly hair and one of the two slaves who could tell time, had stopped by a moment earlier to let him know it was seven o'clock—dinner time. Jonathan left the axe leaning against the woodpile and returned to his shanty. He was sweating heavily and the bucket of water he was allowed to keep nearby was just about empty. Jonathan lifted it to his lips and chugged down the last, tepid cupful. It didn't do much to quench his thirst, but it was all he had.

Jonathan was oddly cheerful. More because the work day was over than anything else. Now there would be a few hours to relax before bed. Late evenings and Sunday afternoons were their only time off. And that was worth a smile or two. Recreation was singing, mostly, since none of the slaves could read or write. Music, though, was allowed. The African chants they brought with them fifty years ago had changed somewhat, but it was still the only way to teach the children a language the whites couldn't understand. It was their sole means of resistance to their lifestyle.

Jonathan strode through the slave quarters strong and haughty. At nineteen, he was easily able to take the hard work. A few children clustered around him, willing him to notice them. One took his bucket, then they all ran off, giggling. They had eaten already. Before the master took ill, they were fed quite well—an investment for the future. Now, however, they were always hungry. Under Edward, only the workers had enough to eat. Not surprisingly, the older slaves shared their food with the youngsters. Edward wasn't aware of it, but he was sowing the seeds of weakness among the very people he wanted to keep strong.

Jonathan entered the plywood shanty he shared with his

parents and two sisters. The latter were both younger than he, one thirteen and one sixteen. The sixteen-year-old lay on a bed in a dingy corner crying. And bleeding from the crotch. Jonathan's mother sat beside her, holding a limp arm around her daughter's shoulders.

Jonathan, his breathing suddenly hard and sharp, looked around the room, his eyebrows furled. "Poppa, what happened?"

Jonathan's father had tears in his eyes, too.

"He wenched her. Just come in here like a storm and dragged her off to some part of the fields."

Jonathan looked around the room for his younger sister. "Where's Anna?"

"Off with Jimbob and his people. She be all right."

"And what about Sirra?" he asked, nodding toward his sister in the corner.

Jonathan's father wiped a tear away. "She live. But inside she dead."

Jonathan wiped away a tear, too. Frustration was a part of life on the plantation. Some nights, all you could do was cry.

The heat the next morning was just as overbearing as the day before. Jonathan stood before the woodpile incapable of getting started. He took a deep breath and grabbed the first log.

Hours later, Edward emerged from the Big House and returned to the rocking chair from which he watched the slaves. "Fan, you pick'ninny bastards." The slave children were already at work.

Jonathan worked on the woodpile for long minutes before provoking Edward. He dropped the axe and took a healthy sip from the tin ladle in his bucket. Edward didn't say anything until Jonathan sat down beneath the huge maple tree towering over the woodpile.

"Hey, niggra, what the hell you doin'?"

Jonathan merely stared back.

"Niggra!"

Edward was not used to this kind of insubordination. He leapt from his chair and strode angrily toward Jonathan, his hands automatically coiling his whip, ready to strike.

"You'd best get yo' ass movin', niggra. You got a lot of work to do." The whip flashed out at Jonathan's left side. But instead of taking it passively like he did yesterday, Jonathan reached out and snagged the end of the whip. The pain in his arm bit hard through the muscle, but he held on and yanked it in toward him.

Edward, unable to resist the pull, fell forward. Jonathan grabbed him by the neck and held him, but didn't squeeze. He had one thought going through his mind.

I want him dead.

Suddenly, Jonathan felt Edward go limp. He pulled the whip from his hand and grabbed Edward by the right arm. There was no resistance.

Jonathan felt a surge run through his hands. It was like nothing he had ever felt before. Powerful. Invigorating.

A moment later, Edward slumped over, dead.

Jonathan, bewildered, stood and stared at his master. He knew he had not applied enough pressure to do that. Somehow, somehow, he had simply *drained* Edward's life away. *He had wished him dead!*

Jonathan had done what he had set out to do, but he had no plan beyond this point. He realized that the children on the porch were staring at him blankly. Something evil had happened and they stood in shock, no more aware than Jonathan of what to do next.

Then Jonathan ran. Back to the slave quarters. There he found only Jimbob, sitting on a stoop whittling a stick. His black felt hat curled down over his eyes. He was too old to work. His only job was to keep the slaves in line.

Jonathan wasn't sure Jimbob was aware he was there, until the old slave suddenly asked, "You got The Gift, ain'tcha?"

"Huh?"

"The Gift. You jest used it, too. C'n tell. It's in yer

eyes."

Jonathan was almost crying. "What I done, Jimbob?"

"Knowed you had it from the day you was aborned. I'se there. Yer eyes had a gleam in 'em that day. It goes away and don't come back till you uses it. I know. I got it, too." Jimbob kept whittling.

"What's it do?"

"Makes you strong and young. And kills."

"You ever use it?"

"Nope. Been Lawd Amighty temptated now an' agin, but ain't never. Don't wanna live forever. Jes' wanna be outta here . . . outta Hansen, outta Virginny, outta this life."

"Then how you know 'bout mah eyes?"

"I seen that look in mah daddy's eyes," Jimbob said quietly as he stopped whittling for a moment. "Sometimes after a raid on another tribe. Once't after the first time slavers come to our village. The time was jest afore a slaver's bullet caught him in the throat. But there was a dead slaver lyin' under him when he went down. Dead from The Gift." Jimbob smiled forlornly as he went back to his whittling.

"Lotsa folks got it?"

"P'rtic'lar few. Even some whites here 'n' there, I'm tol'."

"What I do now, Jimbob?"

"Run. There's some folks what'll help ya. Good whites. Gots to look for 'em, though. You gots to hide at day an' run like a rabbit at night."

"Where these good whites?"

"Don't rightly know. They's aroun' somewheres. You gots to be lucky."

"You come with me, Jimbob?"

"Nossuh. Gots to stay here and keep the Lawd's watch out for our people. 'Sides, someone gots to tell yer folks where you off to."

"You'll take care of 'em, won't ya, Jimbob?"

57

"Don't never worry 'bout that, boy."

As Jonathan stood, a thought struck him. "You know what I did, don't you?"

"May Edward's black soul rest in twisted pieces."

"Where I go now?"

Jimbob stood and faced Jonathan for the first time. "They ain't working the south forty today. You c'n prob'ly sneak out thataway. Circle the plantation quickly and head north. I knowed you learnt real good how to tell the North Star with the he'p o' the Dipper, so's you jest keep it in front of you. If you cain't see the Dipper, then put sunrise on this shoulder"—he tapped Jonathan's right shoulder— "and put sunset on this one." He tapped the left shoulder. "Good luck, boy. Use The Gift wisely."

Tears blinding him, Jonathan ran through the tobacco fields of the south forty without seeing anyone. He slipped through a line of trees and across a dirt road. He was off Hansen Plantation. He sneaked north at night living in barns or under the stars, eating when he could, stealing when he had to, avoiding contact with anyone.

Without knowing it, he crossed over into Pennsylvania. Two weeks after Edward's death, he found himself starting his nightly walk with a bright, full moon just rising. He came to a huge, open meadow, but was too exhausted from hunger to plod through the distant woods that surrounded it, so he stepped out into the grass. Soon the meadow began to make a slight rise. Normally, he hated not being able to see where he was headed, but at this point, he didn't much care. He was trusting to the Lord.

As he neared the crest, the roof of a farmhouse slowly came into view. Jonathan crouched down and crawled to the top of the rise. The farmhouse was just below him and beyond it were fields full of corn. He lay in the grass watching. The house was a somewhat ramshackle building, evidently a dingy gray and in dire need of paint. Lamps were blazing in most of the windows. Four horses were tied to a front railing. Moments later, a group of people stepped out of the front door. Two of them were black. They and two others climbed up on the horses. Three others, including a woman and a child, stood on the porch. Jonathan was close enough to hear their conversation.

"All right, Sammy," one of them was saying to one of the blacks, "you'll be passed along to the next house. The hardest part's over. You oughta make it to Canada within a month or so. Good luck to ya."

"The Lawd be good to ya!" said the black man.

Jonathan noticed the white man's accent was definitely unlike any he had ever heard before. He thanked the Lord that he had somehow stumbled on some of those people who help runaway slaves. Praying that he wasn't making a mistake, he picked himself up from the ground, brushed himself off, and walked down toward the farmhouse.

Three weeks later, he was being sneaked into the town of Ashley Falls. He had spent four days hiding in the Simpson house and as soon as he was rested and fed, he was taken to another home in rural Pennsylvania. From there, he spent brief periods in safehouses throughout New York. They never let him stay long once they learned he was wanted for murder.

"Let me tell you something, boy," Thomas Simpson had told him as he was wolfing down the first hot meal he'd had since he left the plantation, "you're gonna have to run a lot faster than the usual people that come through here. We don't care much what happened down in Virginia, but there's a big group of people out looking for you right about now. I don't know where they are right this minute, but they're out there and you gotta stay two steps ahead of 'em, not just one."

In Ashley Falls, the safehouse was on the edge of town, a fair distance away from the few other homes that made up the tiny village. Years later, Jonathan would return to this house as Father Jonathan. For now, he was ushered into the cellar and hidden in a small room behind a false wall. He didn't know it then, but that room in the Andersen house would be his shelter for another month.

It was in Ashley Falls that he fell less than two steps ahead of the pursuing pack. He was having dinner with Paul Andersen and his wife, both spry, lively people in their early sixties. Mr. Andersen had once been a state senator with dreams of going to Washington to fight slavery. That hadn't worked out—he had a terrible habit of losing the important elections by great majorities. After two tries, he had given up and redirected his fervor to the Underground Railroad. "There are still things we can do to fight this ignominy," he told his wife, Mary. She quickly agreed.

The Andersens, not just concerned with saving bodies, started to teach Jonathan to read and write as soon as he was rested.

"You'll need this eventually, son." Paul Andersen was the first white man to call him "son" rather than "boy."

Jonathan made remarkable progress. Up to third grade level and improving in only a few lessons. Right in the middle of one of those lessons, however, came a terrible pounding at the door. Paul Andersen answered the door. It was a neighbor, a young man.

"What is it, Harold?"

"The Fed'ral boys 're on their way, Paul. We best get Jonathan outta here. I hear they're comin' to see you."

"All right then. Jonathan! You come here, son."

Jonathan joined them at the door. "You go along here with Harold. He'll take care of you until it's safe to bring you back here."

Jonathan understood, and he stepped immediately out into the black night. Harold took him deep into the woods. It rained heavily that night. From a hilltop, Jonathan watched as a number of Federal troopers marched into and out of the Andersen house. They didn't stay long and soon mounted up and rode back down the mountainside. Harold came looking for Jonathan an hour later.

"They hurt anyone?" Jonathan wanted to know.

"Naw, they never do. They're on our side, really. They

got their orders, though, and they'll haul you in if they catch you, but they don' bother no one much more than they have to. They'll be back, though, so you better be ready to run at a moment's notice."

Jonathan nodded. Harold proved correct. Federal troopers returned to Ashley Falls ten times in the following two weeks. Several times, Jonathan fled into the woods. A few times, he hid in the room behind the false wall. No one in Ashley Falls, whether they were even aware of the activities of the neighbors, was immune. "Just a big inconvenience, nothing more," Paul Andersen told him.

"They always come this often?"

Andersen had never lied to Jonathan and he didn't start now. "No, son, they don't."

"Is it on accounta I killed someone?"

"I'm afraid so. But don't you worry. They're not harmin' people. Just lookin' around. But it'd be wise to get you away from here as soon as we can."

By a week after the last search, it was obvious that the troopers had moved elsewhere. It was decided that the time for Jonathan to move on had come. A relatively quiet ride with Harold brought him to an unguarded stretch of the border with Canada. "Well, boy, you're on your own now. You should be okay as long as you stay north of this here line. It mightn't hurt to change your name, neither. Good luck to you."

Harold reached out and shook Jonathan's hand.

"I stayed in Canada for nine years," Father Jonathan continued. "In 1863, I joined the Union Army. I was cashiered out in 1866 carrying an honorable discharge and a full pardon. I returned to the plantation only to find everyone was gone. I still don't know what happened to them all. I never saw any of my family again. Nor any of the other people I grew up with. Edward Hansen was in prison. Don't know how long he stayed there.

"I had no desire to return to Canada; I never really felt I

61

belonged there. With nowhere else to go, I returned here, to Ashley Falls.

"When I came back, I found that the Andersens were both gone. He had died of some disease around 1860 and his lovely wife followed less than six months later." Father Jonathan smiled ironically. "Consumption, folks said, but I know she died of loneliness. My friend Harold was killed at Gettysburg. To this day, I can't help but feel that he died for me. Not for the abolition of slavery, or black people in general, but for me specifically. I know that sounds a little crazy and isn't really true, but still . . .

"As for The Gift that Jimbob warned me about, I did have an occasion to use it again. Several times, in fact. That's how I found out what its power was." His eyes looked into the distance.

The sun rose white and cool over the Mississippi town of Yazoo City that March morning in 1864.

Jonathan stood behind a breastwork shouldering his carbine. His regiment, the Third U.S. Colored Cavalry, was strung out along either side of him awaiting the Confederate charge. It came around ten a.m. and was furious in its intensity. Jonathan's regiment was pushed back, over a road and toward a nearby ditch. Enemy minie balls whistled overhead and all around. More often than Jonathan wished to notice, he heard the nauseating sound of lead tearing through flesh.

The man next to him fell, and Jonathan knelt beside him.

"Billy, where you hit?"

"My laig, Jonathan. You gets outta here."

Jonathan ignored Billy's words and looked at his friend's wound. It probably looked nastier than it really was; the bullet had torn off a large piece of his thigh, and it was bleeding pretty heavily. If he could stop that, Billy would probably live, although gangrene might claim the leg later. But to leave him here would surely mean he'd die at the hands of the Rebels. Not just because he was a Union soldier, either. The color of his skin had something to with it, too.

Hearing a soldier yell, "Get the niggers!" Jonathan grabbed Billy by the collar and dragged him over the edge into a shallow ditch.

A moment later, a Reb came flying over the ridge. He was a young man, but his face displayed an ancient hatred. With a scream, he charged straight at Jonathan.

Jonathan snatched his carbine from the ground and swung it wildly. The butt end caught the Reb's bayonet and sent him spinning off balance. Jonathan jumped up and grabbed the Reb by the neck with one hand and knocked his musket away with the other.

Kill or be killed. I want him dead!

Jonathan felt that almost-forgotten powerful surge run through his body again. The Confederate soldier suddenly went limp and dropped to the ground. Jonathan leaned over the soldier, whose breathing had stopped. Billy lay on the ground nearby; his breathing was laborious and raspy. Jonathan turned to him.

"It's gonna be okay, now, Billy," he said soothingly. "You jest wait and see."

He reached down and cupped the back of his friend's head. Suddenly he felt the charge in his body flow back through his hands.

Billy's eyes fluttered, and he asked, "What's goin' on?"

Jonathan listened for a minute. The Confederates had run past their hiding place, their cries fading into the distance. "I think they're gone. They may be back, though."

Billy suddenly stood and pointed off to the south. "C'mon, we'll hightail it out this way and go 'round 'em."

Jonathan was amazed. "You get back down there! You're still bleedin'!"

Billy looked down at his leg and seemed startled to find it bleeding. He tore off a piece of his shirt and wrapped it around his wound. "Stranges' thing," he mumbled. "Jest

---

all of a sudden got this real shot o' strength. There . . . that'll hold the blood. Now let's head outta here."

They stumbled south, perpendicular to the Confederate advance. They managed to run before the second wave and emerge from the line of breastworks only to find more enemy troops marching along a road in front of them in a long, dusty gray line. They ducked back down behind some trees, watching carefully. Before long, it was obvious that the Rebels were marching away from them, away from the battlefield. From off in the distance, they could hear the bugles and drums of their own army approaching.

"By damn," Jonathan whispered. "We whupped 'em after all."

"Not rightly. They whupped us, then they run into more of us than they is o' them," Billy corrected him.

They settled down among the trees, staying out of sight of any Rebel stragglers, until the Federals arrived. They were taken to a doctor who treated Billy's wound. "Now you say he jest up and run off, jest like that?" The doctor snapped his fingers.

"Yessir," replied Jonathan. "Don't know what shook him like that, but that's what he did, all right," Jonathan answered. "Didn't even hafta he'p him."

"Ain't never seen nothing like that before, lemme tell you. Why, he shouldn't be able to stand 'tall with all the blood and muscle he's lost."

"He gonna be okay, doc?"

"Yeah, he'll live. Hope to God he don't catch gangrene, but even if he does, he only lose the leg, not his life. You boys won't be seein' each other 'til after the war, though."

If you came to Father Jonathan's for dinner, *turn to page 123*.

If you came here after the festival, *turn to page 65*.

LIFE-GIVER

"Fact of the matter is, Lisa, I never saw Billy again at all." Father Jonathan leaned back in his chair, his story now obviously almost over. "Even the name of the battle sounds pretty darn silly—'The Battle of Yazoo City'." He smiled.

"In any event, that little incident at the Battle of Yazoo City gave me my first clue of the power of The Gift. I couldn't ask Jimbob what it was, and as I said, I never saw him again, either, so it really didn't matter, anyway. I had to experiment on my own.

"Now here you are with that same ability. Jimbob was right. You can see a sparkle in the eyes of someone who has just used The Gift. You had it. Dimly. Maybe because you didn't kill Jimmy." Father Jonathan sighed heavily as if a great weight were on his shoulders. "I knew someday I'd find someone like you. Sooner or later . . . "

I sat in silence, feeling like a child caught with his hand in the cookie jar.

"I wish I knew why some of us have it," he continued. "Some sort of mental aberration, I suspect. And I suspect there are actually quite a large number of people who have it and don't know it."

That was curious. "Why?" I asked.

Father Jonathan turned toward me. "How old are you, Lisa?"

"Huh?"

"If I may be so personal."

"Well, twenty-three."

"And in almost a quarter century of life, how many times have you tried to kill someone before today?"

I was beginning to understand his logic. "Never," I said with a shudder.

"Of course not. Until Jimmy became such a threat to you, you had never been in a self-defense situation. Neither have most people. And most people who do kill—for whatever the reason—do it with a weapon. It's pretty rare to try and kill someone with your hands."

"In other words, most people never have an opportunity to find out they have it."

"Correct, my dear. But I know there are a lot us with the latent ability. Jimbob was wrong when he said 'p'rtic'lar few' have it. Particularly few *know* they have it. It was just a matter of time before someone like you arrived here. In fact, over the years, I'm sure some of our mayflies had The Gift. Just never knew. At least, that's my theory."

"What exactly is this Gift?" I wanted to know.

"I'm not exactly sure myself. I've studied and studied, but still don't have any real definitive answer. Apparently, it drains away the 'life force,' if you will, of the victim and then transfers it to ourselves. We in turn can transfer it to others. And it gives them strength and even extends their lives."

"You mean I can keep people from dying?"

"Oh, no. They could be killed in an auto accident for example. But it can help people heal and it can virtually stop them from growing old. However, it cannot bring the dead back to life."

"What about that chanting and the vestments and things? What do they have to do with it?"

"Absolutely nothing. Merely ritualistic claptrap. Theater. For the good of the show, so to speak. The chant, by the way, is an African tribal chant I learned on the plantation. It is suitably ominous and pretentious and unintelligible enough so that it sounds like it belongs to the ceremony, but it doesn't. Only one thing is required."

I already knew what that was. The desire to see the victim die. And Father Jonathan knew that I understood that.

"I came back here because these people once saved me. I felt I owed them something in return for my life, so I have given them theirs to the extent that I can.

"Most of the people from those days are gone now. Over

the years, they died of things The Gift cannot change. But Harry is one of the originals. He's Harold's son, the one who first hid me in the woods that night. You might be surprised to know that Jimmy is actually over eighty years old himself. But to keep them alive means that others must become Life-Givers. Of course, I benefit, too, and I'm not fond of the idea of dying.

"I think the mayfly is an appropriate symbol of that, don't you? It lives only one day a year so that it can pass on the beauty of life to another generation."

I nodded quietly in agreement. Father Jonathan put his drink down and stood.

"This is the Andersen's old home. Most of it has been remodeled . . . several times, in fact . . . over the years, but one portion has never been changed. I'd like to show that to you now, if you'd like."

He took me by the hand and led me to the cellar stairs. He told me more about The Gift as we walked.

"The transferral of life affects different people in different ways. Harry seems somewhat resistant, so he does indeed grow old at a very slow place. Jimmy is very receptive. He stays young. Why, I can't really say."

He led me into the basement and through a twisted maze of corridors. As we got farther from the stairwell, the wood paneling gave way to to plasterboard, to plywood, then to brickwork, and finally to ancient two by fours with a musty odor that stank of long dead secrets.

The corridor now seemed more like a tunnel than a hallway. I had to follow Father Jonathan single file and occasionally had to duck down slightly to avoid low hanging timbers. He stopped in front of a wall of decaying bricks. Father Jonathan stood on one side and, with a great heave, actually pushed it back into the sides of the tunnel. Surprisingly, there was hardly a sound.

Behind the false wall was a tiny room lit by one bare bulb. Beneath the bulb stood Harry, holding a shotgun rather nonchalantly. Slumped in a corner was Jimmy, his head down between his upraised knees.

Father Jonathan spoke to me again. "You see, Jimmy here, even with his great age, still has the impetuosity of youth. I should probably tell you that last year, we had to sacrifice his mother at the festival. She had suddenly decided that the ceremony was immoral even though she was, for many years, the willing recipient of the fruit of The Gift. Isn't that right, Jimmy? Have you ever managed to reconcile her hypocrisy in your own mind, my son?"

Jimmy only nodded dully. He looked dazed and in shock, as if he had just been in auto accident, only there was no blood. I stepped around Father Jonathan and lifted the boy's head. The eyes were glassy, uncomprehending.

"Drugged," Father Jonathan explained. "As you saw, any reasonably healthy human being can slide that door open. So we keep our little mayflies drugged until we need them."

I looked up at Harry. "This is your son. Don't you care what happens to him?"

Harry spat. "He's lived long enough. I been through more wives and sons and daughters than I care to count. Most of 'em got themselves killed one way or another. I got plenty left. One more in the ground ain't gonna bother me none, especially when they been tryin' to drag me along with 'em."

Father Jonathan had an odd look in his eye. "Lisa, please wait outside," he said without looking at me. I stepped back into the ancient corridor and Harry slid the false wall closed, like a nurse closing the curtains to give a hospital patient some privacy.

I slumped back against the dirty wall too tired and sick to hold myself up. Oh, dear God, how could I have such an ability? How was I going to handle it? I can't do this to people . . .

Before the answers came, the false wall opened. Father Jonathan stepped out first, followed by Harry carrying his son's lifeless body. My heart was lead and I wanted to cry, but wouldn't let myself. It made it harder not to. Father Jonathan took me by the arm and spoke to me as we walked down the corridor.

"I'd like to ask a favor of you, Lisa. I'd like you to stay for the Transference of Life tomorrow. I think you'll understand more if you do. So far, you've only seen the evil side of The Gift. There's much more."

I nodded dully. What else could I do? My car was broken down, and I was miles from help. "Okay," I whispered.

He guided me back upstairs the same way you help women at wakes and funerals.

I got sick that night, and spent most of my time in the bathroom, trying to throw up. I hadn't eaten any dinner (despite Father Jonathan's repeated exhortations, how could I?) and I dry heaved for what seemed like hours.

The bathroom was a private one, accessible only from the two bedrooms on either side, but not from the hallway. I was in a guest room on the second floor. Father Jonathan brought me here, then went back downstairs after he settled me in. Apparently, his room was on the first floor. I was grateful for that, although I wasn't really afraid of him anymore. I was afraid of myself. Of what I'd suddenly become. I was a killer. Maybe not literally, but the potential of my awful power sure made me feel like one. I just wanted to leave this horrible town and forget I'd ever been here.

I cried myself to sleep that night when exhaustion finally overcame my sickness

In the morning, I stumbled downstairs after trying my best to fix up my appearance. A quick shower and a feeble attempt to put on make-up and eyeshadow were no help. My hair was wet and stringy. I knew I looked like I had a terrific hangover.

Pulling a chair out from his kitchen table, I dropped into

AMAZING

it wearily.

Father Jonathan smiled. "Would you like some breakfast?"

I could hear eggs and bacon sizzling, but they didn't smell very appetizing. It had nothing to do with his cooking. I shook my head.

"As you wish." He put a cup in front of me anyway. I just stared at it.

He watched me for a few minutes. "Lisa, I know how you feel. This is not an easy thing to learn about oneself, I'm sure." He stepped around behind me and put his hands on my shoulders. I was too apathetic too pull away if he did try to use The Gift. Maybe I was better off joining Jimmy anyway.

But Father Jonathan did nothing of the kind. He just gave me a massage. I had to admit, it felt pretty good to have him rub my shoulders. I rolled my head around my neck to relieve more of the tension.

As he continued, I became more and more relaxed. It was like being hypnotized in a way. Even his speech sounded like a hypnotist's.

"I'll take good care of you, Lisa. We're two of a kind, you know."

I closed my eyes and relaxed even more.

"There's much I can teach you about The Gift. Including an ability that Jimmy and his mother were somewhat resistant to. You're not, though. I can feel that."

His words started fading right about then. After that, all I could remember was him saying, "Stay with me, Lisa, stay with me."

Sometime later, I awoke feeling refreshed. No more than a few minutes could have passed because I was still in the kitchen chair with Father Jonathan behind me.

"Feeling better?" he asked.

"Yes, much."

He smiled again. "Excellent, excellent."

He took me by the hand. "Now, we must discuss your

future."

"I, uh, I don't know . . ."

"You will, I'm sure. Wait until the Transference this afternoon before you decide."

"Yes, I will. I . . . " It was funny how I suddenly found it hard to say no to this man. Last night, I had every intention of leaving Ashley Falls far, far behind. But, now, I wasn't so sure. In fact, I had an irresistable desire to simply be with him.

"I can't let you go, I'm afraid," he said soothingly. "You know too much and you are already too powerful. We must work together now."

His words were certainly logical. I couldn't argue with him. I agreed with him, in fact.

"Good, good. Now I have some work to do before the Transference takes place. There will be a very special ceremony this afternoon as well. Please make yourself at home, Lisa."

I stayed in the kitchen until Father Jonathan was ready to leave. I felt better, and I knew I should be thinking about leaving Ashely Falls, like I planned. But, it was the oddest thing—every time I thought about going, my mind went blank! It seemed like there was a hole in it! Finally, I gave up thinking about leaving at all. It was too much effort now. I was tired. I'd think about it later, after I'd rested.

I stayed in the kitchen until Father Jonathan was ready to leave. By twelve-thirty, Father Jonathan and I were standing once again on the stage at the fairgrounds. The crowd was already beginning to gather in front of us. He was wearing the same black robe he had worn the night before. The "work he had to do" was to make crude alterations on another robe for me. He had time to bring up the hems and take in the sleeves, although his judgement was poor and they were still slightly too large. He hadn't even touched the shoulders. Even in my mind-numbed state, I felt pretty foolish.

"You will help me today, Lisa," he said as he helped me

into the robe. "Just follow my instructions. It won't be difficult."

I nodded.

The crowd watched us in obvious amazement, buzzing with curiosity. I guess it was around one o'clock when Father Jonathan raised his arms. The mob immediately quieted down.

"My children," Father Jonathan bellowed in a great theatrical voice. "Today, we welcome one more with The Gift. She is here to serve you and to aid me. You shall treat her as you do me. Today, she will participate in the Transference of Life to you all."

He then turned toward me and whispered, "Lisa, please face me." I did so. Once again, he put his hands on me again, this time on top of my head. I felt those same feelings of relaxation and subservience come over me as they had earlier at Father Jonathan's. It lasted only a moment before it was replaced by a powerful surge, a strong bolt of pleasurable electricity. Father Jonathan took his hands down. The rush of power was gone and I was sorry that it was.

He whispered to me again. "Lisa, you now have part of the life force I drained from the mayflies yesterday. You can now transfer this to my . . . our . . . people. Just place your hands on the heads of the people as they stand in front of you. A few seconds will suffice."

He turned back to the crowd. "Marilyn Pintriccio! Bring Amy up here! She will have the honor of becoming Lisa's first recipient."

The throng at the front stirred slightly as a woman in her thirties and a young girl about six approached the stage. They climbed the stairs, and Marilyn stood in front of Father Jonathan. He placed his hands on her head as he had done to me, but for a far shorter length of time. Marilyn smiled contentedly and stepped aside.

I looked down. Amy was staring at me, apparently wondering why I hadn't placed my hands on her. She had her blonde hair tied back in cute little pigtails.

"I like you better already, lady. You're a lot prettier than Father Jonathan," she said, smiling. Those near enough to hear, including Father Jonathan, laughed.

Could keeping this little girl six years old alive for as long as possible really be so wrong? Father Jonathan was right—there was a beautiful side to The Gift as well.

I smiled back at the little girl and placed my hands on her head.

And I knew I'd be staying right here in Ashley Falls with a whole new, wonderful life ahead of me.

THE END

FOLLOWED!

"I certainly am glad that you've decided to join in the fun. Permit me to drive you to the fairgrounds," Father Jonathan said.

"Why, thank you." He held the door for me as I climbed into his car. I had to admit one thing about Father Jonathan. He was the most gentlemanly individual I'd run into in an awfully long time.

As he drove the few blocks to the fairgrounds, I asked him about the pins that everyone seemed to be wearing.

"Oh, these," he said, fingering the button on his own lapel. His voice took on an ominous tone, but it was layered inside a smile. "Nasty things happen to those who are caught without one."

"Oh?" Even I could hear the apprehension in my voice.

"Just a local joke. Please forgive me if I startled you."

"What exactly is that thing on the button?"

"The insect, you mean? It's a mayfly. Our festival is in their honor—the Mayfly Festival."

"Isn't a bug a rather odd thing to honor with a festival?"

"Yes, I admit it is indeed. But how much do you know about them?"

It was my turn to smile. "About mayflies? Nothing. Do they keep coming back, like the swallows at Capistrano?"

Father Jonathan laughed. "Well, the festival itself is not really in their honor so much as it is in honor of their life cycle. You see, mayflies hatch in the spring, right around this time, and live only about twenty-four hours or so, just long enough to breed the next generation, then they die. Their progeny pupate for a year until their time comes the following spring. I find it all very philosophical. Their entire life—what we do in seventy years—is crammed into one day."

"It still seems a bit odd to celebrate an insect."

"Perhaps it is. Did you know that the oldest town in

Connecticut holds a festival every year for a fish? The Shad Derby they call it, with a parade and a fair on the town green something like ours. It's in June, when the shad run up the Connecticut River in Windsor. The biggest difference is that they hold a competition for catching the largest shad. It would be a bit silly to try and catch the largest mayfly, but other than that, our festival's not so different."

"I suppose not. But what do the pins signify?"

"Nothing, really. They're just a fund-raising gimmick to pay for the festival."

I nodded politely.

By now, we had driven into a large park filled with tents and display stands. He climbed out of the car and hurried around to my door.

"I'll have to leave you on your own now. I hope you don't mind."

"Not at all."

"Please. Enjoy. I'll return later. I insist that you join me for dinner. I won't take no."

He climbed into his car and drove off before I could answer. Naturally, being a minister, he was supposed to be helpful, but still, he was something special. I was rather looking forward to seeing him later.

Walking through Ashley Fall's Mayfly Festival was really kind of fun. I've always enjoyed homemade crafts and hawkers and silly games. I spent a lot of time at each booth even if I wasn't really interested in what they were doing, simply because I knew I had plenty of time to kill.

I was surprised at the crowd. Much larger than I would have guessed. Every so often, someone would walk through the mob selling those little buttons with the mayfly on them. I had been at the fair probably for about an hour when I was accosted by one of the vendors. He was a young man dressed casually and wearing a clown face.

"Excuse me, miss, you haven't got your button."

"No, that's right, I guess I don't."

"They go to defray the cost of the festival and any left

over goes to charity. They're only a dollar. Won't you please help us out?"

I obviously couldn't resist. "Sure." I dug into my purse for my wallet while he fished into a large basket of buttons.

I had to wait with my dollar in my hand until he apparently found what he was looking for. He held a round button out to me. "Take this one. There aren't too many of this kind. I only give them to pretty girls."

I felt myself blushing a little as I gave him my money. He slipped the bill into his pocket, muttered a cursory "Thank you," and turned away into the crowd before I could thank him for the compliment.

I turned the button over and looked at it carefully. Somehow, it seemed a little different from the ones I had seen earlier. I stared at it, not finding anything at all different about the depiction of the mayfly. The very same piece of artwork that every other button had. I smiled and gave a light-hearted shrug at the vendor's blarney, and clipped the black-and-white button to my shoulder.

The sight of some home-made pickles reminded me that I was hungry, so I searched for the food tent. I expected just hot dogs and potato chips, maybe hamburgers, but the variety of the food I found surprised me. Besides the usuals, there were canolis, pierogis, pizza, bratwurst, steak sandwiches, and even teriyaki-on-a-stick. But it didn't take me long to decide on a large piece of fried dough drenched with melted butter and powdered sugar. You don't get that in New York City.

Although the festival was somewhat larger than I thought it might be, it still wouldn't take more than an afternoon to go through it completely—and slowly. I took my time wandering from booth to booth, absorbing the atmosphere. The vendors in the booths were friendly and seemed ready for a chat. I spent a lot of time watching the little kids, who were just thrilled by the spectacle.

Frankly, I forgot about the trouble with my car for the time being.

———

When I turned at the end of the first row of booths to come back up the second row, I saw for the first time a huge platform lined up perpendicularly to the rows of booths on either side. It rose about six feet off the ground. But unlike a regular stage, there were no backdrop or curtains. Placed at regular intervals around the sides and rear were about a dozen light stanchions. The set-up reminded me of the drawings I'd seen of ancient Greek plays with the torches burning brightly around the edges of the stage, providing more dramatic effect, I think, than spotlights.

The stage at the Ashley Falls Mayfly Festival was built solely of varnished wood and although the underpinnings were masked off with sheets of plywood, I imagined that it must be braced pretty well. It was a good thirty feet wide and probably fifteen or twenty feet deep. They must put on quite a production.

I wandered through the festival some more and saw just about everything there was to see in the booths. It was probably around three that I saw Father Jonathan coming toward me.

"So, my dear, how are you enjoying our little fair?"

"Quite a bit, actually. I can't believe the turn out."

"Oh, yes, the entire town, such as it is, is here. I see you have your button."

I looked down at the mayfly button. "Yes, I got stopped a while back."

Father Jonathan smiled. "You'll be pleased to know that I've run into Jerry Kosinski. After tomorrow, you won't have to worry about your car anymore."

"Oh, that's great. Thank you."

"You're quite welcome, my dear. I was happy to be of assistance. I have to go now and prepare for the ceremony tonight, but as I said earlier, I'd like to have you join me at my house for dinner tonight. Come around five. We'll phone your family then and you can be my special guest for the evening."

How could I refuse those manners? He gave me the

directions to his house, which didn't seem very far. I promised to be prompt.

With nothing particular to do for two hours, I wandered over to a large tent that covered a number of video games. I slipped a quarter into some game that had great graphics of a jet whizzing around a large city. I racked up something like 1,800 points blowing enemy jets out of the sky before I got shot down for a third time. I was about to reload my plane with another twenty-five cents worth of ammunition when I heard a voice behind me.

"Lady, am I glad I ran into you."

It was Jimmy, the boy from the gas station. He had changed into more presentable jeans and a sport shirt and had his hair wetly slicked down. Can't be grubby when you're out to impress the ladies, even at fifteen.

As I stepped away from the video game, he looked at me and frowned. "I see you got your button," he said.

I looked down at it. "Yes, I have. What's the matter? Don't you like it?"

"No, I don't. It's a white one."

"Yeah, so?"

He looked around anxiously. His gaze stopped on an older man playing Asteroids. "We can't talk here."

He started to turn away, but, suddenly angry, I grabbed his arm. "It seems like we can't talk anywhere. What kind of game is this?"

He sighed, frustrated. "Look, meet me in the alley between the rows of booths. Behind the SilverMar Silvercrafts one. But play a game first before you follow me, okay?"

If he had his own game going, he certainly took it seriously. I followed his glance to the booth he was talking about.

"Oh, all right. I'll play your little spy game, but I'm getting pretty tired of it."

He scurried off, away from our designated meeting point. I turned back to my game and saved the U.S. by blowing away 3,547 points worth of hostile hardware. I threw my pocketbook over my shoulder and trudged off after Jimmy.

I found him just where he said he'd be. No greeting, just "Quick, this way."

He grabbed my arm and pulled me into the crowd in the wide aisle leading to the stage.

"Now wait just a minute," I said, digging in my heels.

"You're being followed," he whispered.

"What?"

"I'm serious. Now c'mon."

He dragged me through the crowd in a crazy zigzag pattern, glancing back over his shoulder every once in a while. Somewhere near the fairground's entrance, he stopped.

"Okay, we lost him. I gotta tell you about that button you're wearing, lady. Haven't you noticed it's different from everyone else's?"

"Kind of, but how?"

"It's white. Every other one is some sort of pastel color."

I looked at his. Blue. It was certainly not white, but that didn't prove anything. "I give up. What does that mean?"

"It marks you as an outsider. A potential victim for the ceremony tonight."

"Victim? Oh, come on, Jimmy. Nobody paid me a lick of attention all day."

"Well, uh, of course not. They don't want to tip anything off. But have you seen anyone else wearing a black-and-white button?"

I sighed. "No. I wasn't going around all afternoon looking at people's chests," I said.

"You should have. It might have told you something."

"Yeah, that you have an excellent imagination."

Jimmy looked a little crestfallen. Maybe I was being too harsh on him. "I'm not kidding," he said, dropping his head a little. "The ceremony later tonight is when it all takes place."

"So what happens at this ceremony?" I eyed him suspiciously.

"I haven't got time to tell you that. The guy who was following you is coming back. Over there." He pointed out the man who had been playing Asteroids. He had dark hair and a thick black moustache. He would have looked sinister, except that he was wearing a tattered shirt and a pair of shorts showing bony knees.

"Who is he?" I wanted to know.

"George Miller. Good friend of my dad's and Father Jonathan's. It wouldn't be very smart if they caught us talking. Keep an eye on him if you don't believe me, but don't let him see you doing it. And at five o'clock, meet me back at the gas station. Whatever you do, don't go to Father Jonathan's for dinner."

"How'd you know about that?"

"I overheard you two talking. Oh, yeah. And check out everyone else's buttons while you're at it."

Before I could ask anything more, Jimmy, trying to look casual, sauntered off toward some of the booths. That George Miller was closer now, but all his attention was on some leathercraft items in one of the booths.

I walked toward the SilverMar booth behind Miller. As I pretended to study some belt buckles, Miller moved to another booth on the same side as SilverMar. But he still wasn't watching me. Coincidence, I was sure.

This nonsense was beginning to affect my judgment. I went back to the video games to kill the afternoon. And yes, I do have to admit I looked at a few of the mayfly buttons on my way to the games booth. And no, I didn't see any other black-and-white ones—only pastel. I shook my head, wondering why I was letting myself get sucked into Jimmy's imaginings. Surely, the color of the buttons didn't mean anything. And George Miller was probably up to nothing more than enjoying his afternoon.

A couple of games later, I had reached five digits on Ultimate Invader. Bored with that, I turned to find something else to play.

AMAZING

George Miller was in another corner of the tent playing Pac-Man.

I shuddered suddenly, involuntarily. This was getting pretty damn creepy all of a sudden. Could Jimmy possibly be telling the truth? Was this guy really following me? But why? What was the interest in me for these people? That damn ceremony Jimmy keeps talking about? I shuddered again, wondering what—if anything—I had gotten into.

I decided to give George Miller a good test.

I quickly left the game booth and headed into the crowd. I slipped into the alley between the rows of booths opposite where Jimmy and I had met. It was empty of people because only the backs of the booths faced toward it. I didn't go very far, only a couple of booths in, then ducked around the corner of one of them. Seconds later, George Miller appeared at the end of the alley, obviously looking for something at the other end. He didn't find it (or should I say me?) and, looking worried, he scurried out of sight.

He had to be following me. There was nothing else of interest back here.

What was going on here?

I slipped between the booths and out into the crowd. I couldn't see Miller anywhere as I worked my way toward the entrance, continually looking back over my shoulder. Apparently, I'd lost him in the mob.

It was almost five. I left the grounds and stood under a big flag of a mayfly, trying to decide what to do.

Maybe there was some truth to what Jimmy said after all. The least I could do was try to talk to him again. I could always go to Father Jonathan's a little late. I started walking back to Harry's Service Station. *(Turn to page 143.)*

To say I was confused was the understatement of the decade. But somehow, I still trusted Father Jonathan a lot more than the teenager. I started walking toward Father Jonathan's. *(Turn to page 189.)*

82

FATHER JONATHAN

"If there's anything at all to your story, we'll find it in Father Jonathan's cellar, I imagine," I said.

Jimmy was already walking toward the garage. "I knew you'd see it my way," he called. There was a definite upbeat note in his voice. "I know where the keys to your car are, so wait for me. I'll be right out." He monkeyed with the front door of the building for a minute, then disappeared into the darkness of the garage, leaving the door wide open.

I waited outside, afraid to look around Ashley Falls, cloaked as it was in its black cocoon. I literally felt trapped inside, an unwilling victim of an unnatural metamorphosis. I shivered, wondering what had come over me. I was about to break into a stranger's home—a stranger who, I had to admit, had treated me very well. And what for? To verify a cockamamie story that I really couldn't make myself believe! Yet, I kept seeing the man following me at the fairgrounds, and I kept hearing Harry's words to Jerry Kosinski: I hope Father Jonathan don't get too upset. I know he wants to keep an eye on that girl. And he ain't too crazy about what my son's been up to here, either. Now what did that mean?

The door to the service bay rolled upward. I could barely make out Jimmy's form as he ducked back from the opening. I heard him climb into my car and slam the door shut. A moment later, my Charger pulled out and screeched to a halt beside me.

I climbed into the passenger seat. "This won't screw up the radiator, will it?"

"Naw, I put a temporary patch on it this afternoon. It'll hold for a while."

He pulled into the street and zipped off toward Father Jonathan's house. Although he wasn't going very fast, it was the most hair-raising ride I'd ever taken. He refused to turn on the headlights.

"We'd stick out like a sore thumb with a great big rail-road flare on top of it," he explained.

"Can't they hear us?"

"Probably not. They're pretty far away. But lights'd attract 'em." He swung rapidly around something in the road that I didn't see, slamming me against the armrest and jamming it painfully into my ribs. I gasped.

Jimmy paid no attention. "Actually," he continued, "I think they shut the lights off just for that reason—security, you know? Every once in a while, someone drives into town off the highway during the festival. Their headlights give 'em away. They get hustled out real quick."

"Like your mother?"

"Sometimes. Usually, they just send a guy over in a phony squad car—we're too small for a police force. If we need a cop, they just send us staties from the Chester bar-racks when we need one. Anyway, we got this phony cop and he usually just escorts people back onto the highway on accounta the town ain't safe because of the blackout and he gives 'em a bunch of b.s. about the power company bein' all screwed up and stuff. You know who usually plays the cop?"

"Your father?"

"Nope. Jerry Kosinski."

I settled back in my seat and let my ribs subside to a dull throb. Jimmy was either the best liar I'd ever heard or this town had every angle covered. The next hour should tell which.

Jimmy pulled the car over to the curb, killed the engine, and climbed out. I looked around. There weren't any houses in the area. Nothing, but trees and grass.

"Where are we? I don't see anything around here," I said.

Jimmy had walked around the car and opened my door. I stepped out. "How far away are we?"

"A few blocks. Half a mile or so, I think."

Jimmy led the way through some bushes and into a patch of undeveloped land that in any other town might have been a park if the grass were kept cut. It was sparsely populated by a few odd trees and clumps of bushes.

We trudged on. I more or less kept my head down, trying not to think about everything that happened to me today, but Jimmy was constantly glancing around every which way.

It was obvious that he was scared and whatever you read about fear being catching is right. Suddenly, I was terrified. Terrified of the unknown horrors of this creepy little town and its residents. There was a clammy feeling spreading through my blouse around my armpits, making me shiver even more. Gritting my teeth, I tried to ignore it.

We had been walking for just a few minutes when Jimmy grabbed my arm and yanked me behind a tree and into some nearby bushes.

"What are you doing?" I gasped.

"Shut up!"

Then I heard footsteps coming our way. A moment later, a middle-aged couple walked by. They were laughing and I heard the woman say something about "the ceremony later." They wandered off—toward the fairgrounds, I assumed. Jimmy stood.

"You dragged me off so we wouldn't be seen by some harmless couple walking by? What did you do that for?"

"Lady, I really don't think you quite understand how much trouble we're in. Everyone . . . and I'm not exaggerating one tiny bit . . . in this town is on *their* side. If anybody catches us, they'll just take us straight to Father Jonathan. Nobody wants this little applecart upset. I think you can imagine why."

Sure I could. I had to wonder—if I were a resident of this town, would I be going along with Jimmy or would I just follow the crowd? I mean, assuming Jimmy's story was true, of course.

Not too much later, we arrived at our destination.

Father Jonathan's home was a large, almost mansion-like building. It was white with a dark trim around the windows and doorways and much larger than I would have thought one person needed. The grounds were perfectly manicured, each bush and shrub clipped precisely. There was a feeling of something new, yet very ancient, in that house. We hid in the bushes along one side of the huge yard.

The green Chevrolet was sitting in the driveway looking a little out of place with its surroundings.

"How long are we going to sit here?" I asked.

"Not long. I just want to make sure the coast is clear."

"How can it be? Father Jonathan's inside somewhere."

"Yeah, I know. I just hope we don't run into him."

The kid had a knack for stating the painfully obvious.

He watched for a few minutes more, then decided it was time. "You see that window over there?" He pointed to a small cellar window at ground level some forty feet or so from where we were sitting. We would have to cross about twenty feet of open yard before we'd be able to duck up against the building.

"We can get into the house through that. I've snuck into the house a number of times and I fixed it so he can't lock it."

"How'd you do that?"

"Through the clever use of a couple of screws and some fishing line."

"And he won't be able to lock it because of that?"

"Well, if he hasn't seen it. But I tried it yesterday and it was still open. Betcha he hasn't had time today to go checkin' things."

I absorbed that piece of information and couldn't decide if I wanted that tiny window to be locked or not.

"Okay, let's go." He jumped from the bushes and dashed out into the yard. I was right behind him.

Suddenly, a vehicle swung into the driveway, kicking up gravel and almost catching us standing there. We scrambled back into the bushes on our hands and knees.

I was sure we must have been seen as we lay there in the dirt, hugging the ground, waiting for whoever was in the car to come get us. I was breathing like a sprinter and my heart was pounding into the earth as if it was going to nail me down.

The car screeched to a sudden stop and the doors opened and slammed shut. I think I started saying prayers.

I heard two sets of footsteps moving swiftly toward the front door of the house. So they were going to get Father Jonathan before coming after us. I looked over at Jimmy. He was peering out between the trunks of the bushes. "That's my dad's truck," he whispered.

The door opened and I heard Father Jonathan's mellow voice speaking to the two men. "What are you two doing here?"

Then I heard Jerry Kosinki's voice. "I'm afraid they never came back to the gas station, Father Jonathan. I waited until just before the lights went off and then went back to the fairgrounds."

"Damn." There was a pause. "All right, come on in. We'll figure something out."

The door closed a moment later.

"Don't look good, does it?"

"No, Jimmy, it certainly doesn't."

But how we had managed to avoid being seen was a minor miracle.

"Let's listen!" Jimmy slipped back out through the bushes and sneaked up to the house. He ducked against the house and crept along the side until he came to an open window. I stepped up behind him. We were under the window to whatever room Father Jonathan, Harry, and Jerry were in. I recognized Father Jonathan's voice.

"I'm sure George Miller did everything he could, Jerry. I don't blame him at all for losing her at the festival. Jimmy has obviously warned her."

"They can't be too far away, Father Jonathan," Jerry

87

answered. "Her car is still at the garage. I think we'll catch them."

"Well, I certainly hope so." There was a pause and then Father Jonathan's next words turned my heart cold. "Harry, you understand what this means concerning your son. He'll have to be a part of the ceremony tonight if we find him in time . . . or as soon as we do locate him, whenever that is. There's no other way around this, I'm afraid."

"I understand. He's lived long enough already."

Jimmy turned and looked at me. He didn't say a word. He didn't have to. I closed my eyes. I believed him now. I had to. And, oddly enough, it helped push aside the unnamed fear—at least a little. Now I had something concrete to be afraid of.

Father Jonathan continued, "Okay, we still have about three quarters of an hour before the ceremony begins. I recommend you split up. It's the only way to cover enough ground to give us a chance."

"Jeez, they could be somewhere out in the woods," Harry pointed out. "Jimmy knows 'em pretty well."

"I know, Harry. Let me recommend that you get some people you can trust—"

"That won't be hard." Harry's laugh was demoniacal.

"—and let them know what's going on. We obviously need a little more manpower. Maybe some of them can search the woods before it's too late."

There were a few mutters of general agreement and we heard the bustle of the men standing from their chairs and discussing a couple of details. They moved off to another part of the house and we lost their conversation. Jimmy tapped me on the arm and waved me to follow him once again. We dashed into the backyard and ducked around the corner. Harry and his friend re-entered the pickup truck and drove off. I breathed a great sigh of relief. Jimmy slumped down against the wall, facing the yard.

"You see what I mean, now? This 'Gift' of Father Jonathan's is so important to them that they'll kill anyone who wants to stop them. Even if that means their own damn kids. Or their wives."

I sat beside him and put my arm around his shoulders. I don't really know why I did that, maybe just to show him I cared. Maybe just to say that I was going to see this through with him. I was beginning to think of him almost as a younger brother. He was just sitting there, staring out in a daze. I was surprised to see that his eyes were dry.

I didn't say anything to him and after a couple of minutes, he stood and announced he was ready. We sneaked along the house to the window he had pointed out earlier. I stood beside him watching for any sign of Father Jonathan. Jimmy fiddled with his makeshift latch.

"Something wrong?" I whispered. I could see Jimmy's hands shaking slightly.

"No, I got it."

He didn't, though. It took some moments of fiddling before I heard a slight scraping sound and noticed that Jimmy was leaning partway into the open window.

"Damn!" he cried half aloud.

I bent over. "What's wrong?"

He pulled himself back out into the yard. "I almost dropped it. We'd have been history for sure if I had." He gingerly pulled the glass through the opening and quickly put it on the grass beside him, shaking his right hand vigorously to relieve a cramp.

"I hadda grab it funny." He stopped shaking his hand and flexed the fingers.

"You okay now?"

"Yeah, I think so. How about you? You ready?"

I shuddered. "I guess so."

Jimmy grabbed the window frame with both hands and slipped through easily. I heard him land on the concrete floor of the cellar. Before I tried, though, I poked my head into the basement and looked around. Jimmy may have sneaked in here a dozen times before, but I sure hadn't and I wanted to know what I was getting into. Jimmy stood there staring back at me.

"Don't jump in there that way. You'll land on your head."

"I know that. I just want to see how far I have to jump." It wasn't far.

I pulled back out and repeated Jimmy's maneuver, but much slower. I tried to be graceful, but ended up landing with a very decided thump. I just hoped Father Jonathan, who was still somewhere upstairs, didn't hear me.

Jimmy leaned close and whispered. "I don't suppose I have to tell you to stay quiet, do I?"

I shook my head.

We were in a small room with walls of dull plasterboard. Besides Jimmy and myself, there was nothing else in the room other than a door on the opposite wall. Jimmy stepped up to it and placed his ear against it. Apparently hearing nothing, he took the knob gingerly and opened it slowly. He watched attentively with one eye, then two, as the door gradually, and very quietly, opened wider. Over his shoulder, I could see a hallway composed of the same unpainted plasterboard running in both directions. Jimmy took a quick glance up and down, then stepped into the corridor. He waved me along.

I stepped into the corridor which was illuminated by intermittent pools of light from bare bulbs placed about twenty feet apart. Jimmy led me through a crazy labyrinth of corridors punctuated here and there by a wooden door. However large Father Jonathan's house was, the cellar was even bigger. I suppose it had to be, if what Jimmy had told me about its history was true.

I had the feeling Jimmy didn't really know his way around as much as he had bragged about. Every once in a awhile, he'd stop, look around, then reverse his direction. A couple of times, he re-reversed it.

Eventually, the plasterboard gave way to plywood and later to wooden planks. The tunnel had a musty smell, ancient and ripe.

Suddenly, the corridor just ended. A dead end. Nothing but a wall of sloppy brickwork with oozing gray cement in front of us.

Jimmy stopped and turned back to me. "You're not going to believe this, I'm sure, but behind that's where they keep their victims," he whispered.

"How do they get them behind that wall?" I whispered back.

Jimmy smiled. It was the wide grin of someone who knew a secret. Then he pointed a finger in the air as if to say, "Watch this."

He leaned down and felt along the floor for something. Then he stood and put his left shoulder against one end of the wall. With a slight grunt, he pressed against it. I jumped back startled when the brick wall began to move.

A blast of old, rotten air swept past us. My nose curled involuntarily. Behind the wall was a small room of the same sloppy brickwork. Another bare bulb hung from the ceiling, its harsh light illuminating the eight-foot-square cell. Jimmy stepped into it, looking around in shock.

The room was empty.

"DAMN!"

I poked my head in and looked around apprehensively. Not that it mattered much. I could see the whole thing from the corridor. I sighed.

Jimmy was undeniably upset. "They're gone already! Sonofabitch! He moved 'em!"

I didn't say anything. There was certainly no denying Jimmy's claim that this place was once part of something very secret, like the Underground Railroad. One point in his favor. But, except for the lights that were on all over the place, this room looked like it hadn't been used for anything for a hundred years.

Jimmy, though, seemed to have answer. "They gotta be upstairs. He must be getting 'em ready for the festival."

Bursting past me, he ran back down the hallway. I followed, feeling more and more foolish and trying to think what I'd say if Father Jonathan caught us. Then I went cold again, remembering Harry out there, somewhere, looking for us. I managed to catch up with Jimmy and asked breathlessly, "How does he keep these victims under his control, Jimmy? A bunch of thugs with guns or something?"

"Naw. Drugs, I think. At least they always look drugged."

Just then, the lights went off!

My heart quit beating. I had to cover my mouth to keep from screaming. Next to me, Jimmy swore softly.

"Father Jonathan just turned off the lights. He musta been right ahead of us, taking 'em upstairs!" he muttered.

That thought wasn't very comforting. Then I tried to look on the bright side. At least this meant nobody would be liable to run into us. "You got any idea how to get us out of here?" I whispered.

"Lady, I may know my way around, but I ain't got these damn tunnels memorized."

"Well, do the best you can. We can't stay down here!"

I could sense Jimmy's self-confidence slipping. He suddenly seemed to need a little prodding as if confused by this unexpected setback.

We stumbled along slowly, feeling the walls, sometimes turning when our hands found corners. Soon, the dirt gave way to splinters. I caught a couple in my fingers, but I didn't dare let loose of the wall.

A number of times, Jimmy stopped and tried to get his bearings. Not that it ever really seemed to matter much. He never reversed his direction the way he had earlier.

We seemed lost for a long time, much longer than it had taken to find our way through the older portion of the tunnel. Eventually, we got to the plasterboard walls. Apparently, we were making progress of sorts. We hadn't gone far when Jimmy turned a corner and there was a small pool of dull light in front of us. Relieved, we dashed toward it and found that it was coming from the room we had entered the cellar through.

Now, with his bearings straight, Jimmy became excited. "All right!" He started running and I had to follow the sound of his sneakers. They stopped suddenly in the dark in front of me. Turning a corner I could barely see, I found Jimmy standing at the bottom of a set of stairs outlined in the dim light pouring underneath the door at their head. I could even see Jimmy smiling. My eyes had adjusted faster than I thought, looking around.

We were in a room that Father Jonathan apparently used as an office of some kind. It was comfortably furnished with a sofa, easy chair, and a coffee table of wood that matched the paneling on the walls. The room appeared to continue behind the staircase Jimmy stood at the foot of.

"This leads upstairs," he announced.

"I gathered," I snapped irritably. Now that we were among Father Jonathan's personal possessions, I really felt like an intruder.

When Jimmy reached the head of the stairwell, he laid his ear against the door and listened. Apparently hearing nothing, he tried opening the door. His hand gripped the knob tightly and he paused, taking a deep breath. He turned it slowly and quietly. Peering cautiously through the ever-widening crack, he eventually opened it enough for a body to slip through. Suddenly, like a spirit, he disappeared into Father Jonathan's house.

I held back, afraid. Looking in, I could see a bit of the linoleum floor and a small portion of a kitchen. The opening exposed a little of the dark brown refrigerator.

I carefully stepped to the top stair and took a good look at the rest of the kitchen. It was laid out with modern, wooden cupboards, a microwave, and matching speckled, off-white linoleum on the countertops and floor, as well as the usual appliances. The table was also of wood with chrome legs and a set of tan Naugahyde chairs. Everything was immaculately clean.

I didn't hear anything, so I slipped cautiously into the kitchen. A doorway on the opposite side led to what was apparently the dining room. Jimmy was sneaking along a wall toward another doorway to his left. I guessed that led to the foyer on one side and perhaps a set of stairs to the second floor on the other.

I followed Jimmy, but before I could catch up with him, he had disappeared into the foyer. Seconds later, I was standing at the doorway myself.

I was right about the staircase. I could hear some sounds coming from the second floor somewhere. Shuffling sounds. Jimmy suddenly darted from the foyer and startled me. I jumped back, slapping my right hand to my mouth. I didn't think I'd made a lot of noise, but the shuffling upstairs stopped.

"He's upstairs gettin' ready, I imagine. He has a whole outfit he wears," Jimmy whispered. I nodded back. He turned and stepped back into the foyer. I followed quickly this time.

Slipping through another doorway, we entered Father Jonathan's living room. This certainly wasn't where he had had his little meeting with Jimmy's father and Jerry Kosinski. It was too close to the front of the huge home. There had to be another sitting room, maybe even a study, too, between this room and the back of the house.

But the room wasn't empty. Four people were sitting on a sofa facing us.

They paid no attention to us at all!

"See? See? Didn't I tell you?" Jimmy whispered excitedly. "It's the family that came in this morning to the garage."

They were almost the typical All-American family—two parents, grandfather, a young girl, sitting between her parents. The old man appeared to be asleep rather than drugged, his head hung much lower than the others and his eyes were closed.

The other three watched us dully, uncomprehending.

———

They made no effort to move as Jimmy walked toward them. He stepped up to each, one at a time, and looked deeply into their eyes. They stared right back without blinking.

I stepped up the young girl. She appeared to be around eleven or twelve, with long, wavy brown hair. She wasn't particularly pretty, rather plain. I figured if anyone was resisting the effects of the drug, it would probably be her, the youngest.

"Can you hear me at all? Do you understand me?" I asked softly. There was no response. "Please answer me. Can you hear me?"

"Very well, I'm afraid, my dear," came a familiar voice from behind me. I jerked upright and twisted around, startled at the unexpected response from an unexpected direction. Father Jonathan stood at the foot of the stairs, watching me. He made no effort to approach.

His urbane manner never wavered. "Please be seated, my dear." When I didn't move, he said reassuringly, "I have a little story I think you should hear. Frankly, it's rather long, but I think I can skip certain points that Jimmy, I'm sure, has told you."

Jimmy! Where was he? I didn't want Father Jonathan to think we were both sneaking around in here, so I didn't look around for the teenager right away, but I sort of glanced around.

Hell! Who was I kidding? Father Jonathan obviously wouldn't believe I broke into his house on my own.

I didn't see Jimmy anywhere. Not that it mattered. I don't know which felt worse. Getting caught or the suddenly sickening thought that I had been set up.

"Please, Lisa, be seated."

I turned and walked dejectedly to an easy chair in the corner. My whole body shook. A tear rolled down my cheek. I wiped it away as I sat down, hoping Father Jonathan wouldn't notice.

He waited for me to settle down, then chose an easy

chair facing me. He was wearing a black robe, looking very much like a judge except for the gold piping around the cuffs and collar. He caught me looking over at the people on the sofa.

"Yes, Lisa, they're drugged. Nothing serious. Just a little something to keep them quiet. Now, I'm sure you'll find what I have to say interesting, if you'll just give me a chance."

I said nothing.

Father Jonathan leaned back and cupped his hands under his chin. "You see, this story involves a young slave on a plantation in Virginia some, oh, one hundred and thirty years or so, I guess. This young man had a sister on that plantation—a very pretty kid sister he loved very much. She was sixteen. The master of the house decided she was pretty, as well. He, uh, how can I put this delicately, used her for his own pleasures. Much against her will, I'm afraid. She survived the attack—at least physically. To be quite honest, I never saw her again after that episode. You see, the master didn't survive his lust. It was the first time I used The Gift.

"The Gift, you see, is an ability to drain the life from another human being. I used it first on Edward Hansen after he ravished my sister. I went to him, intending to murder him. I put my hands on Edward Hansen's neck and was about to try to strangle him when I felt an odd tingling up my arms. I felt myself getting stronger and Edward Hansen getting weaker. A moment later, he was dead—much faster than if I had cut off his air supply.

"Before I fled, one of the older slaves, a fellow named Jimbob, explained to me all about The Gift. Of course, I learned much more on my own later, but he told me enough. Part of The Gift is the ability to transfer the victim's lifeforce to others, including, of course, myself. In doing so, it also extends the life of the recipient. Fascinating, is it not?"

He was watching me intently, waiting for a reaction. I

could only shrug my shoulders.

"Naturally, I couldn't remain on the plantation and had to flee. Eventually, I found my way to the Underground Railroad and was shuffled between a number of homes and farms along the eastern seaboard. One of those was right here in this house.

"Indeed, it was here in Ashley Falls that I came closest to getting caught. Searching for escaped slaves wasn't taken very seriously this far north of the Mason-Dixon line unless that slave also happened to be a murderer. Then, it was taken very seriously indeed. The local constabulary returned time and again looking for me. It was much too dangerous to move me on to the next station. Virtually everyone in this town took me in and hid me at one time or another. Sometimes I hid in the woods, sometimes in cellars, sometimes in attics. Of course, back then, there were far fewer homes than there are now.

"I can't really remember how long all of this went on— several weeks, I should think. After a time, the search moved on and it was safe for me to continue. I eventually made my way to Canada."

I couldn't believe what Father Jonathan was telling me. Jimmy's story was the truth after all! It left an aching feeling in the pit of my stomach.

"Didn't any of those people who were helping you care that you were a killer?" I managed to ask.

Father Jonathan smiled. "It's impossible to describe the emotions that slavery aroused. It was so long ago—people today don't understand. The fact is that most of the members of the Underground Railroad didn't care about that. To them, I was just a slave. In fact, when they learned that the man I killed was a slave owner, most of them treated me even more like a hero."

Father Jonathan leaned back, taking his hands away from his face and dropping them on the armrests. He seemed more relaxed now, smiling, and not staring at me quite so intently.

"You see, my dear, I had to return to this lovely village after the War—uh, that would be the Civil War—to repay these kind people for everything they did for me while I was a fugitive. They risked their lives for me and I felt a certain obligation to them. None of my family survived, so I had nowhere to go in any event. I have been the pastor of Ashley Falls ever since."

I looked over at the people sitting on the sofa. They sat unperturbed, not listening to Father Jonathan's story. I took a surreptitious look around the room for Jimmy. I didn't see him. I wondered why Father Jonathan seemed so unconcerned about him. Could he really believe I had come here on my own? Was he so self-confident that he felt no threat from the freakish man-child who had brought me here? Or was this another trap—were Harry and his friends waiting outside hiding in the trees and bushes? Or could it possibly be that Jimmy was a part of all this—that I had indeed been set up? I couldn't force myself to believe that, not the way Jimmy had behaved all day. But still . . . where was he?

I let the thought drop. If Father Jonathan could live to one hundred forty-odd years old, could he read minds, too? I didn't want to find out.

"It's a funny thing about The Gift," he was saying, "it affects people in different ways. Now take Harry. He still ages just a little bit every year. Me, I hardly age at all. There are times when I think your little friend Jimmy actually regresses. He hasn't seemed to mature emotionally despite his chronological age. Some of the children are like that. Others mature quickly, especially after reaching puberty, then slow down in adulthood. I don't try to understand it. I only return it to the people who, in one sense, gave me back my life."

He stopped for breath and said nothing more for several moments, apparently awaiting my response.

"So what about the people whose lives are sacrificed?" I asked, choking. "Don't you feel just a little guilty about them?"

He shook his head. "Not at all. I owe them nothing. I simply close my eyes and see Edward Hansen's ugly face drooling over my sister's body. There is nothing whatsoever to feel guilty about."

"What do they have to do with Edward Hansen?"

"No more than did the tribesmen of Africa when the slavers arrived to kidnap them."

I was incredulous. "That's how you justify this? By equating them with slavetraders?"

Father Jonathan merely smiled. He didn't answer. He pushed himself up from the chair and stood before me. "It's time to prepare you as well, my dear, to become a Mayfly for our festival." One of his hands disappeared deep into the ominous-looking robes and a split second later produced a hypodermic syringe. "Of course," he said, "years ago, we weren't quite so sophisticated about this, but then, it was no problem to just send Harry out to comb the area for vagrants. Nowadays, this makes it easier to control our little mayflies."

He started to approach me, holding the syringe in his right hand, the needle pointing straight up. I stood, looking for a direction to run. He was such a large man that there was nowhere to go that he couldn't reach within a couple of steps. My heart jumped into my throat and lodged there.

I caught a glimpse of Jimmy in the foyer for just a second. I tried to yell to him, but my voice wouldn't come. My jaw just pumped open and shut quietly, sucking in great amounts of air, but accomplishing nothing else. But just as suddenly as I saw him, Jimmy disappeared.

Seconds later came a great clattering from the kitchen. A familiar voice yelled, "Father Jonathan, you bastard!" The sounds of cooking and eating utensils being thrown about grew in intensity.

Father Jonathan turned sharply, his eyes flaring menacingly. "Damn it!" he yelled and made a dive for the kitchen.

His robes flowed after him as he turned the corner from the foyer into the dining room. I heard his footsteps in the kitchen. It dawned on me that Jimmy would need my help, and the thought shook me from my lethargy. Racing into the kitchen after him, I found Jimmy standing in a pile of pots and pans, throwing everything he could reach at Father Jonathan, keeping him at bay.

Father Jonathan stood back a few feet, ducking and holding his left arm over his head, warding off Jimmy's missiles. I didn't know what else to do, so I just ran up to Father Jonathan and kicked him as hard as I could in the small of his back.

He reared up, reaching around his back with his free arm to clutch at the pain in his kidneys. A fork hit him in the face and he roared even louder, but he recovered quickly and spun to face me. He swung for me but missed.

At my feet was a pile of utensils. I grabbed a square frying pan for a weapon. Father Jonathan reached out for me again, and came close to grabbing my shoulder. I swung the frying pan as hard as I could and grimaced as I felt the metal smash into the bone around his knuckles. Father Jonathan yelled out in pain once again.

Jimmy kept up his hailstorm of junk, but unfortunately, we weren't really doing any damage to our adversary—we were just managing to slow him down. I didn't know how long this could go on. Jimmy's ammunition of pots, plates, and other items wouldn't last forever. He had already thrown a toaster that Father Jonathan had ducked easily.

I held the pan out, ready to strike, as the syringe came toward me again. Father Jonathan lunged, but I was able to jump away. His hand brushed my blouse, pushing me off-balance. My foot stepped on a saucepan and it rolled away from under me. My ankle turned and I know I must have winced with the pain. Pitching sideways to the floor, I landed in the pots and pans. Father Jonathan ended up on his knees.

He regained his balance quickly, however, and lunged toward me. I had no time to react as he grabbed my wrist and yanked me toward him. The syringe flashed as he was about to drive it into my arm.

Suddenly, his face twisted in agony. He knelt motionless for many seconds, his left arm still gripping my wrist, the syringe in the air. Eventually, the grip on my wrist gradually eased. The hand holding the syringe fell slowly to the floor. Father Jonathan's distorted features softened and his eyes opened. He dropped the syringe and it rolled away a couple of inches. He leaned over and I could see he was trying to support himself on his hands and knees.

A trickle of blood rolled out of his mouth.

I looked up, horrified, and could now see Jimmy standing over the slumping Father Jonathan. His face was an utter blank. He reached down and grabbed something I couldn't see. He gave a heave and Father Jonathan flinched violently. Suddenly, there was a bloody kitchen knife poised over the robed figure.

Jimmy didn't get a chance to use it again, however. Perhaps using strength from The Gift, Father Jonathan turned himself over, grabbed one of Jimmy's ankles, and flipped him into the air.

The knife flew through the kitchen as Jimmy landed with a thump on his back. Father Jonathan struggled to his feet and stumbled sideways a little. He stared down at Jimmy's still form without recognition, perhaps suffering from shock. He supported himself by leaning on the countertop.

Jimmy's eyes were closed. I was on my own. This time, I reacted quickly. Leaning over, I carefully picked up the syringe. I stood quietly, but swiftly, and held the syringe over my head like a knife. Father Jonathan slowly turned and faced me just before I plunged the needle hard into his neck.

My momentary feeling of triumph abated quickly as he swiped at me, knocking my arm away, and pulling the needle from himself. I don't know how much of the drug drained into him. He tossed it aside, smashing it against the countertop.

He came toward me again. I stumbled back toward the dining room as Father Jonathan came at me, walking in slow, deliberate lurches. I could have escaped easily, but that would have left the job only partially finished. Jimmy and the people on the sofa were still here and helpless.

Father Jonathan spoke for the first time since he had cursed Jimmy. His voice was harsh, raspy, and suddenly old. The mellow tones were gone. "Come back here, Lisa! I have to talk to you!"

I wasn't stupid enough to stop, and I kept backing away through the dining room and once more through the foyer. I heard Father Jonathan's footsteps stamping heavily after me. He lurched around the corner of the living room and stood facing me. His eyes were red, matching the bright blood dripping down his chin and drying on his robes. He seemed to be moving a little slower now, but he was still coming. How long could he continue? How much of an energy reserve did he have?

He backed me past the sofa and toward another corridor leading to the back of the house. I stood in the doorway watching Father Jonathan come at me. He didn't pay any attention to the four people sitting there. They didn't pay attention to him, either.

I stepped back into the corridor. Looking over my shoulder, I saw a line of three or four doors on the left. And a dead end. I ran down the hall. Father Jonathan stepped around the corner a second later. He kept wiping the blood away from his mouth. His voice was growing weaker. "Lisa, please. Come to me."

I opened the first door I came to. Father Jonathan's study, I guessed from the furnishings. Three large bookcases lined the walls. A great mahogany desk filled the center of the room in front of one of the bookcases. Papers and a telephone adorned the desk and to the side was a computer screen with a printer beside it. A pair of large leather

---

easy chairs made a small semi-circle around the desk.

Father Jonathan stumbled closer. I ducked into the room before he reached me. Running to the desk, I yanked open the drawers. I was surprised they were unlocked. And no wonder. There was nothing in any of them. Not even the gun I so desperately hoped to find. The only thing resembling a weapon at all was a wooden letter opener.

Father Jonathan stood in the doorway staring at me. He leaned against the frame, apparently gathering strength. His head sagged. He had all the time he needed to regain his vitality. I could only wait for his inevitable rush at me.

But he didn't move for a long time. He stood and stared. I was beginning to wonder if he actually was regenerating himself or just building the tension to an intolerable level, waiting for me to make some kind of mistake.

I looked around the room once again, unconsciously reading the spines of some of the books on the shelves. Complete works of Shakespeare, Sir Francis Bacon, Edgar Allan Poe, and wide variety of other classics, scientific and literary.

Books—a large number of them.

They weren't very dangerous, but maybe they'd distract Father Jonathan enough to allow me to get past him and back to the kitchen where I might possibly retrieve the kitchen knife. I reached up and grabbed the first book my hand came to. It wasn't nearly as large as some of the others. I jerked it from the case, whirled, and threw it at him. Then another and another. I kept up a barrage just as Jimmy had earlier.

Father Jonathan ducked further back to avoid the reckless onslaught. His hands came back up to protect himself and he yelled something unintelligible. Half-crazed by fear and desperation, I screamed as I threw.

I worked my way around to the bookcase on my right. Father Jonathan was no longer watching me; he was keeping his head down to protect himself.

I just kept grabbing and throwing, grabbing and throwing, grabbing and throwing. I found myself standing almost beside the weakening black man. An oversize but thin picturebook was in my hand.

I didn't throw this one. I stepped up beside Father Jonathan and slammed the spine of the book down as hard as I could on the back of his neck.

I could feel the book hit the soft flesh then slam into the hard bone of the spine just beneath. Father Jonathan's head snapped up for an instant, too brief for me to see his face. He sprawled flat to the floor. I thought I heard a slight moan escape from his lips.

I stood in the doorway staring down at the fallen man. I couldn't tell if he was breathing or not underneath all those robes.

"Lisa! Hey, Lisa!"

Jimmy was calling for me. He seemed to be in the living room. "I'm in here, Jimmy! Around the corner!"

Jimmy popped into the corridor a moment later. He was rubbing the back of his head.

"You okay?" I asked.

"Yeah. But I'll have a headache in the morning." He looked down at my feet. "How about you?"

"I'm okay."

"And him?" He jerked a thumb toward Father Jonathan.

"I don't know. I think he's dead."

Jimmy dropped to one knee and lifted Father Jonathan's head. It came up at an awkward angle that told me his neck was broken. "I think you're right," Jimmy said.

A wave of relief swept over me, followed by a wave of revulsion. I closed my eyes and slumped against the doorway, bracing myself with my right arm.

Jimmy was right behind me. He picked me up by the armpits and made me stand. "C'mon, we can't sit here and wait. I don't know when the crowd'll be back."

He was right, I knew. I gathered what strength I could and followed him. With each step, I felt a little better. It was an odd feeling. The knowledge that I had acted in self-defense was replacing my loathing at having killed someone. My exhilaration at simply being alive was gradually making me stronger.

We had arrived in the living room. The four figures on the sofa hadn't budged. Not even so much as blinked an eyelid as far as I could tell.

"Jimmy, how do they normally get these people to the fairgrounds every year?"

"Oh, they just walk 'em over at the head of the procession."

"They're strong enough to walk?"

"I guess so. As long as they're led."

"C'mon, help me get 'em moving."

We stood the family members up one-by-one. They didn't resist, just stood there. Both of us took two by the wrists and led them from Father Jonathan's house.

Jimmy led us back through the undeveloped land we had come through earlier rather than the streets. I looked around, but couldn't see any sign of the candlelight procession, only lights against the sky in the distance. I felt myself gearing up as my adrenal glands went back to work.

We pulled the family along, not very quietly, and were lucky we didn't run into anyone. Eventually, we reached the car.

We had a real problem, trying to squeeze everyone in. There were buckets seats and a stickshift up front and the rear seats had so little leg room, I once had my eight and ten-year-old nieces complain they had nowhere to put their feet. With four considerably larger people, it was almost impossible. We managed by turning everyone slightly to one side and settling the young girl over everyone else's laps. Thank heavens they were drugged into acquiescence. As it was, I could barely see out of the rearview mirror.

Jimmy slipped into the bucket seat beside me. The car cranked a couple of times, then turned over and roared into life. Jimmy had his head poked out the window.

"Oh, God, they're coming. I can see the lights moving this way."

It was no time to be cautious. I flipped the headlights on and squealed the tires as I pulled into the street. The flickering of Ashley Falls' procession quickly faded away in the distance. Finally, I could truly breathe easily. I concentrated on my driving and, slowly, my shattered nerves returned to some semblance of calm.

With Jimmy's directions, we reached the highway in a matter of minutes. As soon as we pulled onto the entrance, he leaned back and sighed with relief. "Take the Chester exit. There's a State Police barracks just off the highway. We oughta be there in about a half an hour."

I smiled and felt suddenly fatigued. The adrenaline drained out of me once again as if I had sprung a leak. I stifled a yawn.

"You think the police are going to buy this story of yours?"

Jimmy turned to me and his smile grew wider. "Lady, I know exactly how they worked this whole thing, even where they buried the victims up in the hills. When I get done, they'll have so much information about this stinking place, they won't know where to start. I even overheard everything Father Jonathan's told you. And I saw him attack you with the syringe. Nope, lady, as crazy as all this is, I know damn well they'll believe me. Even if it takes a little time."

He slumped back again, obviously content. I heard him murmur, "I just hope Mom knows it's over."

I smiled back at him and I had no doubt he'd persuade the police just as he had me. I stepped harder on the accelerator.

THE END

A FANTASTIC STORY

"If you think I'm leaving here without my car, you're crazy," I told Jimmy. "I don't care how dangerous it is."

"Yeah . . . I don't blame you. It's a nice car."

"Uh, thanks." His reply took me by surprise. He led me around to the front of the service station. I finished the apple and tossed the core into the bag, then crumpled the paper around it. Jimmy took a couple of quick glances up and down the street. I did, too. Neither of us saw anything. The darkness was spooky.

The teenager produced a set of keys from the pocket of his jeans. I noticed for the first time that he was wearing much cleaner clothes than he had been the last time I saw him. He was still in denims but a much nicer pair. He wore a sport shirt with wide red and blue horizontal stripes, like a rugby shirt. Somehow, he seemed more trustworthy now than he had this morning.

We slipped into the office of Harry's Garage and Jimmy told me to wait there. I settled in behind an ancient dull gray desk. On a filthy countertop beside the desk was a crank-handle type cash register.

Jimmy dug a few items out of a drawer beneath the cash register. I saw a tube of some sort, a piece of metal, a flashlight, and something that looked like a basting brush. He clutched them tightly as he stepped into the service area.

My car was in the first bay, but the door was too narrow for me to watch Jimmy work. I saw the flashlight beam go on, and then I heard Jimmy pop open the hood. The beam danced around the room as he worked.

I took a slow look at my surroundings. The office was just as grimy as the restroom. Why wasn't I surprised by that? The dust looked about four inches thick. Oil-stained magazines and catalogs littered the area. If there was any system to his filing methods, I couldn't see it.

"Hey, if you wanna soda or a candy bar, just help yourself," Jimmy called from the other room. "There's a button around back of the machines that lets you get what you want for free."

I looked around. Behind me were a pair of decrepit vending machines I hadn't seen before, just as disgusting and oil-stained as everything else in the room. Lord knows how old the food in there was. While I was grateful for the kid's thoughtfulness, I decided to pass on the offer. I wished I had seen this when Harry had offered me the Coke earlier.

I was about to say "No, thanks," when I caught a glimpse of headlights coming from town.

"Jimmy! There's a car coming!"

The flashlight went off immediately. "Damn! Okay, duck down fast!"

I didn't need to be told. I was already on the floor, crouching behind the counter. The car drove past slowly—very slowly, almost crawling to a stop in front of the station. A third beam stabbed through the blackness at us from the car's side. Someone was playing a searchlight around the garage. In the darkness, with the glare of the beam blinding me, I couldn't tell what kind of car it was, or even its color.

They didn't stop, but they sure did take a good look around. Why was everyone in this godforsaken town poking around this gas station? Was I really that great a prize? The car moved on, and its searchlight beam blinked off.

"That's one of those guys I told you about," Jimmy whispered hoarsely from the other room. "They're still looking for us—or at least you. I guess they figure you won't leave without your car."

I knew insisting on it was dangerous, but I really didn't care if I was playing by their rules. "Well, they've sure got that right."

Jimmy waited a few minutes before I saw the flashlight click back on. I could tell he was being more careful about shielding the beam.

Darkness descended completely as Jimmy worked. Off in the distance, I saw the horizon begin to glow a dull red-orange. It looked like a little dome of light, flickering menacingly and moving toward the north. I read where such lights are sometimes seen just before an earthquake in these hills, and I wouldn't be surprised if that's exactly what it was. But I sure couldn't remember ever hearing that those lights moved.

A short time later, the light in the service bay went off. Jimmy was finished. I could hear him begin moving cautiously around the Charger. He slipped into the office like a shadow.

"It won't be long now. Just gotta let the glue set a few minutes."

I pointed out the window at the strange flickering. It was well north of us now, and darned if it didn't seem like it was turning back again and even getting brighter.

"What's that?" I asked.

"Oh, that's the candlelight procession I told you about. That'll go on for a while yet."

"Is Father Jonathan leading it?"

"No, he's at his house waiting for them."

"Oh."

I hunkered down farther in the gloom and shivered, even though it wasn't really cold out.

Suddenly Jimmy blurted out, "Cripes, I almost forgot something! Wait here and keep your head down." Before I could say anything, he dashed out the door and ran behind the building. I heard his footsteps fade as he apparently headed into the woods. Was he abandoning me. I was beginning to despair of ever leaving this place. I was just about to get in my car, say nuts with Jimmy, and drive off. So what if the service bay was locked shut? I'd just drive right through it and get the damage fixed later. At least I'd be on my way.

I was just about to give it a try when I realized that Jimmy still had my keys. I'd just have to wait for him—if he was coming back.

It took him a long time, but he finally did return. I think I jumped about two feet in the air when I heard him at the door. He wasted no time getting inside and crouching down beside me.

"Where have you been?" It was really a stupid question, because he was carrying a backpack he didn't have before, but it let me express my exasperation.

"Getting this." Predictably enough, he held the backpack up. My eyes must have adjusted to the darkness pretty well by now because I could make it out well enough. It wasn't very large, and it was made of dull blue and orange nylon and predictably grubby.

"What's inside?"

"My stuff."

To a teenager, I suppose that explains everything.

By this time, the procession had moved well to the south. While Jimmy was gone, I had tracked its progress. It seemed to be moving slowly back and forth across town, just as Jimmy had said it would.

"Well, you ready?" he asked.

"I guess so."

He found my wrist with his hand and lifted it up. Then he slapped my keys into my palm. "Don't turn the headlights on."

I stood, brushed myself off, and started walking toward my car.

"And be careful," Jimmy admonished. He unlocked the service bay door and opened it slowly to keep down the noise while I started the car. The engine sounded like an explosion in the silent building as it sparked into life. How could they help but hear it? I slipped the shift into reverse and slowly pulled out.

Once the car was outside, Jimmy pulled the door back down, less cautiously than he had lifted it. There wasn't much need for stealth now, but I knew Jimmy wanted to leave the door down just in case it might buy us a few more seconds if his father's friends drove by again. He jumped into the passenger's seat beside me.

"Okay, let's go. Back toward the highway."

"Okay," I said as I did a quick turn and started to pull into the street. I saw right away that to continue would be a mistake.

In the deep black that was Ashley Falls, it was easy to spot the headlights of another car in that direction. I knew now why Jimmy wanted me to drive off in the dark. It amazed me how far light travels when there's no other light to mask it. I understood what the Great Northeast Blackout must have been like back in 1965, even though I was just a little kid at the time.

"Well, that certainly wasn't a very good choice," I said as I turned the car around.

"This means we'll have to drive right through the middle of town."

Deep down I knew that, but I sure didn't need to hear him say it. And unless I misunderstood what he had been telling me, we were also heading in the direction of Father Jonathan's.

We pulled out again, this time paralleling the path the procession was following. The car behind us was apparently a couple of streets over. Jimmy turned halfway around in his seat and was watching the movement of the headlights. His only comment was "I sure wish they'd turn off."

We must have driven about four blocks, poking along slowly since I had a hard time seeing without the headlights, when Jimmy told me to take a left. He turned and watched me, to make sure I took the right street, then turned back to resume his watch. Suddenly I heard him curse.

"What is it?"

"The car just disappeared. They must have pulled over and killed the lights."

His tone told me he wasn't overly concerned, but I still

would have preferred to know where they were.

We drove in silence for a while, and I decided it was time to find out why we were the prey. "Jimmy, I think you'd better explain what's going on."

He was keeping watch out the back window. "Yeah, I suppose you're right." He settled his chin onto the back of his hand. "I really didn't want to tell you, because you're not going to believe a word of this. Just don't say anything until I'm finished, no matter what you think. Okay?"

"Okay."

"Remember when Father Jonathan mentioned about his father and grandfather living here?"

"I remember."

"Well, that's a crock. There wasn't no Father William or Father Alfred. It was always him—Father Jonathan."

"But that would make him over a hundred years old!"

Jimmy grunted disgustedly. "See? I toldja you wouldn't believe it."

"Sorry. Please go on."

At first, he acted like he didn't want to continue, but he did. "Yeah, he's over a hundred, all right. Something like a hundred and forty or thereabouts. You see, he's got this power. He calls it 'The Gift.' I don't think even he knows how it works, but he sure knows what it does.

"One time, he told me all about how he discovered he had this Gift. He was a slave on a plantation down in Virginia just before the Civil War."

I gasped but didn't say anything, although it was difficult to keep my mouth shut. If Jimmy heard me, it didn't faze him. He just kept right on talking.

"The owner of the plantation had this real bad-news of a son who used to do whatever he liked with the female slaves, especially the young ones. I guess one day, he sorta had his way with some sister of Father Jonathan's. Well, naturally Father Jonathan was pretty upset, so he went after this guy and started to strangle him, only he suddenly found out he didn't need to do that. He just kinda felt himself drawing the guy's life out of him. The way he describes it, it's kinda like a low electric surge that runs up his arm, into his body, and gives him a real rush when it reaches his head. That surge must be the other guy's life energy or whatever.

"Of course, he couldn't just hang around the plantation anymore, so he ran off and eventually hooked up with the Underground Railroad. They took him through Maryland, then Pennsylvania, and finally to New York, where one branch of the Railroad ran through Ashley Falls. Some old geezer—some sorta political bigshot back then—was the head of it. He used to live where Father Jonathan does now."

"What happened to him?"

"I guess he died during the war—the Civil War, of course. Turn right here."

I slowly wheeled the car around the corner.

"Anyway, Father Jonathan says they almost caught up with him a couple of times here, but practically the whole town took turns hiding him—sometimes in their houses, sometimes in the woods. Of course, the authorities up here knew what was going on, and they more or less sympathized with the slaves. In fact, I'd guess that they found ways to let people know when their raids were supposed to take place, so it was really just a matter of making sure the runaways were well hidden and that way they could go back and make their reports and say they never found anything. I don't imagine they really looked very hard.

"It's funny, though. I asked him if the Northerners knew he'd killed a man, and he said a lot of them considered him a hero, especially the ones who were involved with the Underground Railroad. You believe that?"

"Yes . . . I can believe that. Slavery stirred up a lot of emotions that we don't understand anymore."

"I guess so. Hey, pull over here for a minute."

I did so quickly. Jimmy swiftly rolled the window down and stuck his head out the opening, listening. He hauled it back in a minute later. "Okay, go ahead. I thought I heard something. At the light up there, take a left."

I stared into the gloom ahead of me. I could barely make out the ghostly shape of an unlit traffic light a block ahead. I drove off at a snail's pace once more.

Jimmy remained silent. I didn't think he was going to tell me anymore about Father Jonathan. I had to prod him, but then he opened up right away.

"Oh, yeah. Well, they got him to Canada okay, and he spent a few years up there until the war started. Then he joined the Federal Army. I guess they needed warm bodies, so they weren't too particular about checking out a guy's past. Of course, Father Jonathan wanted to earn a pardon if he could. Then, in the fighting in some hellhole out west somewhere, he found himself in a cornfield with a wounded buddy. A Confederate came along and was all ready to take them prisoner when Father Jonathan managed to get a grip on him and use The Gift. And while he was helping his buddy out of the cornfield, he found he could transfer some of the life he took from the Southerner to his friend. The way he describes it, it didn't really heal him, but it gave him enough strength to stay alive and eventually recover.

"After the war, he got his pardon. In fact, I've seen the medal they gave him for saving that guy's life in the cornfield. Of course, he didn't tell them about The Gift. Then when Father Jonathan went back to the plantation to look for his family, it turned out they had been killed by the owners and a bunch of Rebel soldiers right after the Emancipation Proclamation.

"With nowhere else to go, he came back to Ashley Falls. He told me that he considered this his second home after the way they treated him when he was on the run. The townspeople remembered him, of course, and let him take over the house because it was empty by then. And that's just about the time the Mayfly Festival began.

"Father Jonathan wanted an excuse to use The Gift to

---

repay the people who lived here. At first, they only thought The Gift gave you that good feeling I told you about. They used to find people traveling and entice them into town. Then Father Jonathan'd use The Gift on them, especially if they looked like the kind of people that wouldn't have anyone come looking for 'em. Then townspeople would gather around and he'd share it with them. Well, come to find out after doing this for years and years, it turns out that The Gift can actually slow down how fast you age!"

He paused to let me absorb that. I was too shocked to say anything intelligent, so I asked a question instead. His answer almost gave me a heart attack. "So how old are you?"

"I was born in 1905."

I gulped. "Oh." Then something else dawned on me. "For someone in his eighties, you sure act and talk like a teenager."

"Yeah, I know. Seems weird, huh?"

"To say the least."

"Well, part of it is real and part of it is phony. I look about sixteen years old, so for the sake of strangers passing through, I have to act that way—you know, for appearance's sake."

"I suppose."

"And I guess The Gift retards your emotional and psychological growth, too, somehow. Nobody understands it. We just take advantage of it. At least, most of us do."

Jimmy grew silent. Since he had had me stop, he had been facing forward in the seat, but he took time every once in a while during his story to look around. Now his head hung low, apparently deep in thought.

"I take it there are people who don't agree with this festival?"

"One. See, after they found out that nobody in Ashley Falls was getting old very fast, it all became a ritual. In the old days, they just did it when they had the chance. Then cars came along, and it was easier to find victims. So they

115

started this May First festival and gave it some phony religious meaning. It's been going on ever since. Go straight at this intersection."

As we continued on, I asked, "Who is this one person?" From what I'd seen, it certainly wasn't Jimmy's father.

Jimmy sighed. "My mom. I don't know why she changed. She and my dad know Father Jonathan from before the war. Something made her feel guilty. I think it was the part my dad has in the festival—that phony sign and all. Maybe it was because they need more victims 'cause the town keeps growing.

"Does it really feel as good as they say?"

"Oh, yeah. It feels great. I think it's addictive, like drugs. Not just living forever, but the actual physical sensation. It's real hard to quit cold turkey. I been thinking about this for a year."

In a way, I was sorry I wouldn't be able to experience this Gift—that is, if Jimmy's story was true. Suddenly I realized that Jimmy was crying.

"It was hard on my ma. She wanted to live forever, too, just like everyone else in this town. It took a long time for her to confront Father Jonathan, but she finally did. Last year. You know what happened?"

I shook my head in the dark. Jimmy could sense that. He was having trouble talking between the sobs.

"They used The Gift on her at last year's festival. She's buried in the hills along with the rest of them."

He paused, regained his composure, and said, "And that's why I gotta stop 'em this year. But I need help. If I had tried alone, I'd be dead by now."

"How about you? Have you ever felt guilty about it?"

"Yeah, but what could I do? The whole town is in Father Jonathan's hands. I couldn't do much by myself. But when they killed my mother so she wouldn't go to the police, I had to do something."

"Do people really live forever?"

"Not really. It doesn't stop accidents, of course, or heart

---

attacks. It just slows down how fast you get old."

Jimmy had been right about one thing, and I told him so. "I really can't believe a word of this, you know."

"Yeah, I know. You don't have to. Just get me to the police in Chester. That's all I ask. Okay?"

"Fair enough, as long as it doesn't get me killed."

"That's exactly what I'm trying to avoid, lady."

He had me take another right, and for a moment, I thought I could just about make out the lights of the highway ahead. That's when the whole town exploded.

Lights flashed on all around us. They were everywhere—behind us, in front, to the sides. Headlights and searchlights. Somehow, Father Jonathan's henchmen had managed to track us despite our precautions. There was no way to tell how many of them were out there, nor any time to count even if we could have seen them.

"Go, go, go!"

Jimmy seemed almost hysterical. I did as he said, aiming for a spot between two pairs of lights that appeared large enough for the Charger to squeeze through. Surprisingly we made it, amidst a great deal of yelling and screaming. I don't think they expected a girl to try it.

We screeched through the cordon, and I reached down to turn on the lights. Jimmy was yelling "Awright!" as loud as he could.

Then I heard the explosions. There was a shattering of glass behind me, and I instinctively ducked behind the steering wheel. However crazy Jimmy's story had been, there was one thing I couldn't argue about—people were shooting at us. At least if we got to the police, I'd have something concrete to show them. My rear window was shot out.

I zigzagged a little in the street, hoping to throw off their aim. It wasn't much—I didn't want to lose control of the car. It didn't help much, either. I felt at least two more bullets or shotgun shells slam into the car's rear end. I had visions of going up in flames.

We got around a corner and out of their line of sight. I sat up and looked over at Jimmy. He was still hunched over, and I could see he was rummaging through his backpack. He produced a small paring knife. I wondered what good that was going to do us. "See?" he yelled, vindicated. "Those bastards are trying to kill us!"

"So I noticed."

"Listen, stop the car here and let me out. You can get to the highway easily from here. It's right at the end of this street. They're coming after us, I'm sure. I won't be able to hold them off with this, but I sure can slow 'em down enough to let you get away."

"They'll kill you!"

"So what? You know as much about the festival as I do now, and even if you can't bring yourself to tell the cops about it, you sure can show them the bullet holes. They'll investigate and find out what's going on."

Jimmy grabbed the steering wheel and started jerking it back and forth. I had to slow the car down, and as soon as Jimmy felt the speed decrease, he popped the door open and disappeared into the night.

I swung around a long curve that led to the I-87 entrance ramp, and the passenger door slammed shut from the centrifugal force. I stopped the car just before entering the ramp. Rolling my window down, I listened for some indication of what was happening behind me. I expected to hear gunshots. I heard nothing.

Although I wasn't sure exactly what was going on, I was absolutely positive of one thing . . . Jimmy needed help.

That help had better come from the police, I thought, and I roared out onto the highway. (*Turn to page 133.*)

The police would never believe this crazy story, coming from me alone, I thought desperately, and I knew I had to go back and get Jimmy. (*Turn to page 195.*)

THE ROOM IN THE CELLAR

I slipped into a pair of sneakers from my overnight bag and sneaked down the stairs. I looked into the kitchen. No sign of Father Jonathan. I entered the kitchen and found that dinner was still cooking. Perhaps he had just left things to simmer. Certain he'd return momentarily, I quickened my pace.

On the other side of the kitchen was a doorway I hadn't noticed earlier. I opened it. Another stairway led down into the cellar. I took a tentative step, then hurried down.

When I got to the bottom, I expected to find Father Jonathan down there, searching around for a new jar of mayonnaise. The lights were on. Strange. I realized suddenly that I had not heard the moaning since I left the bedroom. I guessed that wherever the sound was coming from, there was only one way up to the second floor—the vents.

I didn't find Father Jonathan in the basement at all. There was a room at the end of the stairs, but it wasn't filled with the canned and jarred goods I expected. Instead, it was a sort of office with wood paneling. An open door directly in front of me led to a long corridor with a series of lights punctuating the darkness in isolated circles. The walls here were of brick, similar to the one I had seen in my brief dream. But they were much neater, much newer than the wall in my nap. Probably just coincidence.

The corridor I was following forked off one branch to the left, one straight ahead of me. And suddenly the walls changed. They were now made of sheet rock rather than brick. I continued straight ahead.

A couple of more tunnels branched off to either side. It seemed a logical assumption that most, if not all, of these branches eventually came back to the hallway I was following. It was probably the main corridor, I guessed. I could sense it looping around in a long left-hand turn. But the lighting system never varied—a bare bulb about every eight feet or so.

Eventually, the plywood gave way to rotted wood plank walls. Now, it really was like going down a tunnel. I don't know why, but I suddenly felt as if I was getting close to the source of the strange moaning. I had obviously reached a very ancient portion of the house. If it had any secrets, they'd be found down here.

I continued on, scared, yet excited at the same time. I hadn't gone far when I noticed that what little of the wood planks had remained over the dirt walls was now gone altogether. Eventually, the lights seemed to come to an end somewhere in the distance. Now, curious and eager to see what was beyond, I began to move faster.

When I reached the point where the lights ceased, I found I had reached the end of the tunnel. A crudely built brick wall faced me, and *it* was almost exactly like the one in the dream! But so what? There were no people here. I had come to dead end, apparently.

But why would there be a brick wall right out of nowhere at the end? I put my ear to the bricks.

The moaning, though faint, was distinctly audible. There were people on the other side! Now how do I get back there?

Maybe my initial impression had been wrong. Maybe this wasn't a wall—maybe it was actually a hidden door of some kind. I looked around for some kind of small latch or a key hole, but found nothing. I tried the simple expedient of pushing on the wall, but that didn't work, either.

"Hey! Hey! Can you hear me in there?" I called. I got no answer. Just as I was about to give up the idea of getting behind the wall, I got some unexpected help.

"If you'll permit me, I'll show you how it opens."

God, how I jumped! Gasping, I turned quickly to see Father Jonathan approaching. He was a long way down the tunnel, but the closed walls carried his voice and made him sound much closer. Even from a distance, however, I could see he was carrying a gun.

His face was stern, with none of the cheerfulness of earlier in the day. I understood now what Jimmy had been trying to warn me about—and save me from. At first, I'd been startled. Now I was terrified. My heart leaped into my throat, pounding furiously.

He waved me to one side. As I watched, he put his shoulder to one side of the brick wall and gave it a heave. It rolled, creaking and protesting, into the opposite wall, disappearing into the dirt beside my right shoulder.

Inside, leaning against the dank walls, were four people. After everything else I had discovered tonight, I was actually surprised that they weren't the people in my dream. They did seem to be in some kind of shock or maybe a trance, however. One of them, a young man probably in his thirties, lay on his side. A young woman, about the same age, sat upright in a corner, her head rolled back, mouth open, eyes closed. Slumped against her was a little girl, eight or nine maybe, half-awake, half-asleep. An older man sat slumped over, his knees drawn up to his face, his head buried into them. Every so often, one of them would make the moaning sounds I had heard upstairs. Father Jonathan anticipated my unasked question.

"Drugs." He waved the gun, and I understood that he wanted me to sit down. I dropped myself between the two drugged men.

"You were very wise to come to my house tonight, my dear. However, I'm sure you'll agree it wasn't very wise to come down here. I hope the abrupt change in my hospitality doesn't upset you too much."

Shivering, I couldn't speak.

"You know, you gave my man George quite a start. Me, too, I might say. He thought he had lost you at the festival. But then, I knew you'd stop over for dinner."

He laughed, then shook his head. "You should have listened to Jimmy. But, of course, that's probably pretty obvious to you now." He paused. "You know, I'm going to do something for you that I've never done for anyone else.

Not these people"—he pointed to the family—"not to any of the others. Don't you feel lucky?"

"Privileged," I said bitterly, my throat dry.

"You should be. It's not everyone who knows why they've been brought to Ashley Falls for the festival. In fact, until just now, it's no one." He chuckled. "Yes, you're the first."

"I know why I'm here. To become a victim—"

"No, you are not a victim! You are a Life-Giver!"

"A what?"

"A Life-Giver. Oh, that's probably impossible for you to understand. At least without hearing the whole story. Are you comfortable?"

The inflection of his last question was startling. He sounded sincerely concerned. Probably planning to keep me off-balance with a small gesture of kindness. I made a mental note to be careful of that.

"Yeah, I guess I'm as comfortable as I'm going to get."

"Good, because this is a very long story." He checked his watch. "But I do have time to tell it."

There were several well-worn, overstuffed chairs in the room. He chose a stickback rocking chair, sat down, then he began his story.

"Perhaps I should begin by telling you how I discovered I had The Gift, Lisa. I wasn't too much younger than you are now. About nineteen, I believe. It was such a long time ago, it's hard to remember."

"Father Jonathan," I interrupted, my curiosity getting the better of me, "if you don't mind my asking, when was that?"

He laughed politely. "I don't mind at all, my dear. It was 1854."

Turn to page 53.

END OF THE TALE

"Fact of the matter is, Lisa, I never saw Billy again at all." Father Jonathan leaned back against the wall, his story now obviously almost over. "In any event, that little incident gave me my first clue to the power of The Gift. I couldn't ask Jimbob what it was, and as I said, I never saw him again, either, so it really didn't matter, anyway. I had to experiment on my own.

"Fortunately, warfare provided me with an opportunity I wouldn't ordinarily have had. If memory serves, there are two other Confederate soldiers lying in their graves because of The Gift."

"What exactly is this Gift?" I asked.

"I'm not exactly sure myself. Apparently, it drains away the 'life force', if you will, of the victim and then transfers it to myself. In turn, I can transfer it to others. It gives them strength and even extends their lives. The transferral of life affects different people in different ways. Harry seems somewhat resistant, so he does indeed grow old at a very slow place. Jimmy is very receptive. He stays young."

"You mean you can keep people from dying?"

"Oh, no. They could be killed in an accident, for example. It can help people heal and it can virtually stop them from growing old, but it cannot bring the dead back to life."

Father Jonathan stood.

"This is the Anderson's old home. Most of it has been remodeled . . . several times, in fact . . . over the years, but this portion has never been changed.

"Oh, yes, one more thing. About the phone call to your family. Would you like to hear today's Dial-A-Joke? That's what I called. Actually, it was rather foolish. I'm sure you won't be missing anything."

I looked up and saw him smiling. I wished I could have spat in his face.

"Of course, you'll have to join us now." He waved the gun around, pointing out the others in the room. "As an honored guest. I'll return for you later."

He left the room and shut the sliding wall, keeping the gun on me until the last second.

I had a watch, but I didn't dare look at it. Time was the last thing I wanted to keep track of. So I couldn't say how much later it was when I heard the door opening again. I don't think it was very long, but then, time seemed twisted in that tiny room. I dropped my head into my upraised knees and tried to pray. I wished I was drugged like the others. The sliding door began to creak open slowly, and I started to cry.

"Damn! I was afraid of this!" a familiar voice muttered.

"Jimmy!" I cried, startled.

"Hey, you're not drugged!" he said with surprise.

"No. He-he had a gun—"

"Yeah. C'mon, we better hustle. They could come back any minute."

"What about them?" I pointed to the family. I'm not sure I felt much better than I did a few seconds ago. The thought of leaving these people behind horrified me.

"We'll have to drag them along, I guess. It's too dangerous to leave them here, especially with my plan."

We picked up the two sleeping men and yanked the two women to their feet. It wasn't as much of a struggle to keep them going as I thought it would be. They were compliant and quietly plodded along where we guided them. Even the two who had seeemed to be asleep awoke enough so that we didn't have to carry them.

Jimmy led us to a room off the hall in the newer part of the basement. We set the family down against one of the walls. Then, from one corner, Jimmy picked up a two-gallon can of gasoline.

"This is why we won't have a lot of time," he said. "Once we set this, we gotta get everyone through there." He pointed out a small, oblong, ground-level window about wide enough for one person at a time.

I followed as he left the room, and we ran down the corridor toward a small room that Father Jonathan apparently used as a spare office. In the middle, directly ahead of us was a staircase leading up.

Reaching the foot of the stairs, Jimmy began spreading the gas on the steps. When the can was empty, he pulled a cigarette and a book of matches from his pocket.

"This oughta give us ten minutes or so to get the hell outta here."

He lit the cigarette and was taking a couple of puffs when the door behind him opened and a deep voice commanded, "Puff it up, sonny boy." The gun in his hand barked once and Jimmy screamed. I stared at him in shocked horror. Half the teenager's right leg was gone! He fell back onto the gas-soaked staircase, his cigarette flying, blood gushing from a stump above his knee. Father Jonathan started coming down the stairs. Looking down, I found the unlit matches at my feet.

Jimmy saw me. "Light 'em! Light 'em!" he screamed.

How could I? He was lying in the middle of the gas puddle!

"Everything will be fine, dear, if you just back away," Father Jonathan was saying.

"Light em! I'm gonna die anyway!"

The blood spurted. Father Jonathan was being cautious, not wanting to slip on the wet stairs. But he had the gun in his hand. I knew I'd never have time to reach down, grab the matchbook, and light it.

The cigarette was rolling around on the floor to my left.

"Light 'em!"

Dear Lord God, I hope he would have died anyway!

Quickly, I reached down and flipped the cigarette at the stairs. Startled by my sudden move, Father Jonathan's shot slammed into the wall behind me. An instant later, he was surrounded by flame.

His screams mingled with Jimmy's. I can't describe the

feeling in my stomach. Turning around, I ran. Long before the screaming stopped, I heard the gun's bullets exploding in their clip. I raced back to the room where we had left the four drugged people.

Already, the vision of Jimmy's twisted face, surrounded by bright orange flames, was haunting me.

I forced the vision from my mind and concentrated on how to rescue the remaining five of us. It probably wouldn't take long for the house to catch fire. I found my way back to the room just as I noticed the smell of burning wood. Smoke was beginning to snake down the hall.

I dashed into the room and closed the door behind me. It was easy enough getting the young girl out the open window, but it was a more of a struggle to get her mother into the yard. Not that she was that heavy, just a little clumsy to lift in her semi-conscious state. I managed somehow.

Now I faced a dilemma: the father or the old man? The old man might be easier to lift, but he had already lived his life. Wouldn't it be better to save the husband and father? I had already played God once tonight and was sick at the thought of having to do it again. Maybe I could still get both.

I dragged the younger man to his feet and tried to lift him. I managed to get his head up to the window, but couldn't push him through. A couple of grunts and hard shoves later, I hadn't made any progress.

"Dammit, pull!" I yelled.

To my amazement, I felt the load in my arms lighten. The man was pulling himself through the window! I helped him by lifting his feet through. A second later, I saw him roll over in the grass. My heart sank. I had been hoping he could help me pull the old man through.

Reaching behind me, I felt the doorknob. It was getting hot. But I thought I still had time.

I pulled the old man from his seat. My arms were tired, but one more effort just might do it. He was indeed lighter than his son or son-in-law or whatever. It still took a lot of work to wrestle him out the opening.

How I pulled myself through, I don't remember. Next thing I knew, I was lying face down on the cool, sweet grass.

I took only a moment to catch my breath. Then I began rounding everybody up, grateful that I had managed to save everybody—at least from the fire. Now to save them—and myself—from the residents of Ashley Falls. I knew there was no way to get out of town tonight. The best I could hope for was to hide until the drug wore off. Then maybe we'd have a chance to steal a car or something.

I got everybody to their feet and moving toward the woods on the other side of the street from Father Jonathan's. The drugged victims were like sheep, needing constant surveillance and rounding up. But as long as I kept cajoling, they kept moving.

We straggled into the brush, and I got them as far as I could from the house when I heard the mob beginning to arrive. I hid everyone in the bushes as well as I could, then ducked behind a tree trunk to watch.

Father Jonathan's house was fully ablaze. A siren wailed in the distance, getting closer. A crowd was gathering on the street, just watching. Three fire engines pulled up, and a crew of firefighters went to work.

Eventually, they brought the fire under control, and the firemen went inside. Some minutes later, a pair of body bags were taken in empty and brought out heavy and lumpy. I swallowed. Hard.

The crowd grew excited as the news spread among the people. They stood there for a long time as the firemen hosed down the ashes. From somewhere, several men arrived and began handing objects out to everyone. Soon, flashlights began poking through the night.

Some of them were coming toward me.

The idea of making a run for it flashed through my mind, but only for a second. These people with me were in no condition to run, and the thought of leaving them was unbearable. I hunkered down in the scrub and prayed for the best. It didn't happen. The young girl moaned, just as I had heard earlier in the bathroom.

"Hey, Harry, look what we got here!"

A flashlight beam lit up the old man. It swept around and found the young girl and her father. Then it spotted me.

"Now, now, now."

A group of people crashed into our hiding spot and manhandled us to our feet, keeping us at gunpoint. Then they dragged us to the street, beneath a streetlight. Even the firemen had stopped working and stood on the lawn, watching. Everyone was staring at me. Their mood was ugly in the extreme. I had an odd feeling of being sorry now, rather than afraid. Sorry that I hadn't been able to save this family and that Jimmy's sacrifice had been useless.

I couldn't see any faces because of the light beams in my face. Voice came from all directions.

"I say just shoot her now, Harry. . . ."

"No, burn her like she did Father Jonathan. . . ."

"Shoot . . . burn . . . shoot . . . burn . . . " The crowd seemed split about halfway. I was so scared and tired and filled with horror that I didn't even much care.

Harry came up and stood next to me. Then he turned and faced the crowd.

"Now listen to me, all of you!" he bellowed. The mob quieted down. "I've already lost a wife and son to this, not to mention a close friend tonight. I think maybe the time has come to end the evil."

"No! . . . We'll all die now. . . . She deserves to die!"

"Wait! Wait! Listen! Is any more killin' gonna do any good? Father Jonathan's gone now! The Gift is gone! We're all gonna die anyway! Is it really worth more killings? Ain't the woods full enough of our graves already?"

One voice came hurling back. "A few more ain't gonna matter, Harry. I say kill 'em now even if The Gift is gone.

'An eye for an eye.' "

The crowd mumbled its agreement.

"You just try it, Steve, and I'll blow your damn fool head off. And anyone else's who tries to hurt these folks."

An uneasy silence ensued for a few moments. It was the classic standoff, but no one in the throng wanted to be the first to die. Suddenly, a woman's voice, high-pitched and somewhat tenuous, came from the darkness.

"Harry's right, all of you. We got a lot of explainin' to do to our Maker, anyhow. I don't feel like makin' it worse."

"Thank you, Dotty," Harry answered.

I felt the tension in the crowd ease. I couldn't see it, of course, but I could sense the gun barrels being lowered.

"I ain't real poetic, but maybe it's time we begin payin' for our sins. I know I gotta lotta mournin' to do," Harry muttered.

The mob seemed chastened. I felt more than heard it breaking up. When we were alone, Harry said softly, "C'mon, help me put them in the back of the pickup and I'll take you to your car."

I had no choice, so I did as he said. He almost had to help me as well as the family walk along. I was so weak with relief, my knees were having a hard time holding me up. We drove back to his garage. It wasn't a long trip. On the way, he told me something I had never thought to question. "I guess Jimmy was driven by revenge. You see, his mother tried to put a stop to this little festival of ours for years. Last year, she almost did. So Father Jonathan, uh, made her one of the mayflies last year, if you know what I mean."

"Yeah, Father Jonathan explained it all to me."

He didn't say anything more and I didn't want to talk about it anymore. But at least now I understood Jimmy's motives and hatred.

Ten minutes later, Harry had a temporary patch on my radiator. "This'll get you home, but get it fixed permanent as soon as you can. Here." He handed me two hundred dollars. "That oughta pay for it. It's the least I can do."

"What about that family?"

"I don't know. I was thinkin' maybe I'd take them to a motel in Chester and leave them overnight. They'll be okay in the mornin'. It'll probably just seem like a bad dream to 'em. I'll have Jerry drive me back or somethin'."

He eyed me and caught the suspicious look on my face. "You can follow me if you like."

An hour later, Harry and Jerry Kosinski drove the family to the Chester Motor Hotel. I followed. Harry paid in advance for a two-day stay for four. Jerry Kosinski and I helped him herd the family, whose name I found out was Hastings, into the room and settled them into the beds. Harry left their car keys and the room key on a night stand. Then we left, and Harry closed the door behind him. I heard it lock automatically.

We parted without saying a word. I'm sure they expected me to go straight to the police, but, somehow, I couldn't. On the way home, I concentrated hard on my driving to keep from going into shock. I stayed at my parents' home overnight on the excuse that it was too late to go into the city, and I phoned in sick to work the next day. That gave me almost thirty-six hours to ponder what I'd been through.

Calling the authorities, I realized, was futile. Would they really believe the story of the Mayfly Festival of Ashley Falls? I had serious doubts. Thinking back on it, I could scarcely believe it had happened myself. And I rationalized that it wouldn't do any good anyway. Those people had to live with their own guilt and no amount of judicial moralizing could absolve that.

It was about a month later that I noticed a small item buried in the back of the *New York Times*.

SUICIDES PLAGUE SMALL CATSKILLS' TOWN

State officials are concerned by a recent surge of suicides in the tiny hilltop town of Ashley Falls in upstate New York. State Police officials report over thirty "definite suicides or suspicious accidental deaths," according to Lieutenant Irwin Caldwell of the Chester barracks.

Caldwell further states that each case is different and apparently unrelated. The first was a local gas station owner, despondent over the loss of his son and a close friend, a minister, in a fire May 1. In a bizarre twist, his wife disappeared exactly a year previously to the day.

"Other than that, the deaths have no explanation," Caldwell says. State health officials, too, were at a loss to explain the phenomenon.

I wasn't.

THE END

SAFE AT LAST . . .

I was safe now. The car settled into a nice, steady, 55 mph. I didn't want to chance blowing that patch off.

There wasn't a lot of traffic on the highway, most of it going north. I found that a little odd. On a Sunday night, you expect people to be heading back to the city. Just a temporary quirk in the traffic pattern, I figured.

The damn pickup truck was on me before I even saw it coming.

I had no doubt whose it was, but where the hell had it come from? I'd never seen it until now! I couldn't believe they were this determined to keep me in Ashley Falls!

The pickup was really moving by the time it pulled up next to me. Automatically, I hit the brakes. The truck shot past and I saw a shotgun poke out of the passenger's window—aimed at me!

God Almighty!

I slipped into the truck's lane and got directly behind the bed. I could see someone maneuvering the gun around for a shot.

There were three heads in the truck's cab. The shortest one, in the middle, bobbed back and forth like one of those ceramic dolls with a spring for a neck. That was Jimmy, I was sure. He was lucky if he was merely unconscious.

The truck's brakelights suddenly went on and I had to jerk the wheel around to avoid hitting it. I swung into the right lane, but that placed me beside the truck again. I gunned the engine to gain speed and when the truck caught up again, I slammed on the brakes, coming to a virtual stop, sending Harry and his passengers shooting past.

They didn't go far before they slowed down themselves. They seemed to be sitting there waiting for me.

I slowed down further and so did they. I was wondering why they hadn't tried taking a potshot at me, when my questions were answered by auto horns. A line of three or four cars whizzed past, their drivers glaring at us angrily. When they were gone, I was alone with the pickup truck.

I stopped my Charger. The pickup swung around backward in a short arc, then sat sideways across the highway, blocking most of it. My only hope for getting past it was to drive on the shoulder of the highway, behind the truck's rear gate. Not wanting to give away my intentions, I slipped the transmission into neutral and slowly began to rev up the engine. At the right moment, I'd drop it into first, aim for the open spot, and pray for the best.

Suddenly, the driver's door opened and Harry's body tumbled out. Another body, smaller, scrambled out behind it. It was Jimmy! I let up on the gas pedal, still watching warily. I couldn't tell what had happened to the third guy.

Jimmy ran over to my car and stood beside my window. Cautiously, I rolled it down quickly.

"How . . . ?"

Jimmy held his knife. "That's how. I got both of them. C'mon, help me get 'em off the road."

Feeling sick, I pulled my Charger into the shoulder. Jimmy was already trying to lift his father's stout body and stuff it back in the truck cab. I couldn't bear to touch him but then realized Jimmy was never going to make it by himself. And what if someone came along? Gritting my teeth, I went to help him and, together, we managed to do it. There was a huge pool of blood all over the front seat. Jerry Kosinski lay against the other door, his neck sliced open.

Jimmy climbed in and backed the truck up a few feet. "Follow me," he called. Numbly, I walked back to my car and waited for him to turn the truck back onto the highway.

He took me a little way down I-87, then pulled off an exit that didn't seem to lead to much except a ribbon of county highway that ran parallel to the interstate. Jimmy surprised me by turning right, back toward Ashley Falls. I'd thought we were going for the police.

I couldn't do much, however, except follow. He didn't drive all the way back to town. After a couple of miles or so, he turned off onto a sidestreet that led to a dirt road going up into the mountains. Nowhere did I see a house. Or even a streetlight.

He led me a long way up the dirt road. Eventually, he stopped the truck and climbed out. Instead of going to the passenger's door to pull the bodies out as I expected, he came directly to my window.

"Well, this is it. I'm l-leavin' 'em here. It'll take Father Jonathan and his b-buddies a l-l-long time to f-find them."

"I should think so. It's pretty isolated." Something about his attitude bothered me. After all, he had just killed his father and another man yet he didn't appear at all upset. Excited, yes, which might explain his sudden stammering, but that certainly was not what I expected.

Suddenly, I felt sick and frightened. I wanted to leave, quickly, but I remembered the gun was still in the truck. The thought of him, behind me. . . . I decided to keep him talking.

"Jimmy, how did you do th-that to them? When I saw you in the truck before, you were bouncing around like a rag doll."

"I was f-faking it. They hit me with a gun b-butt and I was k-kinda d-d-dazed, but I came to a lot f-faster than they thought I d-d-did. Af-t-t-ter th-that, it was e-e-easy. He had it c-coming, the b-b-b-bastard. You know what he was t-tryin' to do?"

I shook my head. I couldn't speak.

"He was t-tryin' to s-s-save it all for himself and his g-g-goddamn friends."

He stuck the knife through the window, barely missing my neck. I snapped back, my heart lurching. "What—"

Jimmy was screaming now, but I knew that, unfortunately, there was no one around to hear him but me.

"Yeah, s-saving 'em for himself," he yelled as he slashed the knife menacingly through the air. "For the d-d-damn festival. But I wasn't g-gonna let 'em get you like they did that l-little b-bitch last year!''

The whole damn town was a killing factory! Most of them did it out of greed, but this little jerk does it because he likes it!!

Horrified, I pulled back as close to my passenger's door as I could. Jimmy was lunging in the window, stretching and stabbing out as far as he could, but I was still just barely out of his reach. Picking up my overnight bag from the floor, I began swinging it at him, hoping something hard inside might hurt him. That didn't happen, but the bag did serve as a useful shield. Jimmy gave up a minute later and ran back to the truck. I slammed the car into reverse and rolled up the window at the same time.

The road was tight and it would take some careful maneuvering to avoid the trees on either side. But I had no choice. My right arm went over the backrest and I began to guide my car back out.

I took a terrific wallop from the front, snapping my head back and slamming my nose into the headrest. It hurt like hell.

Turning, I saw the pickup disengaging itself from my grille. What was that damned kid up to? I couldn't believe he was out there trying to kill me like this . . . that he had spent all that energy to keep me from being killed by this Father Jonathan just so he could do it himself. I suppose living in a society that condoned murder made it easy to enjoy it. I had had doubts about his story, naturally, but they had disappeared the minute I saw the gun. There was no doubt that whatever Jimmy's particular psychosis was, he was extremely dangerous.

The car was still running, so I tried to back up again. I didn't get far when Jimmy rammed into me. He had the advantage of not having to worry about picking his way through the trees. He just plowed on. This time, the damage was too much. Great spouts of steam and hot anti-freeze gushed from the shattered radiator. The engine sounded like every piece of moving metal was crashing against every other piece. The din was horrendous. A moment later, the car stopped moving.

I dove from the automobile and scrambled into the woods. I don't think Jimmy saw me at first because I managed to get a headstart.

I stopped for a moment behind a tree. I couldn't see him but I could hear him, crashing through the brush. I ducked down, hoping he'd just run past.

My prayers were answered.

He passed very close but didn't see me. Picking my way around the tree to keep the trunk between the two of us was a nerve-wracking experience. The slightest noise would give me away, but I didn't have time to be very careful as he ran past. When he disappeared into the bushes atop a slight rise, I ran back for the dirt road and quickly searched the pickup truck. No luck this time. Jimmy had taken the shotgun with him. I started running down the road. A shotgun blast caught me in the shoulder. Not square, just a glancing blow, but the pain was so bad, I didn't want to move. I knew intuitively that I wasn't seriously wounded, but it still hurt worse than anything I'd ever suffered before.

Sobbing, I kept going and managed to get back into the safety of the trees before Jimmy came flying out of the brush.

It wasn't so easy to avoid him this time. He caught me as I fell over a rotten tree stump.

"I wasn't aimin' to k-kill," he informed me. "Ain't my style. I l-like this." He pulled his knife from his back-pocket, then stood above me as I lay on the ground. He was smiling. "Hurt?"

I nodded. Blood was dripping through my clenched fingers.

"It won't for much longer. P-promise."

Suddenly, I didn't feel the pain anymore. Maybe I was going into shock. Or maybe it was just my mind suppressing it as I fought to survive. I needed time, time to recover and regain my strength. "Jimmy," I asked, "why are you doing this?"

"You kn-know why. I like it. M-makes me as important as Father J-jonathan. More important! He kills so everybody c-c-can share his Gift. I kill for n-nobody but me. That m-m-makes it kinda more r-r-r-religious, y'know? L-like a s-s-sacrifice in the Bible or something. Know what I m-mean?"

It was a cockamamie justification, but I nodded in agreement with him anyway.

"Oh, they b-been tryin' to s-s-stop me for years. Of course, they c-couldn't go to the police." Jimmy chuckled. "It's g-g-great. What're they g-gonna say? 'This kid's been k-killing people that we were gonna k-kill. Arrest him.' " He laughed again.

"Look," I said, "let me go and I won't go to the police, either. I promise. I'll give you anything you want."

"You all s-s-say that. I don't care. Can't you s-see that? I j-just like watching the b-b-blood run. That's the problem with the stinking Gift. The b-b-blood don't run."

I had to keep him talking. I had to keep myself talking, my mind off the pain. "What would have happened if I had reached the police in Chester?"

"It w-wouldna have made any d-d-difference."

"Oh, no?" I had an idea. I just had to keep him preoccupied. "What about the buckshot holes in my car?"

"They all would have d-d-denied it. No witnesses. Nobody to b-b-back up your charges including me. S-so what could the c-cops do? They'd investigate, sure, but, believe m-me, lady, they wouldn't f-f-find a thing. Everyone in Ashley Falls'd keep quiet. T-too many secrets here and all of th-th-them bad."

"So why'd you jump out of the car and give me a chance to escape?" I asked, letting my eyes droop a little, like I was on the verge of passing out.

"Hell! That wasn't much of a chance. My only hope of

k-keeping you for myself was to find s-some way to side-track Dad and Jerry. S-so I hadda go with 'em and t-time things j-u-u-ust right. And if you did get away, so what?" He laughed diabolically. "Pretty g-good, huh?"

He was standing over me now, looking down. The shotgun was over his right shoulder, the knife in his left hand. Desperately, I whipped my legs out and scissored his ankles. He went flying into the air, an almost comic look of surprise on his face. He'd obviously thought I was hurt a lot worse.

The knife flew off somewhere, but Jimmy clenched the shotgun tightly until he landed square on the back of his neck. His hand jerked open, and the gun bounced against a nearby rock. Jumping to my feet, I snatched the weapon before the dazed killer's head cleared. I didn't waste any time talking. I squeezed both triggers, but only one went off. And unlike Jimmy, I was aiming to kill.

His body jerked spasmodically a couple of times, fighting death, but losing quickly. I stared at him for a moment, waiting for the shock and guilt to set in. It didn't. I had been duped all day and damn near murdered for it. I had no regrets about surviving. I even wished I had more shotgun shells. It wasn't remorse I felt but a crazy feeling of frustration that I couldn't hurt this bastard any more. I threw the gun on top of him and walked away.

Looking at my wrecked car, I honestly felt more grief over it than I did over killing Jimmy. At least, that's what I thought as I returned to my Charger to retrieve my purse before trying to make it back to the highway. The driver's door was still open and I slumped back into the seat. I really had only intended to grab my pocketbook, but the instant I hit the seat, I dropped my head and cried. And cried. And cried.

But I knew I had to get help. I couldn't take the pickup, because the dead Charger blocked it on the dirt road. So I had to walk. I can't remember much about it. It all kind of faded together in a nightmare of pain.

I finally reached I-87 and began the long trek south. At first, I was going to thumb but thought better of it in the dark. I had taken enough chances already today. I was kind of surprised that the shoulder didn't bother me any more than it did. The pain subsided into a dull throbbing soreness and the wound had, apparently, quit bleeding.

I really don't know what I intended to do. I had some vague idea about getting to Chester, but that was twenty-five miles away. There had to be some little town in between. Someplace with a phone. I decided to take the next exit and see where that led.

I just plodded on, half the time in the shoulder on the highway, half the time in the woods just beyond. Whenever a car went by, I ducked back into the undergrowth. Maybe I was over-reacting, but I didn't want to take the chance that the car might be coming from Ashley Falls.

A mile or two down the road, I found a Motorist Distress Call Box. My hands shook so it took me three tries to dial the number and it was only 911. It was real effort not to sound hysterical to the man on the other end, but I managed. He promised to send a cruiser over right away. I told him I was at Call Box 56.

Sitting on the guard rail waiting for the cruiser gave me time to think over how I was going to explain this to the State Police. Explaining about Jimmy and the two bodies in the pickup truck was not what worried me. But how could I tell them about the Mayfly Festival? They'd never believe Jimmy's crazy tale of The Gift and Father Jonathan. Especially since I had no real proof. I had nothing but the words of a dead man. I was sure they'd think I was crazy at worst, merely hysterical at best.

I saw the cruiser lights approaching off in the distance. Of course, if they found something out during their investigation, well, that'd be a whole lot different, now wouldn't it?

The cruiser pulled up beside me and a tall, broad-shouldered trooper stepped out. "Lisa Ames?"

I stood to sort of greet him. "That's right."

"You're bleeding. You sure you don't need an ambulance?"

"I told the guy on the phone that I wasn't hurt bad."

"May I take a look at that?"

I took my hand down. He gingerly peeled a piece of my blouse away.

"No, you're not hurt too bad, but you are hurt. C'mon, we'll get that taken care of." He opened the door of the cruiser for me.

We hadn't driven too far when he asked, "Now, just what happened to you, miss?"

I have to admit, I didn't say anything about the Mayfly Festival or The Gift, but I sure gave them enough to keep them busy in Ashley Falls for years.

THE END

PURSUIT!

Walking back to the garage was an odd experience. I kept passing people on their way to the fairgrounds, and nearly all of them nodded politely and said "hello." For some reason a "Star Trek" episode popped into my mind—the one where everybody was real friendly until the clocks started chiming and the people all went crazy—screaming, yelling, and smashing things.

I got a creepy feeling as I acknowledged that Miller *had* appeared to be following me. Was he part of some sort of . . . well, weird plot.

Feeling paranoid, I watched carefully behind me as I headed for the service station. I was moving at a fair clip, not quite running but sure wanting to. But George Miller never showed himself again. I had definitely shaken him. Apparently, that was one worry I didn't have anymore.

I found Jimmy sitting on the single step in front of the open office door. I could see a look of relief cross his face as soon as he saw me approaching. He stood as I came closer.

"Boy, am I glad you're here!" he exclaimed.

"Look," I said, feeling silly, "the only reason I'm here at all is because you were right about my being followed at the fair."

"Is he still . . . "

"No, he's gone. I have no idea where he is."

"Probably still poking around the festival looking for you. They'll show up here eventually, though. You can count on that."

"So what do we do?" I asked impatiently.

"For starters, we get out of sight of the road." He took me around back and we dropped down into the grass near the van. "We can't stay here for long."

That was fine with me. The sooner I got out of Ashley Falls, the better.

Jimmy continued. "You don't know how lucky you are

143

that you decided not to go to Father Jonathan's. That man is a killer."

This was just too much! "Oh, come off it!" I scoffed. "He's ten times more a gentleman than anyone else I've ever met."

"I'm serious. And my dad's tied up in it and so's the whole town."

"You are really making it more and more difficult to believe you."

"Well, it gets even crazier."

"What about you? If the whole town's involved, why aren't you?"

"I was. Ain't no more."

"How come?"

" 'Cuz they killed my mother last year."

The flatness of his voice seemed to stab through me. I took a deep breath and looked over at the teenager. He was sitting with his chin dug firmly into his wrists which were crisscrossed on top of his upraised knees.

"What did they do to her?" I finally asked.

Jimmy sighed. "That's the tail end of the whole story. You gotta hear it from the beginning or it don't make any sense at all."

Somehow, I had the feeling it wasn't going to make a lot of sense no matter where he started.

"Okay. Let's hear it."

"Father Jonathan has been around for just about ever. I don't know exactly when he first showed up here in Ashley Falls, but it was sometime before the Civil War."

"What! Are you nuts?"

"Look, I know this is wacko, but hear me out, okay?"

"I'll try." I said, wishing I'd gone to Father Jonathan's.

"Anyway, he came from somewhere in the South. They say he killed a guy on a plantation where he was a slave down there and had to run away. I guess the Underground Railroad— You know what that is, don't you?"

"Of course." I sighed.

"Well, the Underground Railroad picked him up and sent him sneaking up the east coast to Canada. One of those stops was here in Ashley Falls. Of course, back then, there were only about ten or fifteen families in the whole place, so everybody knew everybody else's business. It was no secret he was here. Apparently, they came looking for him and just about everybody in town took turns hiding him till they sent him on north. After the war was over, he must not have had anywhere else to go because he came back and settled in the old Anderson place. He still lives there as a matter of fact. It was the main stop for the Railroad. It's got all kinds of tunnels and stuff underneath it where they used to hide guys."

"How do you know?" I asked.

"I've been down there. Father Jonathan took me, that's how. He told me his father and grandfather lived here. But there wasn't anyone else. It's always been just him, Father Jonathan. I should know, I've been here just about eighty years myself."

I burst out laughing. Then I saw the anger on his face, and gulped. "No, Jimmy, I can't take that. You're telling me I'm listening to an eighty-year-old teenager tell me about a guy who must be around a hundred and fifty?"

The boy picked up a stick and flung it angrily at the old van. It ricocheted off the rear quarter panel and bounced to the ground. "Okay, fine. Don't believe that he kills people so he can keep on living and then somehow passes the life energy, or whatever it is, on to other people so they can live a long time, too. Don't believe that and you know where you're going to end up?"

"No."

"Out in the stinking woods in a tiny little grave surrounded by beautiful pine trees. Is that where you wanna end up?"

I was silent for a moment, feeling chilled. There was something about him. . . . "So where did Father Jonathan get this power, Jimmy?" I asked finally.

"I don't know. I don't think he does, either. He puts his hands on their heads and mutters some African mumbo-jumbo and the next thing you know, bingo, they're lying on that stage with the life sucked out of 'em somehow."

"Then what happens?"

"Then the people go up on the stage and he kind of does everything in reverse. You'd be surprised how old some of the people in this town really are."

I eyed him suspiciously. "I already am! But how does he get away with it? The whole town is in on it, right?"

"Of course."

"And nobody turns him in?"

Jimmy laughed a little ironically. "Of course not. They like the idea of living forever. Well, they don't really live forever because people do get killed in accidents and stuff, but nobody gets very old. Some people, like my dad, do get older a little faster than others, but it's all pretty much the same for everyone in town. It'd be like killing the Golden Goose. Mess with Father Jonathan and everyone else in Ashley Falls is on your ass and they ain't looking for a joy-ride, you know what I mean?"

"Yeah, I guess I do." But I still wasn't convinced.

Jimmy stood and walked to the corner of the building. He took a quick look around and then, apparently satisfied that they weren't in any imminent danger, returned to the grass beside me. He leaned over, plucked a tall blade, and idly stuck it in his mouth.

"There was one person who stood up to him."

I didn't have to ask. I remained quiet and he continued without any urging.

"My mom. She stood up to him. I guess she got sick of what was happening to all those people."

"You mean those people who came in every year to buy your father's gas? Like me," you add, shuddering.

"Yeah. You know, it's kinda funny. I don't imagine she'd have gotten so uptight if Dad hadn't been responsible for drawing the victims in here. Kinda hypocritical."

"I suppose But where did she think the people came from?"

"Closed her eyes to it like most everyone else. Oh, she *knew*, all right, but couldn't force herself to believe it, or was scared to say anything, or probably both. Sorta like the Germans in World War II with the concentration camps, I guess."

I reflected on that a moment. "That's what took her so long to stand up to Father Jonathan, huh?"

"Yeah, partially. And hell, she wanted to live forever, too, y'know. Until she caught 'em all red-handed and then maybe the guilt piled up too high. I don't know. She never had the chance to talk to me about it."

"What happened?"

Jimmy threw a chewed piece of grass back into the yard. He picked up another but, instead of sticking it in his mouth, started tying it into little knots. As he spoke, I noticed that he twisted it tighter and more violently.

"For some reason, she went to Father Jonathan's house on the day of the festival last year. Maybe she was gonna confront him, I don't know. Anyway, while she's standing there, my dad shows up with a carful of peo—"

"Hey, shush!" I hissed urgently.

Jimmy jerked his head up and looked at me. Someone was out front.

"C'mon," he whispered. Grabbing me by the wrist, he yanked me through the grass. The voices we heard were those of two men. They were unlocking the doors to Harry's Garage.

Jimmy scrambled over to the van. He started to open the sliding door but thought better of it as soon as he heard the latch give.

"They'll look in here for sure," he said quietly.

Turning, he took a quick look at the woods beyond us. "We're better off in there." He gripped my arm tighter—it was really painful now—and hauled me into a small copse at the side of a depression.

We scrambled down the slope, trying to be quiet while ducking between the trees. It wasn't easy. The two men, whoever they were, were apparently still inside and couldn't hear us.

My foot hit a rock and I stumbled, twisting my ankle painfully. I pitched headfirst into the undergrowth. Jimmy's arm slammed into a tree as I fell, breaking his hold on me and knocking him off-balance. He fell beside me.

I saw him look up, then he motioned me to keep still. "I hope we're safe here."

Cautiously, I lifted my head. I could see nothing above us but dirt, scrub, and trees. I just prayed that if anyone stood at the top of the ridge and looked down, they'd see the same. We weren't exactly wearing regulation camouflage outfits.

It was very quiet for several long, nerve-racking minutes. Then I heard footsteps softly padding about in the distance. I heard voices again, one of them unmistakably Harry's, but I couldn't make out what they were saying.

Eventually, the footsteps moved closer, but not directly. They were moving back and forth in a zigzag manner as if looking for something. I heard them open a couple of the doors on the van, then shut it up a few moments later.

Suddenly, just as the footsteps were at their loudest, they stopped. Jimmy stuffed my head hard into the ground and nestled his face next to mine. I could hear his breathing in my right ear. The cool freshness of a tuft of grass beneath my nose filtered out some of the stench of his breath.

"Damn, Jerry, I coulda swore they'd come runnin' back here somewhere."

"It was a good guess, Harry. Maybe we just missed 'em."

"I hope Father Jonathan don't get too upset. I know he wants to keep an eye on that girl. And he ain't too crazy about what my son's been up to here, neither."

I couldn't hear Jerry's reply. They turned and walked back to the garage much more swiftly than they had come.

Jimmy waited until he heard an engine start and a car pull out into the street. Then he stood and helped me up.

"It's safe now. They're gone."

I swung my purse at him and caught him square on the arm. He stumbled back more from surprise than because my blow was very powerful.

"Hey!" he said angrily. "What's that for?"

"You grab me one more time and I won't be just winging my purse at you. Understand?"

"Oh. Yeah, sorry."

He began the climb back up the ridge. I was a little apprehensive. "Do we have to go back there?"

" 'Fraid so. This pit don't lead to much except a steep drop about fifty feet down to the highway."

"Uh, can't we just stay down here at least until nightfall anyway? I don't think I want to have to keep running down here if they come back."

Jimmy stopped, turned, and sat down on the ground above me. "Not a half bad idea, lady." He scooted back down on the seat of his pants.

"Besides, you haven't finished telling me about your mother," I said when he reached the point where I was standing.

"Oh, yeah." He leaned back and looked around him. There was no high grass down here, so he scraped a tiny pebble from the dirt and idly rolled it around his fingers like a poor man's Captain Queeg.

"Where was I?"

"Your dad had just shown up at Father Jonathan's with a carful of people and met your mom there."

"Oh, yeah. My mom wanted to know who the people were. My dad told her they had come into the service station looking for gas, but they had serious car trouble that couldn't be fixed until the next day. Sound familiar?"

I swallowed hard and turned away. "Yeah."

"Anyway, my dad told her he was bringing them to Father Jonathan because he couldn't think of anything else

---

149

to do and maybe he could put them up for the night."

"When'd she tell you this?"

"A little later, at supper. My dad was at the festival."

"So when did all this come to a head?"

"At the festival. She saw the same people that my dad was escorting to Father Jonathan's earlier being led up the stairs to the stage. I guess she freaked."

"I should think so."

"Yeah, there was a big fight with a lot of screaming and yelling and stuff. Finally, a bunch of people grabbed my ma and hauled her off in a car. They drove off toward Father Jonathan's. There wasn't much I could do about it."

"You were there?"

"Oh, yeah. It happened at the fairgrounds right in front of everybody."

What an awful feeling, I thought, to see your mother treated that way. "What happened to her?"

"Oh, they told me they took her to a hospital. They still say that. But you wanna know something weird?"

As if I hadn't heard enough already today. "What?"

"They *never told me what hospital she was in!* Now, doesn't that strike you as a little strange? I mean, I can't visit her, can't even send her a card. Nothing. Of course, she ain't in no hospital. Father Johnson killed her just like he kills those people they bring to the festival every year. Just like he wants to do to you. Only he did it quiet, down in his cellar. She's buried with the rest of 'em up on the mountainside."

I saw him try to hide a tear. It was getting late out now and the shadows were beginning to melt together. Dusk was descending, but I could still make out the expression on Jimmy's face—unmistakably one of grief. I let Jimmy sit a minute, afraid to intrude on his thoughts. When he looked up, I had a question to ask him. "How long have you been involved in this?"

"All my life. I just told you."

"No, no. I mean in trying to fight him."

"Oh, just this year. I sorta felt I hadda do something to kinda make up for my mother, you know? My dad said I could come along since I already knew what was going on anyway. I just was supposed to stay out of the way."

I nodded. "Look, it's getting dark out now, so why don't we just head up to the garage, huh?" My voice must have given away my thoughts because Jimmy picked up on them right away.

He stood and brushed off the back of his jeans. "You don't believe me, do you?"

That was an understatement. I didn't reply. Instead, I started climbing back up the slope.

Jimmy scrambled after me and grabbed the back of my blouse, spinning me around. "Hey, lady! I asked you a question."

I didn't know what to say to him. "Jimmy, let's just say that I need a little more proof. That's a pretty wild story you just told me."

His voice softened. "You gotta admit they were following you all afternoon and looking for the both of us just now."

That was true enough. "I'm sure there's a reason for it."

Jimmy chuckled. "Oh, there is, all right. A good one."

Ignoring him, I turned to climb back up the hill to the garage. I reached the crest before Jimmy did and was just pulling myself over, when a flash of white near the building caught my eye. I dropped to the ground. Jimmy crawled up next to me. He heeded my advice about keeping his hands to himself.

"What's up?"

I stared at Harry's Garage, trying to see through the twilight. "I think I saw someone walk around the corner of the building."

"Oh, yeah?" Jimmy squinted into the gloom. "I wouldn't put it past 'em. I'll bet you donuts to dollars that Jerry's still out there. I betcha they tried to trick us into

---

walking out of here."

We waited a few minutes and nothing happened. Just as I was about to admit that maybe I'd been wrong, I heard a noise from the other side of the garage. Seconds later, a figure I didn't recognize stepped around the corner and started poking around the weeds with a flashlight. The arc of the light swung toward us and we ducked back below the groundline. The beam diffused harmlessly above us in the trees.

I peeked over the crest and saw the figure checking his watch. Thrusting the flashlight into his hip pocket, he strolled down the street toward the fairgrounds.

"Jerry Kosinski?" I asked.

"Yup," was the terse reply.

I went cold again. Someone sure wanted us—bad enough to try to trick us out of the woods. I was thankful we'd decided to stay in the copse.

After Jerry's footsteps faded off, we pulled ourselves into the weeds. As we stood, Jimmy asked me a pretty strange question.

"Lady, you ever seen the Aurora Borealis?"

"The Aurora Borealis? No, why? What's that got to do with anything?"

We were walking toward the garage. " 'Cuz you're about to see an artificial one."

"Terrific, kid. First you feed me a story about ritual killings and now you're going to give me an astronomy lesson. You're full of surprises."

We reached the building and were walking toward the pumps. There wasn't a soul in sight along the streets.

"No, really, lady. It's all part of the ceremony. In a couple of minutes, all the streetlights are going to go off. Then watch the sky in the south."

I leaned against one of the pumps and waited. About ten minutes later, true to Jimmy's word, the streetlights flickered and died. Ashley Falls was totally dark. I was just a baby when the Great Northeast Blackout struck in 1965, but I remember my parents telling me about it. It must have been something like this. I had an eerie feeling of foreboding and of being slightly disoriented.

Jimmy poked my elbow with his. "Watch," he said, nodding down the street.

A moment later, the lower southern sky lit up with an odd sort of continual orange flickering. I watched quietly as it remained stationary for several minutes, then began moving slowly toward the northwest, hugging the horizon the whole time. It was rather pretty, really.

"What is that?" I asked Jimmy.

"It's the beginning of the ceremony. They start off with a candlelight parade around town."

"So how come all the houselights are off, too? They're not tied into the streetlights somehow, are they?"

"No, of course not. Everybody turns 'em off for the festival. They like the effect it makes with the candlelight."

"Oh," I nodded in agreement. The effect certainly was impressive from this distance.

"So, what do you think, lady? If you haven't got enough proof to suit you yet, I can take care of that easily enough."

"How?"

"Come with me to Father Jonathan's."

"Have we got enough time? The procession's started already."

"Oh, yeah. No problem. They parade around town for over an hour, picking up more people before they go back to Father Jonathan's and then over to the fairgrounds. I know the route they take, so we can hustle over in your car and they'll never see us. Of course, we'll have to drive with the lights off and park a few blocks away, but I'm sure we'll be okay."

"And what's at Father Jonathan's?"

"A family that came in before you did this morning. In his dungeon."

That shot it. "Dungeon? C'mon now, I can't buy that nonsense."

Jimmy's face fell. "Okay," he mumbled, "so it's not really a dungeon. It's really where they hid slaves before the Civil War. Remember I told you about the Underground Railroad?"

"I remember."

"Like I said, that's where they put 'em until the ceremony tonight. I can show it to you, if you want me to."

I looked Jimmy straight in the eye. His face was guileless but challenging. There was really only one way to verify the truth of his tale. It was a scary idea, but it had to be done.

"Okay. Let's head for Father Jonathan's." (*Turn to page 83.*)

Jimmy's story was the most farfetched thing I'd ever heard. Sorry, but I just couldn't buy it.

"No, we're going back to the fairgrounds so I can find out what's going on over there. Then we'll get to the bottom of this." (*Turn to page 205.*)

HIDE IN HERE, NOW!

Fearful, yet curious, I climbed into the van and closed the door behind me. It was hot and stifling in there. The air was stale. I was beginning to doubt my decision when, sometime later, a commotion began in the service station. Slowly, it made its way around the building.

"All right, where the hell is she?" I heard Harry yell. Doors were being swiftly opened and slammed.

"I don't know, Dad!"

I looked around my little cell. There was nowhere to hide, but I crouched down behind a seat so I couldn't be seen from the front windows.

"You'd better find her, Harry. This is serious." There was no mistaking Father Jonathan's smooth but penetrating voice. It was oddly muffled, as if he didn't want anyone but Harry to hear him. I could tell he was standing near the van's open driver's window. "Check this van," he said much louder. I jumped with a start as he pounded on it a couple of times.

"I'll do it, Father Jonathan," Jimmy volunteered. The rear door opened and I sat face-to-face with the teenager. He looked right at me and shook his head. "She's not in here," he announced as he closed the door.

Harry spoke up then. "Okay, let's check those woods."

I heard three pairs of feet tromp past the van and crunch their way through the undergrowth nearby, spreading out in different directions. A few minutes later, Harry yelled, "She couldn't have gotten this far."

"All right," Father Jonathan yelled back. "But she has to be around here somewhere. Come on up."

The footsteps went past the van again, toward the front of the gas station. A few minutes later, I heard a car drive off. I stayed quiet for about five minutes, then took a cautious look out the driver's window.

At first, I didn't see anything, then I caught a quick flash of movement by a tiny rear window of the garage. I couldn't tell if it was Jimmy or his father. I watched a little while longer and saw the shadow go back and forth a couple more times, but still couldn't tell who it was. My guess was Harry. Jimmy might be inside, too, but I was pretty sure the car that left had been carrying Father Jonathan.

Another car came down the street and pulled into the lot. I saw right away that it wasn't Father Jonathan returning. It was a brown Mazda with two people in it.

Then a second car came from the other end of the street—the direction I had come from the highway. It, too, turned into Harry's Service Station and stopped.

I could faintly hear a number of people scuffling around near the gas pumps and talking together, though I couldn't understand what they were saying. When they started to come around back, I ducked down behind the seat and stayed as still and small as possible.

The first voice I heard was Harry's. "We already searched nearby, but she wasn't anywhere around. She must have headed back toward the highway by going through the woods over that ravine in the back. Can't have got too far—her car's still inside. When she gets to that cliff overlooking the interstate, she'll have nowhere to go anyway."

"What'd you and your son do to scare her, Harry?" an unfamiliar voice snickered.

"Shut yer damn pie hole. Just get out there and find her. George, you and Steve search north. You other guys go south, but all of ya keep within shoutin' distance of each other so's you can close in quickly and help each other. Ya got that?"

It was real weird to listen to plans to capture me, as if I were some dangerous beast.

Everyone melted into the trees. As soon as the last step was gone, the rear door opened again. It was the kid. "Lady, grab your stuff and come with me quick."

What now? I exclaimed inwardly, but I did as he said. As I stepped out, I heard Harry's voice. "Now you guys look 'round real good and I'll be waitin' back at the garage."

Jimmy grabbed my wrist and yanked me into the ladies' room. "Hide in here now." He threw me in, shut the door quickly, and ran back to the station's little office.

I heard Harry trudge up the ravine, pause somewhere out back, then open the door to the van, slamming it quickly in disgust. As he walked past the restroom, I heard him cursing his son.

He burst into the office and began yelling. The sounds coming from inside were amplified by the structure rather than muffled. "What the hell did you do with her? Where'd you hide that broad?"

"I didn't do nothin'."

There was the unmistakable sound of a backhand across a face.

"You're lucky she wasn't in that damn van. How could I have been so stupid to let you check it out? Now where the hell is she?"

"I'm tellin' you, Dad, I don't know."

"Oh, balls. She didn't just go out and run away on her own."

The argument continued for many minutes. Jimmy never admitted helping me. Neither did his father believe him. I could hear Harry throw his son around and beat him, but I never heard a word about why everyone was so interested in finding me. The fight eventually faded down to a quiet truce.

I had to give a lot of credit to the teenager for not giving me away. This was obviously very important to him. But it really bothered me that I didn't have a single, lousy clue why it was so important to him—or everyone else!—that I be located. There was still nothing more than Jimmy's half of the story—if there was any truth to it all. Still, I felt a little better about hiding from Harry and everyone else.

Until I knew why they were so interested in me, how could I trust them? Jimmy, for whatever reason, was not betraying me.

Just sitting there in that tiny room, with nothing to do, made me increasingly nervous. The room was absolutely filthy. Who knows what color the original paint might have been? Right now, everything, including the toilet and the sink, was a dingy gray except for the areas that were rusty. The stench was revolting. But at least no one came to use it.

Time after time I had myself talked into believing that the whole situation was nonsense and that I should just get up and go out there, demanding an explanation. But then the phone would ring and each time it was Father Jonathan checking on the progress of the search. Harry had to give him the same answer every time: "No, Father Jonathan, not yet. They're still out there looking."—pause—"Don't worry—we'll get her."—another pause—"Yeah, the minute I have news."

Late in the afternoon—close to five by my watch—the search parties returned.

"She must be miles from here by now, Harry. We didn't find nothing."

"Hell, we went all the way to the highway and came up empty."

"Hey, Harry, you check this place real good?"

My heart jumped.

"Yeah, me and Father Jonathan checked the place out ourselves. She ain't here."

There were a number of "hmmphs" by way of saying "Isn't that strange?"

"Well, I'll see you all at the festival. Thanks anyway."

"Father Jonathan is gonna be kinda upset with you, ain't he, Harry?"

"Don't worry none about that. I can handle him."

Soon they all left except one guy who stayed behind to help Harry lock up.

"Where's Jimmy?" he asked.

"Aw, I sent him home."

"Listen, I just hope he hasn't screwed up with this dame."

"Me too. We'll find out soon enough."

The doors were locked and Harry and his friend drove off, probably in the pickup I had noticed earlier. I was left alone in Harry's Service Station.

So what now, I thought. What did Jimmy expect me to do now? Break into the gas station somehow and escape in my car? How was I supposed to get in? And how far could my car go with that hole in the radiator?

When I had heard nothing for several minutes, I suddenly couldn't stand being in that disgusting room one moment longer. I slowly turned the knob and opened the door.

The rush of fresh air through the tiny crack was pure heaven. I stuck my nose right into the breeze.

I soon realized there wasn't a soul in sight. Slinging my pocketbook and overnight bag over my shoulders, I stepped out into the daylight.

Stretching my legs was a great relief as well. I just walked around the building for a few minutes enjoying the difference between the outdoors and my little jail cell.

Once my eyes and legs were readjusted to freedom, I settled back against the rear wall of the building, facing the Ford van. Now my stomach spoke up. I hadn't had anything to eat since early this morning when I left Burlington. Even that was only a doughnut and a cup of coffee. I'm not usually a big breakfast eater, so by lunchtime, I'm ravenous. And here it was almost dinnertime. Sitting in that restroom hadn't done much for my appetite, but the fresh air certainly had awoken my stomach.

I supposed the best thing to do would be to wait until nighttime and then see if I couldn't just drive out of town. I'd grab a few gallons of antifreeze from Harry's and if the engine overheated, I'd just toss some into the radiator. I might not get all the way to White Plains, but at least I'd make it far enough to get some help . . . that is, if I could get into the service station in the first place. Maybe I should hunt for a place to break in.

I stood up and decided to start with the little window in the rear wall. I left my bags on the ground beside me.

The window was just about at shoulder height—too high to get in without a boost. There had to be something around here to use. I found a plastic milk crate discarded in the bushes beside the tow truck. It wasn't quite as high as I would have liked, but it was a help. I placed it on the ground just below the window and stepped onto it.

The damn window turned out to be set in cement—no handle, no latch, no hinges. I stood on the crate cursing my luck.

Suddenly, a pickup truck pulled into the lot from the highway. It sounded like Harry's.

I ducked back down quickly and grabbed my bags. I heard the truck stop at the front, then the service door was raised. Harry was apparently dropping something off because I heard him pick up some tools or something from the truck bed and toss them inside the building. They clattered loudly as they landed.

It gave me a moment to grab my bags again. Then I realized that the stupid milk crate looked pretty suspicious there under the window, so I grabbed it and carried it back near the tow truck where I had found it.

Harry finished whatever little chore he had stopped for and I heard him lock up again. I waited with bated breath for him to climb back into the pickup and drive off . . . but he didn't. Nothing but silence. What the devil was he up to?

I heard a door open on the far side of the garage. Harry was taking a look in the ladies' room. I thanked God I'd had the foresight to take my bags with me. He slammed the door shut with a curse. He checked the men's room, then I heard him stomp around the back. It was obvious he was

---

giving the place a once-over, perhaps in the hope that I had returned.

I tiptoed past the tow truck as Harry made his way through the rear lot. He opened the van and checked it out again, slamming the door violently.

I hoped he would turn back and not come this way, but no luck. Apparently, he wanted to check the tow truck too. Hiding underneath it was obviously out of the question, but on the other hand, if I ran out front, I might be seen by a neighbor or someone driving by. Still, it was the only alternative.

I quickly stepped around the corner and stopped dead. Someone was in the pickup truck!

Harry's footsteps were getting closer. I knew I'd have a moment of safety as he stopped to look over the truck, but where was I going to go? The pickup was facing away from me, with its passenger's back to me. It was probably that guy from the search party who had driven off with Harry earlier. I stood frozen.

Just as Harry came around the corner and began poking around the tow truck, the person inside the pickup moved. Jimmy! I ran toward him.

The look of surprise on his face was classic. I thought he was going to have a heart attack. When he got over his shock, he waved me around the opposite corner, back toward the restrooms. I didn't have to be told twice.

Harry didn't spend very long at the other side of the garage, but then, there was nowhere really useful to hide. As he stomped angrily back to the pickup, I ducked around to the back of the building again. Under any other circumstances, it would all have seemed like a game.

The truck coughed into life and drove off, leaving me breathing heavily and my heart pounding like a jackhammer. The adrenalin slowly wore off and my stomach again began to make its presence felt.

"Shutup and wait awhile. There's nothing I can do about it."

It didn't listen. I was still hungry.

I settled back against the wall to wait for nightfall. I didn't want to take a chance of being seen poking around the front doors of the garage while it was still light out. I checked my watch. 5:45. Still some time to go. I wished there was something to do.

After a while, I thought I remembered seeing an old magazine in the van. I was still too nervous to read, really, but I had to do something to relieve the monotony and take my mind off food.

Sure enough, a two-year-old *Redbook* was stuffed into the well next to the side door. I picked it up, returned to my seat, and began reading. Not very many of the articles were interesting, but the fiction was pretty good. The biggest problem was trying to carefully peel the stuck-together pages from each other so I could finish what I was reading.

It's a funny thing about being in danger—no matter how much you've relaxed, there's a part of you that stays keyed up, keeping subconscious guard. I was aware when the light had faded enough to make it difficult to read. I saw when the street lights in Ashley Falls came on. Finally, I heard someone approaching the service station. I tossed the magazine aside and grabbed my bags again, ready to run. My senses were alert, my head cocked upward, listening. I didn't need to listen too hard.

"Lady! Hey, lady!"

I breathed a sigh of relief. It was Jimmy. I pulled myself up and ran to the corner, poking my head around just enough to see him standing in the side lot. He was carrying a brown paper bag and appeared to be alone.

"Back here," I hissed.

He turned and came to me. "Sorry to take so long. I had a hard time gettin' away from my dad."

He must have noticed me looking behind him. "It's okay. There's nobody here but you and me. They're all gettin' ready for the procession. I hadda wait for 'em to take off before I could get over here."

"You're sure you're not being followed? They were pretty suspicious of you this afternoon."

He joined me around back in the gathering dark. "The ceremony's more important." He held out the paper bag. "Here, I brought these. I thought you might be hungry."

I thanked him and took the bag. Inside were a couple of sandwiches, a Pepsi, and a small apple. I could have kissed him. Instead, I thanked him again, this time for my stomach.

"I hope you like bologna."

"Are you kidding? Today, I love bologna." I dug deep into the bag and grabbed a sandwich. The first half was gone in two huge bites.

The kid introduced himself as I ate. "I'm Jimmy," he said simply.

"I know," I mumbled through a mouthful of food. "I heard your father yelling at you. My name is Lisa." I noticed for the first time that he had changed into a blue and red striped rugby-style sports shirt and a pair of crisp, clean bluejeans.

"Hi."

Swallow. Gulp. "Hi."

He waited until I finished off half the apple before he spoke again. "I guess we better talk about getting out of here."

"I guess so. Now what was this about a procession?"

"Oh, part of the festival is a candlelight procession goin' from Father Jonathan's house around town, then back to his house again, then finally over to the fairgrounds. It'll start pretty soon. Most of the town's gathering over there now. We'll have a better chance then."

"That's good." It did, however, raise a question. "What were you doing here earlier with your father when I saw you in the pickup?"

"He took me out to help him take the highway sign down. You know—the one with the cheap gas advertised on it. Well, actually, we don't take the whole sign down,

---

163

just the part that has the price written on it."

I nodded.

"Then my dad wanted to take another look around. There was no way to warn you. I'll tell you, though, you surprised the hell out of me when you came running around that corner."

I laughed. "Yeah, I noticed. You looked like you'd seen a ghost."

Jimmy didn't laugh back. "Bad choice of words, lady."

I took a sip of soda to disguise the eerie feeling that surged through me. He was a little too serious that time.

"You know," I said, "I'm surprised you don't have people backed up to the exit ramp with gas that cheap."

"Yeah, well, this stretch of highway isn't traveled that much. I suppose most people figure it's a rip-off, or an old sign someone forgot to change."

Jimmy looked at the sky. "I figure in another ten minutes or so, it'll be dark enough for us to try and get out of here. By then, they'll all be in the procession."

"Okay. In the meantime, would you mind telling me exactly what's going on here?"

"Later. It's a real long story. I can tell you when we're out of town. I don't have time now."

Suddenly, all the streetlights flickered and died. They had been on for only a few minutes.

"What's that all about?" I asked.

Jimmy was unperturbed. "Part of the procession. It makes the whole thing more dramatic, or so they say. Sort of a tradition."

It definitely made things darker. And spookier.

Jimmy picked up my overnight bag and handed it to me. I followed his lead and picked up my purse. Then he explained our options.

"I can put a temporary patch on your radiator. It'll take a while, but then we can make a run for it."

"I see. How long will this patch last?"

"Don't know. Sometimes two hundred feet, sometimes

---

two hundred miles. Sometimes, they take real good and never come off at all. That's pretty rare, though."

"You mean we may not even get as far as the highway?"

"Well, it's possible. The big problem is that there won't be any other cars on the road in Ashley Falls, so we'll sorta stick out if we leave the headlights on. We'll have to drive out blind. They keep guys sittin' around hidden in their cars with CB sets and if anyone who don't belong here happens to wander into town during the ceremony, they escort him out real quick."

"You mean they keep cops out on the streets?"

"Naw, they're guys like Jerry Kosinsky and my dad and a few others. They rotate every year. No police here but Father Jonathan."

He paused and then added, "I suppose we could walk out, but I didn't think you'd want to leave your car behind."

"You're right. I don't."

"But leaving on foot is safer. A lot safer." His eyes were pleading.

I agreed that we should sneak out of Ashley Falls on foot. I could come back and get my car later. (*If you agree, turn to page 23.*)

I *wanted* that car! We had to try to get it repaired and then take our chances and drive out. (*Turn to page 107.*)

JIMMY'S GIRLFRIENDS

We walked back to the garage in dead silence. Jimmy took the lead, always walking four or five steps ahead of me. He wasn't quite running, but I had to jog a few steps every so often to keep up. The ceremony looked ominous enough, but there was no real explanation for Jimmy's big hurry. We got back to Harry's in just a few minutes. Just like on the way over, we saw absolutely nobody on the streets.

When we got back, Jimmy leaned up against one of the gas pumps.

"Well, lady, we got outta that luckily enough. But if you want my opinion, instead of walking straight into the hornets' nest, I think we oughta head for the woods and avoid them altogether, you know what I mean?"

I had to agree, but wanted to know something. "So how come you came back here?"

"To get something. Wait here a minute."

He dashed off into the woods behind the garage and disappeared for several long minutes. When he returned, he was carrying a backpack. It was filthy with dirt and clumps of moss. In the dark, it appeared to be blue and orange nylon, but I couldn't be sure. He slung it over his shoulders as we left Harry's. I looped my overnight bag over my shoulder, then put my pocketbook over that and followed him.

He took us on a circuitous route through Ashley Falls. First, we headed north back up the same road I taken from the highway. It seemed we had walked almost into the next county when Jimmy took a left and brought us through some side streets heading west. He was sauntering along at his fast clip and I was having some trouble keeping up. I knew I should have taken up jogging.

At one point, I trotted up beside him. "Where are we actually going?"

Jimmy didn't look at me. I noticed he was walking with his head down most of the time as if he was following some sort of inborn radar and didn't need to see where he was headed.

"Over the mountain. Once we top the crest, we'll work our way down the other side and we'll be safe in North Heddon. Then we can go for the police."

I had lagged behind a little again, so I picked up my pace and caught up once more. "Okay, I give. What are we going to the police for?"

"You saw the ceremony. What do you think they're doin' over there? Watching an eighth grade play?"

I had to admit, it looked pretty strange, but I still hadn't actually seen anything illegal. "We didn't stay long enough for me to find out."

Jimmy stopped dead in his tracks. His face was a perfect blank. "Of course not. We didn't want to be their victims like those other people we saw."

"Yeah, but victims for what?"

Jimmy's shoulders drooped and he turned away from me. I could tell he was exasperated by my ignorance.

"If you think they were searching for you just because they like to take long hikes in the woods for their health, you're nuts."

I watched him walk away from me. Yes, it was very true that they had expended an awful lot of energy looking for me this afternoon. But still, there was something in the way Jimmy was evading my questions that had me more than a little curious. I ran up to him and grabbed him by the shoulder, yanking him around.

"Look, I'm tired of playing games with you," I said. "Now I'm not taking another step until you tell me what's going on around here."

Jimmy didn't reply right away. He just stood staring back at me as he mulled over his options. Frankly, if he had just turned around and kept on going, I would have been right behind, but I knew he was trying to figure out whether or not I was bluffing.

Then he surprised me by offering a compromise. "Tell you what. I'll tell you exactly what's up if you keep walking. I don't think you understand just how much danger we're in."

That was fair enough. We trudged on. It didn't take him long to get started.

"Okay, here's the story. This festival they got going is really more like those ancient Roman games where everybody used to go out to the Colosseum and watch people get executed."

"Oh, come on!"

"No, really. They get those people up there on that stage and Father Jonathan gives 'em some kind of ritual mumbo-jumbo and then they off 'em. You ever read that short story 'The Lottery'?"

I had no idea what he was getting to. "Yes. Why?"

"Well, this is that story in reverse. Everyone over twenty-one . . . the drinking age, I think that has something to do with it . . . draws a number from a great big drum and whoever gets the number that matches one that Father Jonathan picks from another drum gets to do the dirty deed."

"I didn't see any drums."

Jimmy stumbled in the dark. "Uh, no, of course not. They keep 'em behind the stage until time for the drawing. Then they haul 'em up and have their little lottery. It's a real honor to win, you know."

"I can imagine," I said sarcastically. "So how do they actually kill those people?"

"With a knife. They slit everybody's throat ear to ear and then they just watch while the victim's life dribbles all over the ground."

"You mean the stage?"

"Yeah. Yeah, the stage. Of course. And eventually it dribbles to the ground. The blood, I mean."

I had visions of the legendary sacrifices of the Aztecs and

Incas. Only to what purpose? To feed the teeming millions as the ancient Mexican Indians allegedly had done? Hardly. Ashley Falls was a town of teeming dozens at best.

Or could it be to appease some crazy concept of a god? For a fruitful harvest or increased fertility or some other such nonsense? Had I fallen into a Stephen King novel? I couldn't believe it. . . .

"Jimmy, why does this happen? They must have some reason . . . "

"Oh, they got reasons up the wazoo. I suggest you keep quiet and save your breath."

"That's not good enough, Jimmy. I want to know why this ritual goes on. What kind of hold does Father Jonathan have over these people?"

"I don't know. Charisma, I guess. He tells them this is what they should do and they do it, no questions asked. It's always been like that. I guess everybody likes it. Bloodlust." He shrugged. "Why'd the Romans like their games? It all prob'ly started innocent enough way back when, then just gradually became more and more violent. I don't know. I wasn't here then."

That didn't sound like much of a justification. I had expected something with a sort of twisted logic to it. Something evil and perverse, maybe, but at least logical within its own context. Instead, all I got from the teenager were vague generalities, and I had the feeling I wouldn't get anything more. I let the matter drop. For now.

We had reached the west side of the town. The houses were getting farther and farther apart. All of them were blacked out—great, ugly tombstones rising out of the front yards of Ashley Falls. It was like walking through a huge graveyard, and I shivered hard several times at the eerieness of the lifeless town.

Jimmy never slackened his pace. If anything, it had quickened as he got closer to the mountain. It was getting more and more difficult to keep up, and even though the night was becoming chilly, I had broken into a sweat.

Jimmy looked as if he could keep going like this forever. Oh, to be fifteen again. I stopped to catch my breath.

It took Jimmy a few steps to notice I had stopped. When he finally did, he turned back to me and I could see a very distinct look of anger cross his face.

"What the hell you doin'? You promised!"

"I know. But I can't go any faster. You have to slow down if you want me to keep up." I realized I was puffing rather hard by now. "And unless I miss my guess, we got quite a climb ahead of us tonight, right?"

"Yeah."

"Well, I'm not fifteen years old anymore, you understand?"

"Okay, okay. But don't wait too long, all right?"

"Yeah, fine. Are you going to slow down a little?"

Jimmy looked around Ashley Falls. We might have been the only two people alive there. "It's dangerous, but I guess we got no choice, huh?"

"Not unless you want to go on alone." Jimmy didn't reply. He stood a few feet away, keeping watch. I dropped my bags to the ground beside me. I hadn't realized until just now how deep they were digging into my left shoulder. I gave my sore muscles a massage. It felt great.

Jimmy was like a cat on a hotplate, bouncing around everywhere, watching everything, and he was obviously relieved when I announced I was ready. Before I had a chance to sling the bags over my right shoulder, he was already halfway down the block or so it seemed. I called to him. He stopped and waited. Just to emphasize that I meant what I said about slowing down, I strolled easily to where he was waiting impatiently.

"I'm not going to be conned into chasing after you. I meant what I said about slowing down."

He nodded sullenly and took off again. This time, he was forced to keep to my pace.

He didn't say anything more about the festival. I didn't push it, either. It was all too fantastic to believe anyway.

Somewhere in there, maybe there was a germ of truth, but most of it seemed like Jimmy's imagination. Maybe there was a very real danger in Ashley Falls. I couldn't deny the events that took place while I was hiding around the garage, but there had to be a better explanation than Father Jonathan's lottery!

We were marching down a deserted road. The blacktop melted into the gloom ahead of us. On both sides, trees loomed overhead. We walked a little way into the scrub. "Hey, isn't there a trail through here somewhere?" I called out.

To my amazement, I couldn't see Jimmy. He was somewhere up ahead, I knew. Even as used to the dark as my eyes were by now, they couldn't see anything in the deeper gloom of the woods. But I could hear his footsteps in the leaves. Suddenly, they stopped.

"Yeah, there is."

I followed his voice and soon found him sitting against a tree. I stood over him and he pointed a thumb over his shoulder. "It's over there a little way. I didn't want to take it right away, but we'll pick it up in a minute."

His voice had taken on a more relaxed tone. He felt safe here. I'm sure he had spent hours up on this mountain and knew it well, like an old friend. I could hear it in his voice as he spoke.

"Sit down."

I was a little surprised that he wanted to rest now, but I took his invitation. He didn't seem tired. I chose a tree facing him to lean against. Gradually, my eyes were able to make out more than just a vague form in the forest.

"This is Carford's Mountain. I used to spend a lot of time hiking around up here. The Indians used to call it 'Penotamee—The Mountain of Tears.' That was because of the waterfall that used to be up here."

"Which is what they named Ashley Falls after, right?"

"Yeah. Some guy named Ashley found 'em and this used to be called Mount Ashley back in colonial days, but the stream eventually dried up and so did the falls. Then I guess some old hermit named Carford moved in and they started calling it after him. That was about a hundred years or so, I guess. I ain't sure. I could show you the clearing where he had his cabin and stuff, if you want. There's not much there now, just a pile of rocks and a shallow pit. Sometimes kids go up there and play.

"I can show you where the falls were, too. It's a pretty neat place, all high cliffs and stuff. I wish I'da had a chance to see 'em. They musta been really neat."

The kid had some sensitivity after all. That shocked me. "Yeah, I'll bet they were. But we wouldn't be able to see much at night, would we?"

"No, I guess you're right. I did bring a flashlight, though."

"So why are we walking around in the dark?"

" 'Cuz we're still too close to town. They'd see it in a minute and come after us real fast. We gotta wait until we're way into the woods."

Jimmy lapsed into silence. I let him enjoy his reverie a few moments before I interrupted him.

"Say, uh, I was kind of wondering a few things about this ceremony you were telling me about."

"Yeah? What about it?"

"How come Father Jonathan never gets turned in? I mean, maybe the townspeople are behind him, but aren't there any cops around?"

"Not in Ashley Falls. It's too small. What we got is a state trooper who drives through about once a month or if there's an accident or something. That's about it. They hide the bodies real good. You wanna know where? Right here on Carford's Mountain, that's where," he said before I could answer. "It's way up by the summit. I'll definitely show you that. We can use the flashlight up there."

I shivered as he continued.

"Naw, they haven't the faintest idea what's going on down there—the cops, I mean. Nobody in town is gonna say a word, either, 'cuz they'd all end up in jail or something."

And that brought up the Sixty-Four Thousand Dollar Question. "So why are you so interested in justice all of a sudden? Aren't you afraid of going to prison yourself?"

"Uh, well, uh, yeah, I guess so. But I mean there's other things . . . "

"Other things? What other things? Drugs?"

Jimmy was getting hesitant again. "No. Nothing like that. It was, uh, my girlfriend, Susie. They, uh, killed her a year ago 'cuz she threatened to squeal."

In spite of myself, I shivered again. If he was lying, he sure was good at it.

"What happened?" I asked. "If you don't mind telling me, that is?"

I heard him throw a few pebbles down the hillside. "No, I don't mind, I guess."

He picked up a few more pebbles. He was playing with them, running them around his fingers, replacing them when he dropped them.

"I guess we went together, oh, six months or so. They didn't like that."

"Who?"

"Oh, you know. Father Jonathan and my dad."

"What could they have had against her?"

I heard him throw a pebble. "She was always trying to stop them. She used to cause them problems. Like yelling during the ceremony and stuff and threatening to go to the cops."

"Did she?"

Jimmy grunted. "Hell, no. She never had the chance."

"How long did this go on?"

"I don't know. Not very."

"What took her so long to speak up?"

"Jeez, she was only fifteen. A lot of people are plenty older'n that and never said nothing at all."

"I guess so. Jimmy, how old are you?"

"Just turned seventeen." He threw another pebble. "I hadda watch, you know."

"Watch what? What are you talking about?"

"Watch them kill her."

He paused. I suppose he was waiting for me to prompt him, but I didn't say anything. It was spooky enough sitting there in the woods in about the blackest night I'd ever seen without listening to murder stories—true or not.

Jimmy reached into his backpack, rummaged around for a minute, then plucked out something I couldn't see. A Bic Lighter flared up in front of his face and I saw that he was lighting a cigarette. I didn't smoke, but this sure seemed like a good time for one if I did.

"She had gone over to Father Jonathan's one day," he said softly, "about a week or so before the festival. She wanted to try to talk him into stopping it. Naturally, he said no. And when he got her into the house, he tried to make love to her.

"See, I know he had his eye on her for a long time. God, she was gorgeous. She had long, brown hair and big huge brown eyes. Just like a deer. And you're probably not going to believe this, but she was a cheerleader. Honest.

"That ol' Father Jonathan, he was watchin' her for a long time, yessir. I seen it in his eyes every time he talked her. Like a big, slobberin' idiot. I mean, you saw how cool he is allatime, right?"

I didn't reply and Jimmy didn't like it this time.

"Right?"

I was taken aback somewhat by the harshness of his raised voice. "Uh, yeah, right. He was very well-spoken."

"Sure, that's the way he is most of the time. But around Susie, he got all excited and stuff and couldn't talk at all. Just stuttered at her like a moron or something. He was like that with all the girls. Never could talk to 'em. Especially the ones he liked."

"So he tried to get her when she went over to his house that night. She wouldn't give in to him, of course. In fact, she just made fun of him. Just laughed at him. 'With you?' she said. She was too damn prissy-faced."

He curled his lips as he said "prissy-faced" and it struck me as being a strange thing to say about one's girlfriend.

"So, uh, I guess she threatened to go to the police right about then, and the next thing I knew, he had her up on the stage at the festival that year."

"How'd he do that?"

Jimmy snuffed his cigarette out violently. "Knocked her out. Got her alone up here in the woods that afternoon and just clocked her with a branch. Then he took her up on that stage and right in front of everybody, he took out a knife and cut her head half off. Right then, her eyes opened and her mouth started goin' up and down tryin' to say something. You know how I knew she was tryin' to talk?"

I didn't dare not answer this time. "No."

" 'Cuz I could see the bubbles from the air in her windpipe in her blood as it poured out, that's how. I was right there, watchin'."

Yeah, I could see that. It was a pretty graphic description. I felt sick.

Jimmy tossed the rest of the pebbles away. They made a sound like a bunch of popguns going off at the same time as they hit the leaves on the ground. He stood up. "C'mon. We wasted enough time."

He picked up his backpack. I slipped my bags over my shoulders once more and followed him.

He wasn't climbing uphill any longer; he had started leading me on a line parallel to the road below us. I assumed he was headed for the trail he had told me about. He took only a couple of steps when he came up short and started cursing.

He pulled his backpack off and went digging through it. He pulled out a flashlight, flicked it on, aimed it at the ground ahead of him, and started walking again.

The light made a sharp beam that bounced crazily off wet leaves and slimy dirt. It didn't help me much since

Jimmy's body masked it, but it helped him make his way with a great degree of certainty.

We hadn't gone very far when Jimmy turned right. I was behind him, and I could tell we had reached the trail.

Jimmy took us uphill quite a distance without saying a word. The trail eventually spilled out into a large, open meadow. I followed Jimmy into the middle of the field and took a look around.

The night was crystal clear. I had never seen so many stars. For the very first time, I could actually make out the Milky Way. It seemed impossible to think that just below us, in the town of Ashley Falls, a grisly scene was being played out.

Jimmy had turned his back to me and was looking down at the valley. He had turned off the flashlight.

"Hey, watch this," he said.

I turned myself and stared off in the blackness. I had no idea what I was supposed to be watching for. It was quiet now, and all I could hear were the insects and creatures of the forest.

The ribbon of the highway was clearly visible miles and miles off. A small trickle of vehicles was making its way in both directions of I-87.

Nothing occurred for a very long time. I had to wonder why Jimmy had suddenly abandoned his hurry-up attitude. Now, he was taking his time, stopping when he wanted to and absorbing the atmosphere of the night in the woods.

Suddenly, I thought I saw a flicker of light off in the distance. I stared harder, thinking maybe my eyes were playing tricks on me. That turned out not to be the case. There was another flicker, then from the same spot, a tiny twinkle. Then another and another. A whole cityful of streetlights blazed up in numerous zigzag patterns. The Mayfly Festival of Ashley Falls was ending and the town was returning to life. It was an awe-inspiring sight from the mountain.

Jimmy watched quietly for several minutes after the show had ended and it was obvious that Ashley Falls had returned to normal. After a while, he broke his silence.

"What do you think? Pretty neat, huh?"

"I have to admit I've never seen anything quite like it before."

"You get to see it once a year, that's all. Like fireworks. C'mon, I want to show you the falls."

He flipped the flashlight on and started walking off to the left. He picked up a trail at the edge of the meadow, but I had no way of knowing if it was a continuation of the one we had just left or a different one altogether.

We trudged on for a few hundred yards before Jimmy stopped. "Down there."

He was using his flashlight as a pointer.

"Here it is, the world-famous Ashley Falls," he announced. "The 'Mountain of Tears,' as the Indians put it. Now as dead and forgotten as Ashley himself."

It seemed we were at the top of the now-empty falls and were, in fact, standing right in the dry stream bed. I couldn't see much over the cliff because Jimmy's light simply didn't penetrate very far. I was sure, however, that we were standing at the top of a very long drop.

Jimmy swung the light around and found a good-sized branch lying on the ground. He waved the light over it so I could see how big it was, then, picking it up, he threw it over the edge.

I half-expected not to hear anything at all, but I guess that comes from watching too much televsion. In fact, the branch hit the ground long before I thought it would. But the noise it made in the brush below was small indeed. I was suitably impressed.

"About fifty yards or so, I guess," Jimmy explained. "Enough to hurt you real bad." He reached out and grabbed my arm, giving it a sudden jerk toward the cliff. My stomach lurched. I screamed, grabbing at Jimmy frantically. He snapped me back quickly, laughing loudly at my expense.

"Just curing your hiccups," he snickered.

"That wasn't funny, you little bastard!"

Still snickering, he wandered off into the woods. As angry as I was, I had no choice but to follow.

He went back to the meadow. This time, he didn't stop and continued straight through to another corner. He had picked up his pace slightly, but I had no problem keeping up. He unerringly found yet another pathway leading through the trees. We got to a point where the trail went off to the right and seemed to skirt the summit. I was growing tired. Jimmy stopped and waited for me to catch up.

"Don't worry, once we get going downhill, you'll find the walking easier."

"Don't you think we've spent enough time wandering around here? Shouldn't we get a move on?"

"We're fine. They'll never catch us now. There's something I want to show you first before we leave."

I sighed.

He plowed into the brush, leaving me to make my own path behind him. We were going downhill, back toward Ashley Falls. I didn't like that idea, but Jimmy was right—it was easier going downhill.

Something alive fell in my hair and I swatted at it, hitting it with the back of my hand. It went flying into the leaves. I couldn't tell what it was and, frankly, I didn't want to know. It was all I could do to stop shivering.

We walked quite a distance before Jimmy brought us to a halt.

"We're here. This is it."

I looked around. It didn't look like much of anything to me. Just another little patch of woods and scrub.

"This is what?"

"This is the burial ground. All the victims are buried here."

"It doesn't look like much to me."

"Of course not. You think it'd be smart to bury 'em out

there in the meadow with tombstones all over?"

"How far does it go?"

"Oh, not far. People are buried on top of other people so a whole lot of space isn't used up. Susie's here."

This was beyond spooky. This was downright scary as hell. First, there was the big effort they spent looking for me, then those poor people standing on the stage, then this crazy trek all over the Mountain of Tears. Finally, I find myself standing in a hidden graveyard, overlooking the unmarked burial sites of people who were murdered in public with the full consent of an entire town.

Could this really all be happening?

Jimmy was playing the role of tour guide and relishing it. His flashlight stabbed out here and there as he indicated various points of interest.

"H-h-here's where Susie was b-buried. Over h-here is Anne. R-r-r-right here are M-m-mary and another girl whose name I don't r-r-remember."

"Jimmy, who are these girls?"

"Huh? Oh, o-o-old g-girlfriends."

"All of them? You only mentioned Susie."

Then it dawned on me that he was stuttering.

He turned quickly and poked the flashlight beam directly in my eyes, dazzling me for an instant. Just before he flipped the flashlight off, I saw the dull outline of a branch in his right hand.

I couldn't see a thing except a bright yellow orb. Somewhere in the back of my mind, something was telling me to run. Turning, I stumbled through bushes and branches. I kept my left arm over my face and used my right arm to feel out for tree trunks. I just plowed through in panic, oblivious of the pain.

I heard Jimmy behind me, laughing. At first, I didn't understand why he didn't just come right after me. Then I realized he was playing a deadly game of cat-and-mouse. Everything was in his favor—he knew the terrain and had the flashlight. And he didn't let me get too far away before he started coming after me. I heard his footsteps crunching down onto the forest floor.

My eyes weren't quite as dazzled as a moment ago and I stopped just for a second to see if I could make Jimmy out. His flashlight gave him away.

Then he stopped. Could it be he had lost track of me as well? Had his overconfidence gotten the best of him? I saw the flashlight go on and poke around through the woods nearby. I circled around a tree and its trunk shielded me.

Jimmy was moving very slowly now, obviously aware that I must be nearby, and not wanting to make another mistake. His steps were slow and deliberate in contrast to pounding going on in my chest.

Jimmy's light flashed past my hiding place and kept going. It danced along in a great, sweeping semi-circle, then came slowly back. I heard him cursing softly.

He took a couple more steps and then stopped. The light went off.

What in God's name was he up to? I think my breathing stopped. It was downright cold up here, but I was sweating anyway. I didn't dare budge, afraid that the tiniest creak would give me away.

It gave me time to reflect on what Jimmy had done. That whole story about Father Jonathan was obviously a lie. Now I understood. It had hit me first when I heard him stammering. He—not Father Jonathan—had killed all those young girls. He had simply substituted the black minister for himself in his story.

How could I have been so damn gullible?

Long, tense minutes floated by. Jimmy had chosen a terrific way to panic me.

But if I could be, oh, so quiet . . .

A short, slow, deliberate step . . .

Then another . . .

I crooked one leg and slipped off the shoe from my right foot, then my left. I didn't want to take the chance of them making any noise as I put them on the ground, so I tied the laces together—a task made a lot more difficult than it should it have been by the blackness of the forest and shaking of my hands. Once they were tied together, I hung them around my neck.

Stepping out tentatively, I slipped my toes under the leaves to the ground beneath. I could feel the slime of the dirt through the bottom of my stockings. I prayed that I wouldn't feel anything move under my feet.

Walking so slowly made it difficult to keep my balance. It was almost impossible to judge my steps in the dark. I felt like I was walking a tightrope; one slip and . . .

I got the hang of it after a dozen strides or so and it got considerably easier after that. I couldn't hear Jimmy make a sound nor did he turn the flashlight back on. I must have been using muscles that had long lain dormant because I started feeling an unaccustomed soreness in the fronts of my thighs. Another large tree loomed up ahead of me. Six or eight careful, painstaking paces later, I was able to slip behind it.

There was no way to tell, of course, but I guessed I had put maybe forty or fifty feet between me and Jimmy. If I had had any idea where I was, I probably would have just run for it. I supposed if I went to my right, downhill, I'd eventually end up back in Ashley Falls. Not knowing where Jimmy was, though, made it a difficult decision.

"Screw this! I'm coming after you, bitch!"

He was a lot closer than I thought. The light went on and I heard him crashing through the forest again. He was moving in a zigzag pattern on a kind of diagonal between where I was hiding and the summit. I listened to him with bated breath, aware that if he kept going in that direction, he'd eventually pass me by, maybe even cross over the summit. And then I'd run for it.

Suddenly, he stopped, turned, and the flashlight beam came bouncing in my direction. I slipped around to put the tree trunk between us again.

Jimmy didn't see me and started off once more, searching an area nearby, but not putting me in any immediate danger. After a time, he moved off to another part of the woods.

I waited until I could barely see his light. It was a good thing I hadn't put my shoes back on. I was already heading downhill, so my course of action was pretty obvious. With far more confidence than I'd had when I first tried skulking away, I started to put more distance between me and my pursuer.

I got no more than three steps when something sharp and extremely painful jabbed its way through my stocking and into the tender ball of my left foot. I screamed and fell into a prickle bush, causing me to yell even more.

I heard an exultant cry of victory coming from further up the mountain. Jimmy was following the sounds of my scream. I scrambled from the brush, and that helped him home in on me.

Pulling myself up, I started running, but my foot hurt so badly, I couldn't limp along very fast. My only hope was to play dead. I dropped to my knees and rolled behind a tree stump just before Jimmy's flashlight found me. Or so I thought. He must have caught a glimpse of me, though, because he came straight toward me. But he wasn't slowing down. Perhaps he figured I'd kept going. I had him! In another second, he'd be running past me.

I whipped the shoes off my shoulders and clobbered Jimmy square in the face. He staggered back with an oath and his flashlight flew into the air, landing somewhere just below us and going out. I couldn't tell what happened to the branch he was carrying. He fell into the prickle bush and began cursing even louder. Standing, I hobbled downhill as fast as I could.

I was making so much noise, I couldn't hear what Jimmy was up to behind me. I never heard him get close enough to swing the branch. . . . .

Sometime later, I awoke. At first, I felt nothing but exhausted, as if I'd spent the last five days wide awake.

Tiny little circles of black, brown, and gray swam in front of my eyes. Gradually, the tired feeling lifted and was replaced by a feeling of nausea. There was a tremendous ache in the back of my head. I tried to reach up and rub it, but couldn't. My hands wouldn't move. It took me a long time to realize that they were tied behind my back. It took an even longer time to realize that they were wrapped around the trunk of a small tree. I was on my knees, slumping forward, and bits of forest were digging into my flesh.

It seemed like my whole body was in pain, but all I could think of was that my head itched where I'd been hit.

"It's about time you woke up."

It was Jimmy, of course. Just the sound of his voice was sickening. I looked up and was a little surprised that I could actually see him. Dimly, perhaps, but definitely. Then I saw that he had arranged a few candles around us. He had tied me up in the same area as the unmarked graveyard.

"I'll bet you got a lot of questions, huh?" he asked.

I mumbled some sort of affirmative answer. The words just didn't want to come out.

"Well, we're in no hurry. And I sure don't want you to die not knowing."

He settled back quietly. My head slowly cleared. A few minutes later, I shook off the last of the cobwebs. Unfortunately, the more I woke up, the harsher the pain became.

"Feeling better?" Jimmy taunted.

"Oh, yeah." I took a deep breath. "Now untie my hands and let's forget this nonsense."

He laughed. "Nonsense, is it?"

He pulled himself up from his seat on the forest floor and came to me. He crouched down, holding his face just a couple of inches from mine. His breath was revolting.

"Kiss me, Lisa? Huh? Kiss me?"

He leaned hard into me and brutally shoved his lips onto mine. His tongue penetrated my mouth. I jerked away, a grunt of disgust in my throat. He grabbed my jaw and forced my head forward, sealing the obscene kiss once more. I rolled up what saliva I could and spat in his mouth. He slammed my head back against the tree.

"Oh, ain't you the d-d-damn p-p-prissy-faced one? Just like the r-rest. Think you're just too d-damn good, d-d-don't you?"

He strode back to his seat, agitiated. "D-d-don't you?"

"No, Jimmy, I don't." My words were weary, unconvincing.

"Yeah? Then why won't you k-kiss me?"

I was beginning to think that maybe it had been a mistake to resist him. It's a sort of standard piece of advice that in New York, you let the rapist do what he wants—as revolting as the idea of actually yielding may be. A mugger probably won't kill you if you do what he says. But the first sign of defiance would bring you a bullet to the head or a knife in your ribs. A swift belt in the chops at the very least. And here I'd violated that rule. So far, I'd only managed to get Jimmy riled. It was probably too late, but I had to try and calm him down.

"Jimmy, please. Don't do this to yourself. It's only because you're younger than I am. Really."

"Hell! Is that why you s-spit at me? And what about th-th-the others? What was their excuse?"

"What others? Susie? She was your girlfriend, wasn't she?" My head cleared enough to realize that my only hope lay in keeping him talking, even if that meant talking about his lies. If I could stall long enough, maybe I could work my hands free. With a great deal of luck, maybe someone would come up here.

"Susie? Oh, sure, she was my g-girlfriend all right. When she wasn't with that idiot M-matt Latham. Maybe I shoulda k-k-killed him instead. You know what? Sh-she never wanted t-to k-k-kiss me, either. Just l-laughed at me. So I m-made her, just l-like I did you. And just like you're g-gonna get another k-k-kiss later."

I had to keep him talking. "And Anne and Mary?"

"Same th-thing. Anne was a townie l-like Susie, but M-mary and that other one I c-c-c-can't remember were strangers like you. They didn't like me, either."

"I like you, Jimmy. I really do. You just need some help, that's all."

That was a mistake. "No, I don't!! I'm doing what I like! I got l-lotsa girlfriends now! Th-th-they're all right here!"

I had to find a different tack, something that might calm him down. I wasn't sure this was it, but what did I have to lose? "What about your mother, Jimmy? Don't you think of her when you do this?"

He did calm down a bit, leaning back against his tree. "Oh, yeah, alla time. Alla damn time."

"Where is she, Jimmy?"

He took a deep breath. "Dead."

Oh, God! My head slumped to my chest in frustration. Was there anything else I could say wrong?

"I found her one day after school. Hung herself in the basement. You know, it didn't hit me much back then. Of course, I was just a kid." He paused and I could tell he was counting back. "Third grade. I was eight. You know what I remember most about it? Her neck. It was all welted up and red. I saw it when the cops took her down. I wasn't supposed to, but I was watching from the doorway. My dad didn't see me. They took her down and she had these big red marks all around."

He made a gesture around his neck as if to say her throat was cut.

"She had n-no right, y' know? N-no right at all!!"

He threw a handful of dirt at me striking me in the face. I couldn't see it coming and it caught me in the eyes. I screamed out in pain for a moment. Then I just plain screamed. Loud and hard, just like in the movies. It echoed off the hillside.

Jimmy smiled at me. "Go ahead. Scream all you want.

———
186

There's no one around. Ain't no one gonna hear you. Nobody heard the others scream, either. Oh, they'll look all over hell for you, but they won't find you. Not now. Not ever. I won. Again."

He laughed some more, then grew silent. I couldn't let him stay that way. I understood all too well how his pain had eventually manifested itself.

"Jimmy, they must know what you're doing. That's why your father and his friends were looking for me so hard all day."

"Oh, sure, they know. No, actually, they d-don't. They *think*. They th-th-think I'm d-doing it, but they don't know for sure. Can't p-prove it because there's no b-bodies or nothing. Ol' Father Jonathan, n-n-n-now he's a clever one. Always talkin' about getting me p-professional help. B-but it ain't gonna b-bring my mother back, now is it?"

"Of course not, Jimmy, but . . . "

"So now I collect g-girlfriends. Since I can't have a m-mother, I have those. And k-k-keep 'em up here. Where no one else can have 'em. P-pretty neat, huh?"

I had reached a state almost of dullness where the ache in my muscles and the burning in my eyes hardly differentiated themselves any longer. How much time had I bought? How much more would I need? As much as I struggled, I hadn't been able to loosen the ropes that held my hands. Not a bit. It would take hours to free myself. And even if I did, I doubted I was strong enough to fight him off.

How could I have been so damn stupid? Good Lord, couldn't You please send someone up here?

I heard Jimmy stand up and I lifted my head to watch him. He flipped the flashlight on and held it under his chin pointing upward. He was grinning like a skeleton.

He stood like that for a few moments, watching me. I wasn't sure what he was up to, but I knew hope was flickering. As long as he didn't touch me again . . .

Then he shoved the light into his backpack and pulled

something out. I couldn't see what it was.

"You sh-sh-shoulda stayed at the festival. You know what you c-coulda been watchin'? You coulda w-watched them th-throw pies in the faces of th-the p-people you saw on th-the stage. You know why? 'C-cuz they g-got caught at the f-festival without th-the stupid buttons. That's why!"

He laughed viciously. "Honest t-to God. Pretty g-good story I t-told you about Father Jonathan, too, huh? Had you b-b-believing every phony word of it."

He walked toward me as he spoke and I noticed a glint of silver coming from his right hand. It was a paring knife.

I started to whimper as he held the blade against my left ear. "No, no, please don't, Jimmy. Please don't hurt me. Take my money. Anything. No, don't."

The blade slashed rapidly across my soft flesh. I expected a lot of pain, but instead, there was only a feeling of warmth around my neck as Jimmy drew the knife across throat. The warm feeling was followed by a feeling of intense cold starting back in my feet and working its way up my legs.

I began to weep softly. I knew I'd become one of Jimmy's girlfriends as soon as the cold reached my head. . .

THE END

AT HOME WITH FATHER JONATHAN

I turned right outside the the fairgrounds and began walking toward Father Jonathan's house. It was a little farther than I thought it would be, and it took me almost half an hour to get there. But it gave me a chance to see more of Ashley Falls.

The town itself was unremarkable, pretty much a typical small town in the northeast—wood frame houses, mostly Cape Cods and saltboxes with a smattering of newer ranches thrown in.

Father Jonathan's house, however, was quite different. I knew it was his home as soon as it came into view. I didn't have to bother checking the name on the mailbox.

All the other houses in town were average-sized suburban buildings, Father Jonathan's was a mansion—huge, white, monumental in scope, and totally incongruous to its surroundings.

It stood alone, in a great park of a perfectly manicured lawn. The driveway was long and straight, running between two hedgerows up to the right side of the house. I followed it onto a small sidewalk of garden tiles leading to the front door and rang the bell.

Father Jonathan answered quickly, and I apologized for being late.

He stepped aside to allow me in. "Not your fault at all, my dear. I should have warned you that it was a much longer walk than it sounds. The important thing is that you're here."

He took me into the kitchen where he was fixing dinner, motioning me to a well-appointed kitchen set—eight tan Naugahyde chairs and a wooden table all on gleaming chrome legs. A moment later, he had a cup of coffee in front of me.

"I hope you're not a vegetarian," he said. "I've taken the liberty of preparing the menu on my own. I hope you don't mind."

How could I? This Father Jonathan was one of the most thoughtful people I'd ever met! "Of course not," I told him.

He smiled that big, ingratiating grin. "Fine, fine. Now, I would imagine you're anxious to contact your family."

To be quite honest, I'd forgotten about that.

"Oh, yes, please."

"I thought so. Tell you what. I'll make you a deal."

I was suddenly suspicious again. "Oh? What might that be?"

"You give me the phone number, then go on upstairs to the guest room and freshen up. In the meantime, I would consider it a privilege to make the call for you."

His smile and manners never wavered. I smiled back. "That sounds like a pretty good bargain to me. I get to rest and you get to do all the work."

He laughed. "That is quite astute. What's the number?"

I gave it to him and then he asked for my parents' names. He wrote them on a piece of gummy note paper and stuck it on the refrigerator door. "That's fine. Now if you'll please come with me . . . "

He took me upstairs to a huge second floor. The guest room was off to the right somewhere away from the kitchen.

"Now here's the Honeymoon Suite. I hope you'll find it to your liking."

He opened the door to a great, canopied bed—white and frilly and spotless. Around it was a stereo ensemble, a color television, a recliner, even a small desk and chair set. It seemed incredibly extravagant for a single man's guest room. He must have guessed my thoughts because he added, "I occasionally have relatives visit. I like to keep this room for my nieces when they come up from Virginia."

"They must love it. Teenagers, I suppose, judging from

the way you have it furnished."

"An excellent guess. Thirteen and sixteen, actually. Now, the washroom is right over there." He pointed to a door in the corner of the room. "There's another guest room on the other side, but of course, no one is in there. I'll take care of contacting your parents now, and if there's anything at all you need, Lisa, please do not hesitate a second to ask."

I looped my overnight bag off my shoulder. "You'll be the first to know."

"Excellent, excellent. Dinner will be in about forty-five minutes. See you then."

I smiled and nodded as he turned and left the room.

I listened to his footsteps going down the hall and, when they faded, I dropped the overnight bag onto the over-stuffed bed. Then I followed him cautiously. I saw him go back to the kitchen. He stayed there for what I thought was a pretty long time and I was beginning to think he had forgotten about the phone call. Then I heard him dial a number and ask for my mother. He gave her the circumstances of my tardiness, explained that I would be just fine, and gave her his own phone number and address. "You needn't worry. Lisa is resting for a short time as I fix her dinner. She'll be on her way again tomorrow. I'll have her call just before she leaves."

He hung up a moment later, and I quietly retraced my steps to the guest room, feeling ashamed. How could I have mistrusted him like that? And how could I have let myself get taken in by that teenage jerk?

The idea of freshening up a bit before dinner was really appealing. Kicking off my shoes, I laid down on the bed, spreading my arms and legs and just reveling in the sheer luxury of it. I think I almost fell asleep because I had one of those quick little dreams you get bubbling just below your conscious—the kind that are easy to remember when you suddenly pop awake moments afterward.

I saw a group of people I didn't know—a small group,

perhaps a family of five or six. I couldn't tell how many there were for certain, but their ages seemed quite varied, from eight or ten years old to over sixty. They looked as if they'd just been through an earthquake. They were leaning against a brick wall, but there was no way of knowing whether it was part of a building or not.

They just sat there, rocking back and forth as if in shock, moaning. Some of them were bleeding from the mouth and some had trickles of blood running down their temples and over their cheeks. It was so odd, but really only half-vivid. Only their peculiar moaning, like some kind of funeral dirge, really stuck in my mind.

Horrified, I awoke with a jerk. The moaning remained burned in my mind as the image of their faces gradually faded. I shook off the cobwebs and checked my watch. I had been asleep only about ten minutes. Still plenty of time to freshen up.

I entered the bathroom which was not quite as luxurious as the bedroom. I found enough towels, though, to dry off a small army.

Digging through my carryall, I pulled out some eyeliner, shadow, and make-up. I had just leaned into the mirror above the wash basin and begun to patch up the spots where my old liner had started to fade when I heard the moaning again. And now, I wasn't asleep!

I turned away, trying to ascertain where the sound was coming from. Then it faded as quickly as it had come. Shrugging, I told myself I had an overactive imagination.

I was just about finished when the moaning sound returned. This time, I was sure of it.

It rose and fell in volume from very soft to very distinct. I wondered if Father Jonathan could hear them, too. I listened for some sign that he might be coming upstairs, but I heard nothing

The moaning ceased. I sat still and did nothing more than listen intently. The funeral lament—or was it someone in pain?—returned seconds later.

And damned if it didn't seem to be coming from the very walls themselves!

I put my ear to some tiles near the bathtub. The sound was amplified through the walls. There were a number of voices, but it was impossible to say how many.

I drew back in alarm. Had my dream been real?

Looking around the bathroom, I saw a tiny vent near the ceiling. Could the sound be coming from there? By standing on the edge of the tub, I could get a little closer to it, although I couldn't quite reach it. But I was close enough to realize that the sounds were indeed coming from the vent.

I jumped back off the tub siding and re-entered the bedroom. Sure enough, the moaning seemed to be coming from an upper corner near the ceiling in that room, too. It was the corner of the wall separating the bathroom. The canopy of the bed, however, muffled it somewhat.

I was afraid to pull on the bed for fear that Father Jonathan would hear it dragging on the floor, even though I knew the kitchen was on the other side of the house.

Instead, I tried to stick my head behind the bed and look up in the corner, but there wasn't enough room. Frustrated, I went to the end of the bed and took a hard grip. Slowly, I dragged it a few inches. I managed to do it very quietly and just enough to give my head clearance.

I stuck my head behind the bed once again and I saw it. Another tiny little vent. The moaning had stopped in the meantime.

Father Jonathan's dinner would be ready soon, but maybe there was still time to look around a little if I wanted to. I *had* to investigate the sounds. (*Turn to page 119.*)

But then I thought maybe I should wait for dinner and confront Father Jonathan with everything I've seen (and heard!) today. (*Turn to page 29.*)

DEATH ON WHEELS

I spun the car around wildly and roared back into Ashley Falls. Jimmy, his father, and the other fellow were exactly where I had left them. Except that the two older men were manhandling the youth into the pickup truck. When they heard me coming, they looked up in surprise. Jimmy tried desperately to use the moment to break free, but as soon as they felt him struggling, they tightened their grip. Jimmy couldn't budge.

I didn't slow down a bit. I aimed straight at the group of them. When they saw I wasn't going to stop, Harry and his friend dove for safety; Harry behind the truck, his friend off to the left somewhere. Jimmy himself had sense enough to climb quickly into the truck bed.

I whizzed by expecting gunshots again, but there was only the sound of my tires squealing on the asphalt. Slamming on the brakes, I spun my car back around. Jimmy was in a footrace with his father for the truck cab. The two of them clenched together in a wrestling match near the driver's door. I didn't have to be told where I could find the shotgun. I hit the gas and drove to the passenger's door. Harry's buddy made a half-hearted attempt to run for the same door, but as soon as he saw me coming, he retreated. The car screeched to a halt.

I dove out, leaving the engine running. Sure enough, the shotgun was lying across the seat, pointing toward Jimmy and his father. Quickly, I reached in for it. I was just a half-second too late. A large, hairy hand grabbed the muzzle and snapped it out of my fingertips.

Jimmy hadn't let go of his father. In fact, now it would be too dangerous to do so. His best bet was to stay as close to his father's body as possible.

I looked around quickly but saw no sign of Harry's partner. The thought struck me that he had gone off for reinforcements, but I didn't have time to dwell on that. I ran around the front of the truck and came up behind Harry. I had no weapon, so I just drew my right hand back behind my head and swung it as hard as I could in the best tradition of Bruce Lee.

I caught Harry square in the nape in the neck. He shot bolt upright for a second as if I had put an electrical charge through him. The shotgun went off harmlessly to the side, then dropped to the pavement. Harry and his son slumped to the ground in a great heap, the gun beneath them. Harry rolled over and his head flopped lazily at my feet. His eyes were half-shut. I had dazed him a lot more than I thought I could. Then I saw that Jimmy was pushing him over and crawling out from beneath him. The teenager picked up the shotgun.

"C'mon, let's get the hell out of here."

I didn't need to be told twice. We clambered into the Charger. I caught a glimpse of Harry struggling to his feet.

I slammed the transmission into gear and left a little rubber on the pavement. The Charger only had a four-cylinder engine, but they were four pretty powerful cylinders. We were doing fifty in a few short seconds. Jimmy was grinning ear-to-ear.

"Why'd you come back?" he asked.

I swung the car around a tight left turn, back toward the highway. "Damned if I know."

"I thought I saw your father getting back into his truck," I told him. "You better keep an eye out for him."

"Yeah," Jimmy replied tersely.

What I hadn't expected was having to keep an eye out for trouble in front of us. Just as we were nearing the entrance ramp, I saw a roadblock of a pair of automobiles hastily forming. I caught a glimpse of a T-shirt I recognized. Harry's friend. The reinforcements hadn't been too far away. I hit the brakes hard, fishtailing my car sideways. A quick jerk rocked the stickshift into reverse and I swiftly backed the car up a few feet. Jimmy spun around, a look of concern on his face. He looked over at the highway ramp

———

and immediately understood.

"Damn."

I must have been a little panicky. The stickshift jammed and I couldn't get it into first gear right away. A little jostling did the trick. I pulled away from the roadblock. In the rearview mirror, I saw a bunch of bodies scrambling into the two cars.

Now if we could just avoid Jimmy's father coming back at us.

I took the first intersection I found and went zipping down a sidestreet. Another intersection came up and I swung through it, too, hoping to weave a zigzag pattern that would permit us to escape. After a short time, Jimmy started giving me directions.

"Right here! Left at the light. . . . "

I figured he knew the town, so I'd better do what he said. I was scared to death of hitting something or running off the road in the dark because I still had my headlights off. But we lucked out. We didn't collide with anything and our pursuers lost us.

Jimmy had me pull over into a little sidestreet that was partially obscured by trees.

"What did we stop here for?" I asked.

"I don't see much sense in driving around just for the hell of it. Maybe I can see where they are from the top of that ridge over there."

He pointed out a shadow in the night that I could barely make out. We were somewhere on the outskirts of Ashley Falls. A small crest loomed over us. I could see Jimmy's point. With all the lights off, their headlights would stand right out from a distance.

Jimmy piled out, leaving the shotgun behind. The courtesy light blinked on and off, blinding me slightly. I couldn't see anything outside the car for a few seconds until the dazzle in my eyes faded. It was more than a little spooky sitting in that car by myself. I shivered, then put my right hand on the gun. It made me feel better.

Jimmy came back to the car and opened the door. Even though I knew he was out there and expected him back any time, it startled me. I jumped involuntarily. Thank God I didn't have my finger on the trigger!

He climbed in quickly and gave his report. "Well, I think we're safe here, but we do gotta coupla problems."

"No kidding!"

"I couldn't see them anywhere. They probably headed back to the highway to wait. I don't think they'd drive around without any lights. It'd make it too difficult to find us. Now our other problem is that we're nowhere near the highway."

"That's bad? That means we're probably nowhere near them, too."

"Yeah, I know. But you wanna try drivin' over this stupid mountain with no lights?"

"Huh?"

"It's the only way out and we can't turn on the headlights 'cuz they'll come chasin' straight after us. We might as well put up a big sign that says 'Here we are.' Besides, there're a whole lot of places where there ain't no fence or wall to keep you from goin' over the cliff."

"But how could they catch us if they're on the other side of town?"

"We don't know if that's where they are for sure. They may be right behind us for all we know. Just wanna play it safe, y'know?"

I shrugged my shoulders. I suppose that made some sense—as much as anything else I'd heard today—but I still didn't like this idiotic cloak-and-dagger stuff. Jimmy's imagination was too much. But I had to go along with him. After all, they *had* shot at me!

"So what do we do? We're not going to walk. I already told you I'm not leaving without the car."

"Where do you hide a tree?"

I don't know if Jimmy could see the incredulous look on my face. "What the hell are you talking about?"

"Where do you hide a tree?" he repeated.

"How the hell do I know? All over the place, but right now, I don't give a damn about . . . "

"All over the place, right!"

"What?"

"Don't you remember that old trick about hiding a tree in the forest?"

"Yeah, so? This car isn't a tree."

"No, but we can sort of do the same thing. What we do is wait for the festival to get over with and all the street-lights to come back on. People will go home and when the traffic picks up again afterward, we'll just kind of melt into the crowd going home."

"Fine, Jimmy, except that I'm sure they'd recognize my car."

"That'd be harder at night, even with the lights on."

"Maybe. But that won't get us past the roadblock."

He grew silent and thoughtful. "I guess you're right. But it would get us closer to the highway," he added hope-fully.

It was my turn to be quiet and thoughtful. Driving over the mountain was out of the question—at least in the dark. And crossing Ashley Falls wouldn't do much good, either. But we couldn't sit here all night.

"How about this," I suggested. "We wait it out like you said. But instead of heading for the highway, we drive over the mountain."

Jimmy pondered that. "With the lights on?"

"Of course."

"It might work. Except that nobody'd be going home that way. They'd still see us."

"Can they really see the lights going up and down the mountain all the way across town?"

"Oh, yeah. You oughta see some of the pictures photog-raphers get up here at night with all the red and white lights twisting up and down. It's pretty neat. And believe me, lady, tonight they're gonna know you and me are the only ones up there. We just gotta hope they're too far away to catch us."

"What's on the other side?"

"North Heddon. At the bottom of the hill."

"Is it safe there?"

"Oh, yeah."

I shrugged my shoulders. "It's the best shot we got."

I felt more than saw Jimmy clutch the shotgun tightly. "I know."

We settled back to wait.

"How long will this take, Jimmy?"

"Another hour or so."

"What are they doing over there?"

"Oh, they got all kinds of rituals that go along with this. It's all a big deal."

"They, uh, get victims down here to do this to?"

"Oh, hell, yeah. With the cheap gas sign. There was a whole family that came in about two or three hours before you did. I wasn't at the garage when they drove in, so I couldn't do anything for 'em. I saw 'em walking off with Father Jonathan a little later."

I wanted to ask him more about his mother, but I thought better of it. I didn't feel I could intrude that way. Instead, for the first time, he showed some interest in me.

"So what's your name?"

"Lisa. Lisa Ames."

"Where you from?"

"Manhattan."

He asked me a few more questions about my job, my background, New York City, and things like that. I felt like I was on a blind date. When his curiosity seemed satisfied, he slumped back quietly. I used the opportunity to question him a little, but I wasn't making smalltalk. "Jimmy, what else can you tell me about The Gift you claim Father Jonathan has?"

"Not much, really. I don't know that much about it. Just want to stop it, that's all."

"Do you know how it works?"

"Nope. Some sort of psychic crap, I guess."

"How do you plan to prove this to the State Police?"

"Oh, I got proof up the wazoo. Don't worry about that."

"Other than people taking a few potshots at us and chasing us all over the place, which admittedly is pretty serious stuff, I don't see anything," I argued. "Is your proof in that backpack?"

"Hell, no. It's in the woods. Remember I told you they got my mother buried up there somewhere?" He pointed off into the wooded mountainside.

"Yeah."

"Well, Lisa Ames, I know where all the gravesites are."

I shivered.

"It's a good thing I came back then, isn't it?" I said thoughtfully. "I couldn't have taken the police to those sites."

Jimmy nodded. "I guess so. I hadn't thought of that. I was just worried about getting you safely outta here."

I knew then how much it meant to him to stop Father Jonathan.

"Of course," he continued with a smile, "that doesn't include the fact that I would have been up there myself if you hadn't come back. Yeah, I guess it is a good thing you did. Thanks. I almost forgot how much I owed you."

I smiled back. "We're even, then. You risked your life for me, too, don't forget."

He held his hand out and I shook it vigorously. The bond formed by earlier events was now official. We laughed heartily, feeling some relief. Not that anything was very funny, but the simple fact of still being alive made it seem pretty joyous right about then.

When the lights finally went on, we almost jumped in surprise. Jimmy grew excited. "It's almost time. They'll be going home soon."

"How long should we wait?"

"Until we see a car or two drive by here. Then we'll just blend in. What you wanna do is drive down about a mile and a half, two miles. There's a road that goes off to the right. Hadley Road. It's the road that goes over the mountain. It's hell to drive, so be careful."

Ten or fifteen minutes later, the first car went past. It didn't take our street but went through the intersection behind us. Shortly thereafter, two more went by.

"Okay, it should be safe now."

I nodded in agreement and started the car. The engine sounded louder than normal and I was certain it would bring the entire population of the town down on us. Nothing of the sort happened. The drive to Hadley Road was uneventful except that I almost missed it. Jimmy pointed it out just in time as he realized I hadn't seen it.

Jimmy had sure been right about what a pain this road was. It snaked back and forth in tight, twisting S-curves that were so close together, it almost seemed that we were turning back on the stretch we had just driven. At some points, there were sections of stone walls as barriers in the curves. In some spots, there were guard rails and others had pieces of old telephone poles stuck in the ground.

And in a lot of places, there was nothing. Not even reflectors on those tin sticks.

"You know," I commented, "I can't believe the state would leave a dangerous road like this so unprotected."

"It's pretty backwoods up here, Lisa. Somebody goes off the road once, takes some barriers with him, and then they don't bother fixing it until some other drunken idiot goes flying through the open part. The state's more worried about keeping traffic going through New York City. A lot more people are affected by that than by some hill in Ashley Falls."

We eased around yet another curve only to find a pickup truck sitting in the dark, facing toward us, blocking the road. Its headlights went on instantly. They were on highbeam and I was suddenly blinded.

"Jeez!" Jimmy yelled.

It sat there unmoving. I braked my car to a stop only about ten yards away. But I knew I couldn't stay there. That CB antenna on top of Harry's cab was broadcasting our position. "Hang on," I told my passenger.

I slammed the Charger into first and headed straight at the pickup. Let Harry think I was crazy enough to chance a head-on collision. The truck jerked to my left at the last second. I took the right side of the road, but my calculations of the margin of error weren't as good as I thought. I scraped the side of my car all along the driver's side of Harry's truck as we passed. Both sideview mirrors shattered in the night air. But at least I had gotten behind him and now he was facing the wrong direction—back downhill.

It took Harry a long time to turn around so he could chase us. We opened up something of a lead on the mountain road but didn't hold it for long. Harry's familiarity with the road gave him the edge.

We weren't far from the summit when I felt a heavy bash on my rear bumper. It was Harry, of course, trying to run me off the road. I had to struggle desperately to control the car, slowing down and allowing Harry to hit me again. This time, he drove me sideways into a guard rail. I slid along, further wrecking the already bashed-up left side. The rail, though, put me back on the road.

I hit the accelerator as hard as I dared once I'd regained control. It was an awful struggle, mentally and physically, slamming my feet back and forth from gas to brake. I just wanted to be able to floor it and get the hell out of there, but had to temper that feeling with the need to keep on that twisting mountain road.

The whole time, I was too busy to pay the least bit of attention to Jimmy. I caught a quick glimpse of him leaning out the passenger's window. The lights behind me started zigzagging back and forth in the rearview mirror.

Now why was Harry doing that?

He rammed me a third time, but not as hard as the first

two because of his zigzagging. I laid off the brake and cut the wheel slightly, letting the car fishtail back into control.

Suddenly, I found out why Jimmy was hanging out the window. And why his father was all over the road a second ago. Harry's truck had pulled up close and fast, this time to nail me good. Then I heard the bark of the gun. It's odd how far behind me it sounded. There was an awful screeching sound. I watched as Harry's pickup canted at an awkward angle, blown tire making a hideous squeal.

"Nice shot, kid!" I caught myself shouting.

The pickup lost speed rapidly and ran up the side of the mountain, then careened back down onto the pavement and sliding all the way across the road. The truck slammed obliquely into a sawed-off telephone pole barrier, smashing up the left headlights and the grille on that side.

Then it tilted over sideways, flipped over two more of the barriers, and disappeared into a wooded ravine. I expected to hear an explosion, but that didn't happen.

I slowed the car down to a crawl. The adrenaline was gone now and my nerves were taking over. My hands shook so, I could barely hold the Charger straight.

Jimmy had pulled himself back into the car. The shotgun was lying on his lap. His eyes were shut, his face twisted in grief and shock.

"Some shot," I said. He didn't respond. "You had to do it, you know. There was no other way."

Jimmy's voice could barely be described as a whisper. "Yeah, I know." He threw the shotgun out the window. It bounced on the road a couple of times and came to rest in a clump of bushes. "C'mon, let's get this trip over with."

I took several deep breaths to calm my nerves somewhat, and then, relieved that it was finally all over, I drove us over the crest of that unnamed foothill and into North Heddon.

THE END

THE CEREMONY

"That's a real dumb move, lady," Jimmy told me.

That very well may be, but sometimes chances just had to be taken. I had to wonder where all this sudden courage was coming from. The old saying about curiosity and felines popped into my mind.

"I don't care. It's the only way I'm going to find out the truth about what's going on around here."

"I already told you what's going on around here."

I shook my head. "You've got quite an imagination, Jimmy. I want to see it for myself."

"You're going no matter what, huh?"

I had already stood and was throwing my bags over my shoulders. That was enough of an answer for him. He stood up, too.

"Then at least let me come along to keep an eye on you."

I couldn't stop him from coming if I wanted to.

"All right."

"Wait here a minute, though."

He ran off into the woods before I could reply. I could hear him scrambling through the brush. I prayed Jerry Kosinski wouldn't return.

Jimmy's rumbling through the undergrowth grew more and more faint. It was obvious that he had wandered a long way into the wooded lot. I hadn't the vaguest idea what he was going after. When I suddenly thought that this was my chance to take off without him, I realized that I didn't trust him too much either.

I scampered around the corner of the garage and began to retrace my steps back to the fairgrounds. Ashley Falls was ominously quiet. Dead. I'd never seen a town so utterly devoid of life.

Although my eyes had pretty much adjusted to the dark, the moon was nothing more than a cold sliver in the black sky and it was almost impossible to make anything out. I simply could not see anything at the fairgrounds. There were no lights except for a few glass sconces on six-foot poles around the edges of the stage at the far end. The candles inside them were lit, casting an eerie glow. It was totally silent.

I crossed the street and entered the grounds. The main concourse was empty, and I strolled down it, half-expecting a gunshot to ring out from the darkness around me, but that didn't happen. I trembled. I had to get my imagination out of overdrive.

I began looking for somewhere to hide so I could watch whatever was going to happen here later. I had some vague thought of hiding beneath the stage, if I could get under there, because it was someplace they certainly wouldn't expect me to be. Examining the stage closely, I couldn't see any hinges on it anywhere nor were any of the plywood sheets loose. I had to discard that idea.

I would have to hide somewhere outside the fairgrounds, maybe in the shadows of one of those unlit houses, where I could both be safe and have a good view.

I ran back to the entrance of the grounds. There were some buildings right across the street, but the views from most of them were obscured by trees.

Wandering around, I found a large oak tree just outside the Anchor fence that enclosed the fairgrounds. It was perfect. I hunkered down behind it and waited.

Sometime later, I heard the sound of footsteps coming from behind me. Startled, I stared out into the night while at the same time putting the tree trunk between me and the direction of the sound. In a moment, I saw Jimmy's ghost-like form appear. I breathed a sigh of relief. "Psst, hey Jimmy! I'm over here!" I whispered loudly.

"Yeah, I kind of figured you would be. It's the best place to watch the ceremony. But you're a real dolt for running off like that."

He was standing there with some kind of knapsack in his hands. It was filthy. Clumps of dirt and moss clung to the sides and he was brushing it off as he talked. "I didn't think it would take that long to find this thing. I hadda hard time in the dark."

"What's in that?"

Jimmy shrugged. "My stuff."

I smiled at him, remembering the days when that phrase covered a lot of ground for me, too. It hadn't been all that long ago.

Then a thought struck me.

"You know something, Jimmy, I was just wondering if maybe there was something you could do for my car."

"Like what? Take its temperature?"

"Don't be funny. I mean plug the hole somehow. At least temporarily."

"Yeah, actually, I could put a patch on it. No guarantee how long it'll last, though."

I looked off in the distance. The flickering orange lights that told me where the procession was seemed to be a long way from returning to Father Jonathan's.

"You think maybe we have time to put that patch on now?"

Jimmy looked up from his knapsack at the glow across town. "Nope. Takes a long time."

"How long?"

"Unh, I dunno. Hours if it don't take right away. At least an hour even if it does."

He seemed to be hemming and hawing.

"You ever done one?"

"Me? No, never. That's another reason why it'd take so long."

"You know, it might be a good idea to have some means of transportation out of here." I was beginning to get exasperated.

"I guess."

He sat down beside me, still plucking dirt from his backpack. It appeared to be made of nylon, but I had no way of guessing what the original colors might have been.

———

"Don't you think we oughta do something about it?" I persisted.

"Yeah, yeah, yeah. We got plenty of time. See, lady, if we go back to the garage right about now, we're runnin' the risk of havin' them come back and finding us putzin' a round. But if we wait until the ceremony begins, then we're much safer. That is, if I can figure out how to put the patch on."

"Do you at least know what materials to use?"

"Yeah, I know that. And I know something else, too. That this is a pretty damn stupid place to be right about now. We oughta hide somewhere else."

"You just said we shouldn't go back to the garage."

"No, not to the garage, but somewhere *else*."

"How can I watch the ceremony?"

"You can't. And you shouldn't anyway. It's not real pretty."

"I'll take my chances."

The orange glow of the candlelight procession was moving closer. For a minute, I was afraid that it was heading right at us. Then I saw that it was going to veer away to my left, passing the other side of the fairgrounds by a couple of blocks.

"You know something, I think I'm going to take a look at this procession of yours," I said.

Suddenly, Jimmy panicked. He jumped to his feet and almost began yelling. After a couple of syllables, he lowered his voice. "That's about as stupid an idea as I've ever heard. You're gonna end up in the middle of it and you won't want to, believe me!"

His hands reached out for me, but I ducked back, avoiding his grasp.

"What the hell is your problem?"

He dropped his arms and hung his head sheepishly. "Okay, look, if you insist on taking dumb chances like that, fine, but I'm coming with you to keep you out of trouble."

It was a statement, not a request for permission. He didn't even say "Okay?" For the second time that night, I gave in to the inevitable.

"Yeah, sure."

I bent over quickly to pick up my bags. The procession was moving slowly, but if we didn't move right away, it would pass us by. I took off at a jog, throwing the bags over my shoulder. My haste took Jimmy by surprise. He whispered a loud, irritated "Hey!" and chased after me.

I didn't slacken my pace, forcing him to sprint briefly to catch up. He didn't say anything as he pulled up beside me and slowed to match my gait. We slipped through a couple of backyards and dashed quickly over a couple of streets in the eerie blackness that was Ashley Falls.

We crept into the shadows of a clump of bushes, Jimmy on my right. Most of the procession had already gone by, which bothered me a little because I wanted to see who was leading it. I wished I had thought of chasing after it a little sooner.

Frankly, there wasn't much to see. It was kind of pretty, actually. The street was filled curb-to-curb with people trudging on. Naturally enough, it was quite a gay atmosphere. People were laughing and joking, kids playing.

Apparently it was true, what Jimmy had said about the entire town turning out. Parents carried or pushed stroller-borne infants too young or too sleepy to walk. Older, gray-haired people walked by, there were even a couple of people in wheelchairs.

But what struck me most was the total lack of a *sinister* feeling. If this was indeed what Jimmy claimed it was, then the townspeople certainly found ritual murder amusing!

We crouched, waiting until the end of the procession went by. It had hardly been worth the effort. I waited until the last of the parade turned a corner and disappeared. Then I stood and stared at the intersection. The odd glow that the candles produced in the night sky was no longer the ominous spectacle it had been. Now, it was just a bright spot in the night, indicating that a large group of people were having a good time.

"Well, Jimmy, that certainly wasn't very horrifying."

"Yeah, well, I don't think you understand what's going on around here."

Hearing him rummaging through his backpack, I turned back to see what he was going after when a pair of headlights loomed up down the street. Someone in a pickup truck had been following the procession. A spotlight was waving back and forth from the driver's side, a smaller beam waving out the passenger's side. I scrambled back into the bushes. Jimmy quickly gave up his search.

He grabbed the back of my neck and shoved my face hard into the grass. The pickup drove by slowly. I was able to lift my head enough to watch the spotlight. It stabbed through the night around us, an evil eye searching out its prey. I could almost feel it poke into the bushes around us.

The windows of the pickup must have been open. I heard two men talking as they drove by. I couldn't be sure of what they said, but I thought I heard one of them mutter "that damn son of mine . . . " and then something unintelligible as the truck passed, taking the searchlight with it. It turned the corner and continued following after the crowd.

Jimmy stayed on the ground for a long time after that and wouldn't let me move. He had crawled half on top of me and seemed inclined to stay!

"Get off me and let me *go*!" I blurted out.

He rolled over.

"Do I really have to beat the daylights out of you to make it sink in? Keep your damn hands off me!" I sat up, drawing my knees to my chin. I doubted I was really strong enough to 'beat the daylights out of him,' but I really didn't think it would be necessary anyway. I was pretty sure I got my point across.

"See what I mean?" he asked, ignoring my anger. "They're still out there looking for us. Don't that tell you somethin'? And one of their biggest tricks is to have

———

another car running along behind the first one to catch people nappin'. They're pretty damn clever, ain't they?"

I leaned over and looked past his shoulder. If there was another car coming, it wouldn't be here until Tuesday.

"Oh, give it a rest," I said as I stood up. In fact if Jimmy's dad hadn't just driven by obviously looking for us, I would have caught up with the procession and joined it myself. Then I could have had Father Jonathan explain what was going on. But despite Jimmy's strange behavior, I decided it was still best to keep a low profile and my eyes wide open. I started back to my hiding place to wait for the ceremony, whatever it may be, to begin.

Jimmy scampered up beside me.

"You still don't believe me, do you? Isn't it enough that they've been searching for us all day? And they *still* haven't given up? Where're you goin'?"

"Back to that tree. I intend to see what's going to happen at that festival later."

"You *can't*!"

He grabbed my arm and I snatched it right back. I turned and faced him. Even in the dark, I'm sure he could see the anger in my face.

"Now, look! You're not dealing with some high school sweetie-pie. You keep your damn hands off me and we'll get along just fine. I'm going to watch that ceremony, or festival, or whatever the hell it is, and you, young man, are simply not going to stop me."

He looked as if no one had ever spoken to him like that. His head drooped, crestfallen. "Okay, okay. Sorry."

Sulking, he poked along behind me.

We returned to the shadows of the tree to await the rest of the festival. Jimmy seemed anxious, nervously fidgeting with his back pack. I can't say I blamed him. I was more than a little spooked myself.

I had the impression that it was quite a long walk to and from Father Jonathan's house, but that just may have been from the circuitous route the procession had taken through town. Of course, Jimmy and I had spent part of the time ducking from the automobile and its occupants. Perhaps that had taken longer than I thought. In any event, the parade took just a few minutes to return to the fairgrounds. The whole time, Jimmy seemed on the verge of saying something—or maybe doing something—but he didn't. He just kept fussing and fretting.

The townspeople piled into the fairgrounds. This time, I could see very clearly who was leading them—Father Jonathan. He took the lead, holding a candle himself. He was wearing long, black robes with gold or silver embroidery—I couldn't tell exactly in the uncertain orange light—around the cuffs and collar. I expected him to be carrying a book, but he wasn't. He, too, was grinning, obviously enjoying himself.

Behind him came six people who were notable for their lack of candles. There were four men and two women. They appeared to range in age from the mid-fifties or so down to around the late teens. Nor was there anything remarkable in their clothing. They were dressed in pretty much the same kind of casual blue jeans or corduroys and sport shirts or blouses as everyone else in Ashley Falls that night.

They were jostled and cajoled good-naturedly by the marchers behind them.

Somehow, this just didn't have the look of impending murder.

The crowd filed in behind them in a great, seemingly endless wave. As each entered the fairgrounds, each person blew out his candle. I soon found out why. In order to get everyone into the grounds, it was necessary for the mob to pack together tightly. It would have been far too easy to accidentally set someone's hair or clothing on fire.

Father Jonathan walked up onto the stage and stood dead center, facing out toward the crowd, waiting for the end of the procession to surge its way into the back of the space between the rows of booths. The six people who had followed him stood beside him, three to the left and three to his right. They were ringed by those sconces which gave out more light than it had seemed at first. I could very clearly make out seven smiling faces.

I turned to Jimmy. "You know, those people seem pretty damn happy for so-called murder victims."

Jimmy just glared at me.

A moment after the last of the procession turned into the fairgrounds, the headlights poked their way toward us again. I stood immobile, surprised. Jimmy touched me lightly and nudged me. I dropped to the ground behind the tree trunk. This time, I wasn't upset with him. I had been caught napping.

It was Harry again. His searchlight swept past us much as it had earlier. We hugged the ground tight and the beam went over us. This time, I could see the figure in the passenger's seat. He was waving the flashlight around the lawns on the other side of the truck.

The pickup cruised past, stopped at the end of the street, and stayed there, unmoving. Its searchlight went out. Even the flashlight was turned off. Jimmy and I sat tensely, watching. A moment later, it took off again and turned another corner.

I turned back to the ceremony. Father Jonathan was giving a speech.

"So, for this year, dear friends, we have chosen six-year-old Amy Pintriccio to do the honors on our neighbors who were caught by the ever-vigilant Jerry Kosinski."

I watched curiously as a young girl mounted the stairs. Behind her was a somewhat older woman—her mother, I guessed—carrying a number of square, shallow boxes. She put them on the edge of the stage and her daughter opened the top and withdrew a pie!

As she approached the first "victim," Father Jonathan said, "Bill Harberry, this is the second year in a row you have been caught without your Mayfly pin. I should think you might have learned your lesson by now."

"I don't care, Father Jonathan. Hell, I like cream pie!"

The crowd roared with laughter as six-year-old Amy, aided by a boost from Father Jonathan, hit Bill Harberry square in the face.

I stared totally dumbfounded at the events in the fair-grounds. It took several seconds for my anger to boil up enough to force verbal expression.

"*This* is the evil ceremony you've been trying so hard to keep me from watching? What kind of trick is this?"

"This kind," was the answer I got.

I turned to face Jimmy. He was standing inches from my chin, holding a large, silver blade at the flesh of my neck.

"What th—"

"Sh-shutup!" he whispered harshly, stuffing his hand over my mouth. "Stay sh-shut up and you won't g-g-get cut!"

He slowly pulled his hand away, testing my willingness to be quiet. I kept silent. Screaming wouldn't save me. Help was too far away. I needed time. . . .

"G-good. Now c-come with me," he growled. He grabbed the collar of my blouse and dragged me across the street and into the shadows of the houses and trees opposite the fairgrounds. I didn't struggle or try to break loose. That blade was just too damn sharp to test Jimmy's exper-tise with it.

He eventually brought me to a wooded lot somewhere nearby—half the time dragging me and half the time push-ing me. We couldn't have gone too far from the fair-grounds, but with all of Ashley Falls watching whatever was going on at the festival, we were as isolated as if we had gone a mile into the forest of the surrounding mountains. Jimmy threw me to the ground.

"Christ, are you a p-p-p-pain," he told me. He was talk-ing through his teeth, barely moving his lips. His stam-mering was becoming more pronounced as he became more excited.

"I n-never had th-this much t-trouble with any of the

others. Every d-damn time I went to g-g-get my old joy-stick here, you were off somewhere l-l-like a s-s-stinking jackrabbit." He waved the knife around as he called it his "joystick." It was a long butcher's knife with a thick, sharp, nonserrated blade.

"What's this all about, Jimmy?" I managed to speak calmly, hoping to figure out what he intended.

He leaned against a tree and his voice took on a cocky tone. "You know, in a way, I'm g-glad you were such a p-pain. The challenge makes it even s-s-sweeter." He was waving the blade nonchalantly. "B-b-but you had to see the damn festival! N-n-nothing's happening th-there. All the action's r-r-right here with you and me, in case you hadn't g-g-guessed. Usually, I d-d-do this up in the moun-tains. Then I d-d-on't have the d-drag the b-bodies around. I just b-bury 'em where they d-drop." He chuck-led and sounded proud of his cleverness.

I felt my blood run cold.

"But you're g-gonna be a p-p-problem. Somehow, I'm g-gonna hafta drag you outta here and up the m-mountain. I already g-got an idea how. I'll m-manage. It'll just be a l-little more exciting than usual."

My only chance was to stall for time. "Why not just take me up there, Jimmy?"

"Naw, t-too dangerous. We'd hafta g-go all the way through t-town and it's t-t-too likely they'd find us. I ain't that st-stupid. No, you're g-gonna die right here, and l-later, when everyone's gone home, I'll c-come b-b-back and d-drag your b-body from the b-bushes, then take you to your new home."

He chuckled again.

"How many of us are there?" I asked.

"Oh, th-th-three or four. My g-girlfriends, I c-c-all them. Every year, I f-find some stupid l-little bitch like you and k-k-kill her. And you know why I d-do that?"

I shook my head, unable to speak.

"B-because I *l-like* it."

———

215

He slipped the blade across the side of his thumb. I assume he did so to draw blood, but whether he was trying to impress me by being macho, or just wanted to indulge in a little fantasy, I couldn't say.

He was walking toward me now and I scrambled back through the undergrowth, scraping my hands on the rocks and pebbles beneath me. Jimmy stared at me like a cobra watching a mongoose.

He made no attempt to close the distance between us, he just kept coming slowly, one deliberate step after another, the knife held blade down in his right hand. A moment later, I found out why he didn't simply just rush me. He had maneuvered me against a large clump of bushes. I quickly glanced in both directions and saw that it was too large to get around before Jimmy would have a chance to grab me. Pulling my feet up underneath my legs, I crouched, coiled like an animal. My hands were clenched in the loose dirt beside me.

Jimmy got close and raised his arm overhead, about to strike. His eyes were wide, bright, and excited, his face glowing in evil triumph. His teeth glinted slightly through his huge grin.

Jesus, God, Lord, he *did* enjoy this!

I threw up a handful of gravel and dirt into his face. Some of it caught him in the eyes and some flew into his open mouth. He choked, then screamed.

I stood immediately and kicked him in the groin. He fell, clutching himself, cursing me loudly. The knife had flown off somewhere into the undergrowth and there was no hope of finding it in the dark. I stood over him, unsure of what to do for a moment. I realized Jimmy's pain was gradually subsiding and that he was slowly regaining his feet.

I kicked him in the thigh and ran. My blow had knocked him over, but he recovered immediately and gave chase.

I had no idea where I was headed. I was just trying to put a lot of distance between me and Jimmy. I expected to end up flat on my face after twisting my ankle on a rock or in a small depression.

In the distance, I could see streetlights trying to come back to life. They weren't strong enough to help me see, but at least they gave something to run for.

I could hear Jimmy behind me, plowing through the bushes. I knew he could outrun me in a flat-out footrace, but the undergrowth seemed to slow him down considerably. And maybe, I though, just maybe, it was still quite painful for him to run.

The streetlights came on full and bright as I emerged from the wooded scrubland. Ahead of me lay a large, open park. Beyond it was a residential street. Maybe if I could make it that far . . .

I didn't hesitate a step as I broke cover and dashed straight for what I prayed was safety.

Just as I had almost reached the sidewalk, I saw a pair of headlights turn the corner and drive down the street toward me! The searchlight was waving off into the park. God bless that Harry! He was everywhere! I must have slowed down a pace or two in my excitement because just then, Jimmy got me with a rolling leg tackle. We both grunted as we hit the ground hard and actually bounced a couple of inches off the turf.

I flipped over onto my back and kicked and kicked and kicked like a swimmer training for the backstroke.

I caught Jimmy in the face a couple of times and he broke his grip to protect himself. I pulled myself to my feet quickly and ran into the street. Jimmy recovered almost as quickly and was on my heels again. With nowhere else to go, I darted in front of the pickup truck and turned toward it, waving my arms frantically over my head. "Hey! Hey!"

There was plenty of room for Harry to come to a stop, but I must have startled him. He swerved hard to my right and flew past me. I could have sworn he never touched the brakes. Damned if he didn't actually seem to accelerate!

The pickup truck slammed with a horrifying thud into the teenager behind me. Jimmy's body flew almost fifty feet, bouncing like a boneless canvas dummy down the asphalt. Sickened, I fell in a lump in the middle of the street, too numbed to care if I was next.

Harry stepped from the cab of his truck as his friend (it was George Miller) scrambled from the passenger's door. The two of them stood beside the truck for a long time, staring down the street at Jimmy's corpse as if they expected it to stand up and say "I'm okay," then brush itself off. Long moments later, the collective shock subsided a bit and Harry walked slowly over to me, his head down.

He stood above me and softly uttered words that appalled me more than anything Jimmy had ever said.

"I was aimin' for him."

There were tears in his eyes.

Sometime later, I found myself at Father Jonathan's house. I was seated in a large, overstuffed sofa. The room itself was large and airy, mansion-like in its dimensions. A number of matching chairs were placed around the walls. Wood and glass end tables and a coffee table framed the couch I was sitting in.

A large group of strangers was wandering in and out of the room, some carrying food, most carrying cups, all of them talking in low, hushed tones. I couldn't make out their words. But there were no police anywhere.

It was odd how I came to be aware of my surroundings. It had come to me slowly, like a curtain being raised on a dream. I saw the people, the furniture, the living room. But none of it registered right away. It just started to make sense piece by piece, none of it related in any way until the very end—when the whole picture came to life.

I looked down and found a cup of coffee in my hands. It was half empty. I didn't remember drinking any of it. I lifted it to my lips and took a sip. It was still warm. I don't really like coffee much, but this particular cup was the perfect tonic for the situation.

Father Jonathan worked his way through the crowd from another room. He was no longer his usual smiling self. Instead, his face had a grim look as he walked to the sofa and sat beside me. His black judicial-like robes were gone and he was wearing a tan dress shirt and black corduroy trousers.

"Lisa, my dear," he said, "how are you feeling?"

I nodded affirmatively.

"Is there anything you'd like?"

I shook my head no.

"It seems we owe you something of an apology."

I sipped the coffee and said softly, "How about an explanation instead?"

"Yes, indeed, you are due that first."

He had a cup in his own hand and sipped from it. It was coffee, too.

He took a deep breath, then began. "Jimmy, you see, has . . . had . . . a rather tragic problem. He more or less took the idea of the Mayfly Festival a little too literally."

I stared at him, aghast. "You mean you *knew* about his killings?"

Father Jonathan hemmed and hawed. "We, uh, take care of our own here in Ashley Falls, Lisa. We're too small to even have a State Police barracks any closer than thirty miles away. We thought we had the problem under control. It had happened once before, several years ago."

"That's not what he told me."

Father Jonathan seemed genuinely surprised. "Oh, really? What did he tell you?"

I told him about the hidden graveyard and Jimmy's boast of three or four others.

"Oh, dear. That is distressing news. I don't suppose he told you where the gravesite is?"

"No."

"No matter. It's probably the same place he buried that

219

first poor girl. We'll look into it, of course. I just wish I understood more about his psychosis. I suspect it had something to do with his mother's suicide some years ago. That's when he started exhibiting anti-social behavior. Over time, it escalated into more and more violent activities. He always had trouble in school. But I had no idea about any other murders . . ."

Father Jonathan shook his head sadly. I then told him the story Jimmy had told me about the Mayfly Festival. He smiled sardonically.

"He would have been a wonderful writer, so full of imagination. No, I'm afraid there's no more truth to 'The Gift' than there is to the Man on the Moon. And Harry's sign for inexpensive gas is no more a lure for victims than a sign for a restaurant. What he told you about occasionally receiving cheap gasoline is the truth. He may seem gruff, but he is an honorable man."

There was an ominous, unstated thought behind that sentence.

"And you're not going to turn him into the police, are you?"

Father Jonathan was staring into his coffee cup, holding it with both hands. It looked as if he were going to shake it, turn it over, and then read *Reply hazy. Try again later,* floating in water under a little plastic window.

"Lisa, what good would that do? He's lost a wife already and now a son he cared for very much. He told me he drove into Jimmy on purpose, 'to end his misery,' he said. No, he's been through enough. Indeed, I'm afraid he may be next. I fear he may try to follow in his wife's footsteps, so to speak. Especially since he tried so hard today to keep you out of Jimmy's clutches only to have events work out the way they did."

He had a point, I suppose. But I saw the look in Harry's eyes as he stood over me in the street. If anyone knew about Jimmy's later victims, it was his father. I trembled at the thought. Perhaps guilt, too, might just drive him to what Father Jonathan feared.

Father Jonathan stood. "I've already aranged for your car to be repaired first thing tomorrow morning. If you feel up to it, you can leave then. If not, feel free to stay as long as you'd like. In the middle of this crowd somewhere is Doctor Myers. He's already given Harry a tranquilizer upstairs. I'll have him give you a shot to help you sleep if you'd like."

I would like very much. Deep, deep dreamless sleep was what I needed.

The nightmare was over.

THE END

ABOUT THE AUTHOR

The owner of an advertising and public relations firm, Lee Enderlin lives in Connecticut, where he's getting fat on a steady diet of Stephen King novels. He gets his ideas from his dog, Budweiser, who is an excellent observer of the human condition. Unfortunately, the dog can't type, so Lee has to do all the work.

A 1973 graduate of Notre Dame, Lee has been writing for six years. His work has appeared in most of the major gaming magazines, as well as military history magazines, and his fiction has appeared in PHANTASY magazine.